The Uncommon Prison of Henry V Henry

SIMON BULLIVANT

Ouen Press

Published in Great Britain in 2018
by Ouen Press

Suite One, Ingles Manor, Castle Hill Avenue
Folkestone, Kent, UK
www.ouenpress.com

ISBN: 978-0-9956299-7-4

Printed by CreateSpace, SC, USA

A CIP catalogue record of this book is available from the British Library.

Cover Design: Ouen Press, Main illustration: istock/kamisoka

To Sam and Joseph

.

CONTENTS

ACKNOWLEDGMENTS

Thanks to my brother, Matthew, for his enthusiasm; to El, for her unflagging support and encouragement; to Andrew Gordon from David Higham, who first believed in Henry; and to Paula Comley for showing faith.

CHAPTER ONE

It wasn't till I'd struggled past all the stuff on the stairs that I could see there was a leaflet on the doormat. So much for it being the newspapers. Where were they? Hadn't I told the newsagent's no later than half-nine? I like to have my morning papers by half-nine. Any later and they aren't really morning papers, are they?

I reckoned it was closer to twenty-to-ten. It's a good thing I don't have to go to work. Imagine if I had to leave the house by half-nine every morning. What would I do then? I'd be spending every evening just catching up with things. So it's not such a lot to ask, is it, for the papers to arrive on time? Especially when there are important things going on. Yet here I was again, left in the lurch.

It sometimes feels like they do it on purpose. Making you wait; trying to upset you. Three times this week it's happened now. I've complained at the shop but the newsagent just laughed and said it wasn't his fault. He blamed the summer holidays. Said the kids didn't wake up so early when they didn't have to go to school. I felt powerless. But what could I do? When I tried to take matters into my own hands, it all went wrong. I'd lain there in wait for the paperboy – crouched behind the front door, darting out at the first flap of the letterbox. And just as the papers started raining down on my head I jumped up and opened the door. But instead of apologising the boy had given me an earful back, hadn't he? And a lot more besides. And not long after, the boy's father had shown up, snarling and jabbing his finger and calling me all sorts of names. He had daggers on his arm and swirling black lines that poked out from under his shirt and curled up to his ear. It's strange what some people choose to do.

I picked up the neatly folded leaflet and wiped away a few beads of sweat. *Are you ready for the paperless office?* it said. I don't know, I thought. But it's always better to be prepared, isn't it? I can't properly use my office room at the moment, but I will do one day, when I get on top of things, and it would be good to have useful information at my fingertips. You can't have too much information, I know that much. The slip of paper had two phone numbers on it, something to do with computers, and a contact name – Jamal. There was no telling when any of it – the numbers or Jamal himself – might come in handy. I don't actually own a computer, you see. But even if I never call Jamal it's useful scrap paper, and paper is expensive these days. So it would be foolish to throw it away. Best to keep it somewhere safe.

I thought I'd put it with the other slips of paper for the time being. There's several piles half-way up the stairs amongst the overflow of magazines. It's not the best place for them but they won't stay there forever. When I'm not quite so busy I've got plans to sort them all out. I'm going to put the Chinese restaurant menus in one location and those from the curry houses in another. Then I'll need somewhere else for the little taxi-cards and the flyers from the local builders. Perhaps some sort of cupboard or shelf. But there isn't really time for that now. There's more important matters to be concerned about. Because things have been happening, haven't they? Things that I need to know about. That's why the papers are so important.

Of course Jamal's flyer wasn't the only thing that had landed on my doormat. There was a letter from the electricity company. A serious one. I knew it was serious because I could see the coloured writing through the window. I was tempted to leave it unopened. I know what coloured writing means. Those bills always follow the regular ones. The regular bills tell you what money you have to pay, but if you don't pay they send you a coloured one that tells you off. I sighed when I tore it open and saw what it said. I'd forgotten to pay. It wasn't my fault really, I had meant to pay. I just hadn't got round to it. Most likely the original bill had got buried under a power-tool catalogue somewhere or an advert for wicker furniture. Still, it's no use looking for it now. The same thing had happened with the phone, and they'd been very quick to disconnect me then, hadn't they?

The service will be terminated immediately unless
full and prompt payment is received forthwith.

I have to turn sideways to negotiate the narrow hallway. It's piled high with boxes, bags and bin-liners, each crammed full of all manner of things. Once upon a time I knew what every one of them contained. But when you get a lot of bags and cardboard boxes it becomes harder to keep track of everything. There's coat-hangers in one of the bags, I'm pretty sure of that. And willow-pattern plates and picture frames with glass in and plastic flowerpots. And there's some velvet curtains that'll be good as new as soon as they've had a repair. Plus no end of other useful things. They just need some organising, that's all.

It's a tight squeeze by the kitchen, and I have to stop to catch my breath by the door frame. The pain in my chest is playing up. It often gives me trouble first thing in the morning. What had Dr Singh said? *You need to exercise, Mr Henry.'* And she'd wagged her finger at me and told me I might be forty-two, but I had the heart of a sixty-five-year-old. Then she'd prescribed me capsules. I can't say I'm fond of them. The tablets I quite liked – they came in brown-glass bottles stuffed with cotton wool. But they don't give me those anymore. Now my medication comes shrink-wrapped, and looks like little rows of brightly-coloured coffins. Of course I could always improve things and transfer my capsules into a brown-glass bottle. I had the good sense to put some by long ago. It might take me a while to remember where they are, but I'll find them in the end.

It's hot in the kitchen. The sun is already high and beating through the windows. There is a blind, which could have stopped the glare. But it hangs at an angle half-way up and the cord's broken and anyway I can't reach it, what with all the things in the way. I'm not keen on the summer. Summer means heat and with the heat comes the flies: fat ones in the kitchen, which appear from who knows where, and tiny little ones that hover like a cloud above the bags of fruit.

I try and make a space among all the things on the kitchen worktop, fill the kettle and wait for it to boil. The television sits in its own little space, chattering away about loft conversions and potential and knocking through. It's not the sort of programme that interests me really. But the news will be on soon. It's wasteful, of course, leaving the television on around the clock, and I do hate waste. But I'd made the mistake before of turning it off and then when I'd tried to switch it back on again it wouldn't work properly and I was lost without my television. And the man from the shop who came to look at it was rude and said some unkind things about the house and didn't finish the job. And when I asked when they were coming back, someone else was rude and said they wouldn't be round again and why didn't I try someone else. But I didn't try anyone else. I got a new television instead which stays on all the time, but that isn't such a problem nowadays because the picture doesn't turn into a whistle at one o'clock in the morning. I felt a bit sorry for the old set really, just standing there not doing anything, but in the end it just sort of disappeared under clothes or bags or something. Sooner or later I'll get it repaired though and then I might take it upstairs. It'll be good to have a television upstairs as well as in the kitchen. Just as soon as I've sorted things out and cleared some proper space.

It occurs to me that Jamal might prove useful, what with all his phone numbers and computer jargon. Someone like that might know about televisions. Perhaps Jamal wouldn't be so rude about my house. But his leaflet only said computers, didn't it? There was no mention of television sets. And I couldn't be certain but I didn't think any cards had come through the door offering TV repairs. There wasn't one of those in the piles on the stairs. But then I heard a voice on the television and I stopped thinking about Jamal and his computers and remembered the girl again. Not that I'd forgotten her. How could I?

It's been four days since I first saw the news on television. A girl had gone missing. The first twenty-four hours were critical, so the experts all said. Missing children usually turned up safe and well within twenty four hours or so. But one day had become the next and when the girl hadn't reappeared her parents had begun to get anxious and make appeals and I'd started to worry. And after that the story had just continued to grow until each new bulletin began with the latest updates about missing Lorna Coulson. So I'd spent hour after hour wedged between the boxes, devouring the papers and watching the news reports. Then yesterday I'd been struggling with a bag upstairs when I'd heard the theme tune come blaring from the kitchen. It had taken me by surprise, because it hadn't been time for the news. I know when all the bulletins are on and a theme tune at a strange time could only mean that something significant was happening.

By the time I'd reached the television I could see that a press conference had started. There was a table, microphones, Lorna's parents and that bald police officer. My first reaction had been a familiar tingling sensation, quickly followed by a sense of panic. I had to tape the press conference, to keep an account – but the video recorder was on standby and there were no fresh tapes to hand. It made me feel hot and cold at the same time because I had no blank tapes left and the bald police officer had started to speak and what was I going to do now? Because I hadn't got a blank tape and I didn't know when I'd be able to buy any more because it's not so easy to find them these days. There was an old one lying on a bag close by, but I knew there was something on it though I wasn't sure exactly what it was. And I didn't want to record over it without checking first, because what if it was important? There are all sorts of things on my tapes and once you've recorded over something you can never get it back, can you? It's gone for ever. But there was nothing written on the label and it would take too long to look and see what it was. And by the time I'd managed to dig up another tape the press conference would probably have finished. So I didn't really have any other option but to use it. And when I stuck in the tape and pressed the record button my heart had started fluttering and I felt that terrible prickling sensation I get in my face.

'We only want her to come home,' the girl's mother had said. 'Just a phone call. Anything.'

Her father had said very little between his sips of water. They were watching him, I thought. That's what the police did. They watched you. If they suspected someone of carrying out a heinous crime they'd often put them in front of the cameras and look for tell-tale signs. Sipping too much water was one of them. So was saying too much, or not saying enough. And people would watch and see the father crying and say, *'She's dead of course. And I bet the dad did it. He'll have killed her. Those are crocodile tears.'* And if he wasn't crying then they'd say, *'Well, why isn't the father upset? That's not right, is it? Has he no feelings? He ought to be in floods of tears. That must mean she's dead. And he'll have done it. You can bet your life.'* That's what people would have been thinking.

Click. The kettle juddered to a standstill. Cups, cups. Why are there never any clean cups? I had to fish one from the bowl of dirty washing and rinse it under the tap with my finger. I ought to get some hooks really to hang all the cups on. Perhaps a shelf or two for the plates and things when I've got a moment. It doesn't do to leave them all in the sink. What would my mother have thought? I'm pretty sure she'd never have left dirty mugs in the sink.

I heard the letterbox flapping and the familiar sounding thud that meant the papers had arrived. So I abandoned my tea and scurried as best I could to the door. Even before I'd negotiated the passageway I could see the familiar smiling face on the front page. A second or two later I was able to read the headline. *Missing Lorna – Fresh Hope*, it said. If only that were true, I thought.

I take two newspapers every day – the *Telegraph* and the *Mirror*. Both ends of the spectrum, I like to think. I'm quite sure there isn't anybody else who takes just the *Telegraph* and the *Mirror*. But that's because I'm not like everybody else. I'm one of that rare band of people who is independently minded – who can distinguish fact from bias. Nobody tells Henry V. Henry what to think. Not that I care all that much for either paper. The *Telegraph* is too big and unwieldy for one thing. Other papers have shrunk in size, but not the *Telegraph*. It's still huge and not at all easy to read in my little den. It also makes for difficult storage. The *Mirror* on the other hand is too full of idle chatter for my liking; too full of news about famous people I don't much care for and whose function I don't really understand. But at least you can trust the newspapers. The papers are a permanent record, aren't they? Something you can touch and hold and file away for future reference. Where's the substance to Jamal's computer universe? There's so much misinformation on the internet. Not to mention pornography. From what I can gather it's awash with filth.

I took my tea and papers and sat on an old sofa cushion wedged on the floor in between two big cardboard boxes. Was there still hope for poor Lorna Coulson, they speculated. *The schoolgirl had been missing since Monday... It wasn't like her... We want her to come home... Everyone loved Lorna... Loved,* I noted. *Vanished into thin air... Scouring the local area...* It was all so familiar. Apart from the names I'd read it all before. My eyes skimmed over the words and the perspiration ran down my face. My heartbeat quickened with each turn of the page. No, I thought. There was no hope for poor Lorna. She wouldn't be coming home again. I just knew.

The television programmes changed from property speculation to talk of snuff boxes and forgotten treasures in the attic. I was so engrossed in my newspapers I didn't hear a word of it and my tea went cold. I was only stirred by the familiar drumbeat and a newsreader's voice that confirmed poor Lorna was now tragic Lorna. They'd found her body. And suddenly my papers looked like tatty old rags with their smiling photographs of the still alive schoolgirl. There was no point reading any more about hope. The hope had gone and the news had moved on.

I knew at once what I needed to do. There was no question about it. I had to go and see things for myself. It meant taking the train, of course, with its noise and chaos and all those people. But there was no other way. All I had to find out were the times of the trains, but that wasn't a problem. I had a timetable somewhere. I wasn't sure where exactly, but it was somewhere. Everything was somewhere.

CHAPTER TWO

It took me much longer to get there than I expected. The information on my timetable was out of date. The 11.28 no longer ran. The 11.28 was now the 11.54. That meant an extra twenty-six minutes of waiting, so my mind started to wander. It was the usual thing. I worried that I'd forgotten to lock the front door. Should I go back and check? And while I was there, make sure that the video was working properly? I'd left in a hurry so I might not have pressed the record button. I couldn't remember. I'd been distracted, hadn't I? I'd spent too long looking for the timetable and then my favourite black and yellow scarf and that had got me flustered. I couldn't very well leave home without either. I found them both eventually, but all that searching had cost me time and I'd lost concentration.

So I paced up and down the platform and agonised over my options as each second ticked by on the clock. If I went home, I'd miss the 11.54, because twenty-six, or now twenty minutes, was nowhere near long enough to do all the necessary checks and then return. I'd be hard pressed to make the 12.21. And of course there was no guarantee I wouldn't find myself back on the platform feeling exactly the same as I did now. I'd learned that before, to my cost. So instead of going home I tried to visualise locking the door behind me. That was a technique I'd seen on television. Unfortunately, when I closed my eyes all I could see was somebody on the doorstep about to enter my house. And what would the neighbours be doing while I was being broken into? Helping themselves to my possessions, most likely. Just like they took things from my front garden. Or they might be having a good snoop around my unprotected house.

To try and distract myself from this awful prospect I went off in search of some up-to-date timetables. I found them in a plastic holder near the ticket office, under the banner of a new service provider. The times all tallied with the digital display – 11.21, 11.54, 12.21 (slow service), 12.54. So I took two new timetables and after some deliberation dropped the old one into a bin. I told myself there was no point keeping it, but it still upset me and I tried hard to look away as I let it go. It's best that way. If I peeked in the bin and the timetable caught my eye there was always a chance I might be overcome with an urge to fish it out again.

Eighteen minutes later I was standing in a corridor, shaking backwards and forwards. Occasionally the train would squeal and break, and me and my fellow passengers would slam into one another like skittles. Some of them seemed to regard it with amusement, but I didn't. I don't enjoy being pressed against people, squashed and squeezed and unable to escape. It was stuffy in the corridor too, and awkward standing by the toilet, which whooshed and hissed as people went in and out. A man to my left, standing next to the carriage door, said that for the price of his ticket he could have bought two decent seats at the theatre, with first-class entertainment as well as comfort. Then he said it was a shame the doors no longer had windows which opened, and he launched a tirade against the safety-first culture that had deprived us all of fresh air. Like everyone else, I looked away. I was in no mood to talk to people. In any case, I most certainly had no desire for a window. I never liked the old doors with their opening windows. Those windows had meant temptation and risk. After all, what had there been to stop me or anyone else reaching through and unfastening the door as the train thundered along the tracks? Or pulling it down all the way and leaning outside, just to see what it felt like, knowing that at any second the gale-force wind could become the sudden impact of a bridge or a passing train? Apart from my common sense, there'd been nothing to stop me at all. That's why I prefer trains the way they are now. They might be a little unpleasant and lacking in home comforts – but at least they're safe.

The passengers thinned out after an hour or so and I found myself a seat. Every now and then I kept thinking about my video and how it might not be recording the news. Assuming my house was still safe, that is. Even if I hadn't suffered the misfortune of a power cut there was always the possibility that the tape had jammed. It had happened to me before. It looked like the machine had vomited a ribbon of crinkled black tape onto the floor.

I find travelling long distances very stressful although it is sometimes necessary. As well as all the things I've got to worry about at home, every single second I spend travelling is like being in an information desert, deprived of access to television. Because the news never stands still, even when you can't see or hear it. By now they might have arrested a suspect. Perhaps the quiet father with the parched throat. Or the neighbour who'd been so eager to help. There was one of those after Shannon Armitage had been killed. The press got very interested, but he was never charged by the police. Nobody was.

If the train journey was cramped, the ride from the station was equally uncomfortable. But as the bus bounced its way along the rutted A-road I felt pride at my foresight. I'd had the good sense to write down names and places before I'd set out, hadn't I? Not everybody would have thought of that. It was a good job I wasn't impetuous. Just imagine if I'd charged out of the front door without doing my homework. How would I have had any idea where to go? An impetuous man would have been forced to ask awkward questions. *Which bus do I catch to the murder site please? Where Lorna Coulson was found. That's right – Tragic Murdered Lorna.'* It wouldn't do to say that. Not around here.

The site in question was a patch of waste ground a few miles out of town. It was all that remained of a long abandoned plan to build a business park or some such. Left-over concrete bags had turned to rocks, while shrubs and weeds had spotted their chance and colonised the wasted tarmac. I'd seen far too many places like that before, on TV, on my journeys, or staring through the windows of passing vehicles. It was the kind of spot where people dumped old mattresses, or murdered teenagers. A small mound of cellophane-wrapped flowers, some messages and a few stuffed toys lay heaped by a hedge at the roadside. I walked past without reading any of them. As I crossed the pockmarked ground, I spotted an upturned plastic tray that had once been used for carrying loaves of bread and wondered why it had been thrown away. People still need bread, don't they? If I'd been nearer home, or owned a car, I might well have taken the tray for myself. It would have been the perfect thing to store my books in – the ones in the garden that still needed sorting. But I continued past it.

A small crowd of perhaps a dozen adults were huddled together some distance from the parked vehicles. As I approached I could see they were respectfully standing behind the barrier of police tape. Beyond the crowd, and the thin blue and white line, the ground sloped away to a wooded ditch which had been partially cleared. A few uniformed policemen were combing the area. Some plain-clothes officers and people in lab-coats were engaged in conversation near the customary white tent. So that's where Tragic Lorna had come to rest, I thought. I presumed she was no longer inside but had been wrapped up in plastic to preserve her dignity. They never let someone like me see the body, of course. Only murderers and forensic scientists and people walking their dogs at odd times of day ever got to see the actual body. It reminded me of the place where Pauline Furber's body had been found. How could it not remind me? That site had been my first one, after all. They'd called Pauline a Tragic as well. Not like Siobhan. Siobhan had been just as Tragic as Pauline. Perhaps more so. Not that the press had called her that. Siobhan hadn't even merited an adjective. They'd found her, printed her story and forgotten her just as quickly. I hadn't forgotten her though. I'd never forget. I had a brooch as a reminder.

I took my place in the huddle without any acknowledgement from the others. I'd have been surprised if they had done. Chatter is disrespectful and respect is why we'd all made the pilgrimage. We can show our consideration by our presence alone. So I stood amongst them for three-quarters of an hour, while we watched the goings-on down below or stared at the white cloth tent. It was an odd crowd. Who knew where any of them had come from? There was a couple with a flask of tea and matching wellingtons; a man with a cloth cap; a middle-aged man who munched quietly on some foil-wrapped sandwiches; an elderly woman with two small dogs that got tangled up in one another's leads; a man of indeterminate age with a neatly trimmed ginger moustache. There was also a young woman who couldn't keep still and spent the time pushing a child's pram backwards and forwards. Some of them I'd seen before, others were unfamiliar.

After an hour a bald-headed man emerged from the tent and began clambering up the rough slope.

'That's the DI,' somebody said.

I recognised him as the same police officer who'd conducted the press conference. He'll have seen the body, I thought. I watched the man negotiate the tape and clean something from his shoes. I was so busy looking at him I didn't notice the young uniformed officer who approached us.

'Can you all stand back please?' he said. 'Keep back behind the line.'

I shuffled away from the edge, together with Sandwiches, Ginger Whiskers, Cloth Cap, the Flask pair, Miss Two Dogs and most of the others. But one woman held her ground and continued peering down the bank. She wore a black woollen cap, which was pulled tight over her head. Some wispy blonde hair poked out from underneath it.

'Miss?'

'We're not doing anything wrong,' she said.

'We just need you to keep back,' repeated the constable.

He walked towards her.

'It's all so upside down though isn't it?' She turned towards some of the other observers before staring at me, though I looked away. 'Isn't it?'

But the others said nothing. I said nothing.

'A girl's been murdered and what are you doing to help?' She implored the constable now, who kept silent.

A female officer in plain clothes came over to them.

'Are you having trouble, Constable?'

She had short dark hair and pierced ears. She stood close to me and faced the young officer across the blue and white divide.

'No, ma'am. It's just they were taking a little time to move away.'

They? I thought. I'd done as I was told. Stepped two paces back, clear behind the tape. I wasn't the guilty party.

'Anyone would think it was us who were the criminals,' said the woman.

I looked at her. She was weather-beaten beneath her tattered hat. And I could tell she was angry; very angry. At first glance she looked to be about Susan's age, then I could see she was closer to forty. I thought for a second she might be the *Grieving Mother of Tragic Lorna*, but then I recalled the press conference and the woman who spoke with quiet dignity about her missing daughter. This wasn't her. An aunt then? But whoever she was, why was she behaving like that? It made me feel very uncomfortable.

'I've a good idea to report him for harassment,' said the woman.

She pointed at the young constable.

'He's just trying to do his job,' said the plain-clothes officer.

'What's his name?'

'I'm Detective Sergeant Wyatt.' She turned to the others. 'Can you all move further back please? There really isn't anything to see.'

I took a few more steps back but I noticed that once again the woman with the woollen hat did not. It made me wince when I looked at her. Why did she want to upset the police? It didn't make sense.

'You've no right to do this,' she protested. 'We're behind your precious tape, aren't we? And this is common land.'

Once again she implored us. I forgot to look away and met her gaze.

'There's a police investigation going on,' said Wyatt. 'I was hoping you might understand.'

'But can't we pay our respects?'

Some distance away a car started.

'Did you know Lorna Coulson?' asked Wyatt. 'Any of you?'

I could hear the car behind me.

'Not personally,' said the woman. 'But she was known by God.'

Wyatt acknowledged the car, looked right past me and smiled.

'I saw that,' said the woman. 'You're making fun of me. But God does see everything whether you think it's funny or not. And there will be judgement in heaven you know. For all of us.'

She reached down to the rucksack which lay at her feet. The young constable took a step towards her, stumbling slightly down the bank.

'Don't do anything you'll regret,' he said as he slipped.

But before he could add another word the woman had pulled a bunch of white carnations from her bag, which she flung one by one beyond the police tape. She muttered to herself as she did so.

Wyatt walked slowly towards the car.

'I'm not contaminating your precious site, I hope.'

'It's a free country,' said the detective sergeant. She raised a hand in the direction of the police constable, who was kneeling by the nearest of the flowers. He dropped the one he held in his hand.

A police siren sounded and Ginger Whiskers, Pram Girl, Miss Two Dogs and all the others scuttled away like rats. The woman, her work presumably done, collected her bag and left. I stayed behind. I wasn't going to leave until I'd found a little souvenir to take home with me. So I crouched down and pretended to look at the scattered flowers, hoping that I'd find something. I trusted that no-one was looking at me. If they'd known what I was doing they wouldn't have liked it at all. But if they did see me, nobody said a word. There was a strange-coloured stone I could have picked up. I've done that in the past. They don't make for attractive mementoes, but having some sort of reminder is the important thing. And I was about to make do with the stone when I caught sight of something glinting in the weeds, just beyond the boundary of the tape. My heart skipped a beat thinking it might be an ear-ring or an item of jewellery, but when I saw exactly what it was it almost made me faint. It was a neatly folded sheet of foil-backed paper, no doubt containing a discarded piece of chewing gum. I tried to act as normally as I could, even though I didn't feel normal at all. I felt light-headed and sick and with good reason. Because I'd found a piece of foil-wrapped chewing gum six months ago at the spot where Shannon Armitage was murdered.

CHAPTER THREE

The house was safe.

'A forty-three-year-old man has been remanded in police custody this evening.'

There'd been no break in; no power cuts; no pile of crinkled black tape.

'Held in connection with the murder of missing schoolgirl Lorna Coulson.'

The video recorder had worked perfectly. By the fifth time of watching I knew the words of the news report off by heart.

'Police refused to confirm the man's identity as David James Coulson, the dead girl's father.'

It was him though. I felt quite certain about that. It couldn't have been anybody else. Lorna's father was forty-three, the *Telegraph* and the *Mirror* had both said so. David James Coulson, forty-three. The fact that they didn't call him Mr Coulson and referred to him by his full name indicated that he was a suspect. They only ever did that when someone was in trouble.

'The suspect is currently being held at an undisclosed location for further questioning.'

An undisclosed location. I knew that meant the police station, but that they didn't want to say which one. I watched the tape back, again and again, always being careful to check each time that a fresh news bulletin hadn't started.

'All the police will say is that he's a local man who was known to the deceased.'

He'd done it before as well. The chewing gum I'd found was proof.

The six o'clock bulletin confirmed my suspicions. The arrested man was named as David James Coulson, father of Lorna and a planning officer for the local council.

He'd have known where to go. When it came to killing his daughter and disposing of her body, a planning officer would be aware of all the disused plots of land and waste ground that were awaiting redevelopment. It made me shudder to think of it. What could make someone do such a terrible thing? I'd seen the site. It was no place for anyone to have spent the last moments of their life – least of all while suffering at the hands of their father. So it was good to think I had something to keep Lorna Coulson's memory alive.

The newsreader gave a warning about flash photography before footage appeared showing David James Coulson under a blanket, being escorted into a police van. And then the vehicle was driven away at top speed, lights flashing, past the photographers and a small crowd of people, who suddenly rushed forward and tried to beat their hands on the side.

And that was when I saw her. I played back the tape just to make certain, but there was no mistake. It was the woman I'd seen near the murder site – the one who'd thrown the white carnations and caused trouble. She was at the front of the mob rushing forward, yelling something as she flung herself at the speeding van. She stumbled as she did so and fell to the ground. What might she have done to David James Coulson, I wondered? Would she and the others have torn him limb from limb? It was frightening to see.

There was a noise from the back garden. I paused the tape. The image of the speeding police van jerked and flickered on the screen. Someone yelled, and then I heard the cracking of a pane of glass.

'Hello,' I called out. I hoped that the sound of my voice would be enough to frighten people away. 'Who is it?'

But I knew exactly who it was. It was those boys again. Only more brazen than the last time.

'Hello?'

I heard one of them laugh as more glass shattered. I had several sheets of glass in the back garden. Most of them were propped against an upturned bath. I'd gathered them from a skip when the house down the road had had their windows done. I'd never be able to use them for anything now.

I clambered past a pile of things and struggled towards the back door.

'Go away,' I called out while I fumbled for the key. 'You've no right to be on my property.'

Another sheet of glass splintered, and I could hear laughing and cheering. Was it the paper-boy and his friend? The one I'd confronted? I couldn't take the law into my own hands – not after what happened last time. Still, I ought to say something. But what if there weren't just two of them? And supposing they stopped throwing stones at the glass and turned on me instead?

I tugged at the stiff door which finally yielded. But no sooner had I stepped outside than the boys melted away, scrambling over the wall, jeering and calling me names. It didn't need an examination of the windows to confirm my suspicions. Almost all of the sheets had been destroyed. What a waste of good glass, I thought. Perhaps I ought to have a word with the boy's father. In the meantime, it might be worth checking to see what other damage they'd done.

There was a banging at the front of the house. I jumped at the sudden noise. The boys must have rushed round to attack the windows there. The stocktaking would have to wait. I hurried back through the kitchen door, shoved it roughly behind me, and squeezed my way to the front. I could see at once from the outline it wasn't the boys. It was a man of some size.

'Hello?' I called through the frosted pane.

'Take away any rubbish sir,' came the reply. 'House clearance.'

'There's no rubbish,' I said.

'In the garden sir.'

'No thank you.'

'It's no trouble sir.'

'It's not rubbish. Please leave it alone.'

o0o

The news next morning was little different. David James Coulson was still being questioned by police. By Detective Sergeant Wyatt, I presumed. And the other one – Detective Inspector Hillyard. I didn't much care for the look of him. He seemed like one of those old-fashioned policemen, the kind who got results but didn't much care how they went about it. I dreaded to think what would happen if I should end up on the wrong side of DI Hillyard. I'd probably confess to anything.

The *Mirror* carried a lot of quotes from Hillyard, as well as a couple from DS Wyatt and a profile of David James Coulson. The focus was still on Lorna. There was no mention of Shannon Armitage anywhere. None of them seemed to know what I knew, that David James Coulson had thrown away chewing gum as he disposed of the girls' bodies. I took a sip of tea while I read, but soon abandoned it. Powdered milk is no substitute for the real thing. But the shops had been shut when I'd got back from the murder site, and in the summer heat the milk had turned in my absence. I'd tipped the curdled remains into the sink and the smell of rancid milk still filled the kitchen. It wasn't particularly nice but I knew well enough that the smell would pass eventually, smothered by something else. Sour milk is always a risk at this time of year, especially as I haven't got the hang of my new fridge yet. Why are fridges so complicated now? They never used to be. I'd be tempted to get rid of this new fridge once I've got my old one repaired. In the meantime though it stood outside the back door, mould flecked and battered by the elements.

I started reading the *Telegraph* but I'd hardly got anywhere when I was disturbed by a gentle tapping at the front door. I tensed. It was the boys again, wasn't it? Not content with invading my back garden they were now assaulting me from the front. They used to enjoy pressing my buzzer when I had a doorbell. And they pressed it and pressed it until the batteries gave up the ghost and it made a feeble noise from behind a pile of bags. After that I refused to replace the dead batteries. I'm no fool. That would only invite them to do the same thing all over again. There was another knock. I wanted to call out – to tell them I wasn't at home. But I knew they'd only make fun of me if I said anything like that. The knocking carried on.

'Leave me alone,' I called out.

Would they smash the windows like they'd smashed those spare sheets of glass at the back?

'Mr Henry?'

A voice now. It didn't sound like the boys but you could never tell.

'Go away,' I said.

'Mr Henry?'

'I don't want anything cleared away.'

'I need to talk to you Mr Henry.'

It was a man's voice. Now that I listened I could hear that he wasn't the same man I'd just sent away. I crept out of the kitchen, stood behind a stack of boxes and craned my neck towards the front door.

'Who are you?' I said.

No reply.

'Who's there?'

'Mr Henry?' Two eyes then a mouth appeared at the letter box. 'Stephen Shields, Environmental Health.'

'No,' I said.

'I do need to speak to you Mr Henry,' said Mr Shields from Environmental Health. 'I'd prefer not to do it like this.'

'I can't now,' I said. 'I'm in the middle of something.'

'I can wait,' said the voice at the letterbox. 'My next appointment's not till eleven.'

The news came on at eleven.

'No,' I said.

'It won't take any time Mr Henry. You have my word on that.'

Things always took time, I thought. How many people had come to the front door promising they wouldn't take up my time?

'Are you getting the best deal from your gas supplier?' 'Are you paying too much for your electricity?' 'How do you feel about your current phone provider?' 'Can you answer a few questions for us?' 'It'll only take a few minutes.'

That's what they always said, time after time.

'No,' I said again from behind a box full of old shoes and cleaning products.

'I can make it a little later if you're busy. Shall we say half eleven?'

'People won't leave me alone,' I said.

'That's why I'm here Mr Henry.' The mouth returned to the letterbox. 'I can help.'

'I don't need your sort of help.'

I came out from behind my box and stood in the hallway, wedged in the space between the staircase and a mound of stuffed bags.

'I'm not here to cause problems Mr Henry. Quite the opposite.'

'What do you want then?' I said.

'I need to talk to you.'

The letterbox flapped open again and a plastic identification card dangled through.

'I shouldn't really do this,' said the man from Environmental Health. 'Somebody pulled at it once and I smashed my head against their front door.'

'Oh dear,' I said. 'Why would anyone do a thing like that?'

'You get some very odd people Mr Henry.' He removed the card. 'So would you mind opening the door for me, just for a minute?'

'I can't. Perhaps in a few days. When I've sorted some things out.'

'Well we do have people who can help you with that Mr Henry. Properly trained people.'

'No.' I could hear the music coming from the kitchen.

'Mr Henry.'

'It's the news,' I said and went back to my little den. Sitting down was a difficult manoeuvre and as I lowered myself my arm caught the cup, spilling lukewarm tea all over my trousers.

'Now look what you've made me do,' I muttered.

There was another knock at the door, louder this time.

'Mr Henry.'

'Go away,' I shouted.

It felt like something was happening in the Lorna Coulson case. The suspect who'd been arrested was still being questioned said DS Wyatt. But significant leads were being pursued. Perhaps that meant Shannon

Armitage. I liked Wyatt. She certainly didn't look as stern as her superior.

'Significant leads were being pursued.'

That meant the police were just wrapping up the loose ends and Lorna's father would be charged with her murder soon. Perhaps even in time for the one o'clock news. That's what had happened with Colin Bianchi. The police had talked about significant leads and in a matter of hours his uncle had been charged. I had a small toy I'd recovered from the burnt out remains. Whenever I saw the little helicopter I always thought of Colin.

I needed to get a fresh videotape in time for the next news. The current one only had about ninety minutes of recording time left. The woman with the woollen hat might be there as well, standing outside the police station. I wouldn't want to miss that.

When the news turned to foreign affairs I stood up. My legs were soaked with cold tea and it was uncomfortable, so I thought I'd change my trousers. I had another pair upstairs. The wet fabric stuck to my skin as I wriggled through the gap in the hallway.

'Mr Henry.'

I stopped. I couldn't see any shape behind the frosted glass in the front door. But I knew I hadn't imagined the voice.

'Mr Henry?'

'Are you still there?' I called back.

There was no answer.

'Please go away,' I said.

'I can see you like Dan Brown.'

I felt a tightness in my chest. I remembered I hadn't taken my capsules.

'You've got three copies of the *Da Vinci Code*.'

'Leave my books alone.'

My heart was thumping now. This was worse than the children in my back garden.

'It can't be doing them any good being out here – open to the sun and the rain. And what's going to happen in winter? The snow's going to ruin them. Mind you, we normally just get freezing cold rain, don't we?'

I opened the front door. A young man, perhaps in his early twenties, was bent over a box of paperback books.

'I'm getting a tarpaulin,' I said.

'That's only a temporary solution though.'

'Until I've got time to sort them out.'

'My mistake – four *Da Vinci Codes*.'

'Why can't you leave me alone?' I asked. 'You wouldn't like it if I interfered with your things.'

'I'm not here to interfere Mr Henry, but I'm afraid a complaint has been made and we're duty bound to investigate it.'

'It's the neighbours isn't it?' I thought about the paperboy's father – the one with the tattoo on his neck and the crossed daggers on his forearm. I looked out at the street and the nearby houses.

'I'm not obliged to say at this stage who raised the complaint Mr Henry. I'm sure you understand that.'

'It isn't fair you know.'

The man from Environmental Health ran his finger along the books.

'They don't respect my property. The local kids come into my back garden and mess about with my things. I had some glass smashed this morning. I don't suppose they told you that, did they? I'm a prisoner in my own home.'

'I'm not here to take sides Mr Henry.'

'Running over everything like rats.'

'Some people are concerned about the health aspects.'

'Well that's rubbish for a start,' I said. 'What health aspects? There's nothing unhealthy about books, is there?'

'Not everyone wants a pile of books and – things – outside their house.'

'It's not outside anyone's house is it? It's outside mine. Now if you've finished will you go away please, I'm very busy.'

I went back inside and closed the door behind me.

'We can't leave it like this I'm afraid Mr Henry,' said Stephen Shields from Environmental Health. 'I'd rather we didn't invoke the statutory powers, but if you fail to reduce the accumulation then we'll have to. What you choose to do inside your own home is your business of course, but once it spills outside then it can affect the lives of others. That's when we sometimes have to take action.'

'It's not affecting anyone's life,' I said.

'When people don't co-operate.'

'Are you finished?' I said. I could feel my pulse starting to race. This wasn't what Dr Singh had recommended for my health. 'You want me to throw all my things away, don't you? Is that what people want?'

'You don't need all these books.'

'How do you know what I need?'

'And this clothes rack. Shouldn't it be indoors?'

'Leave it alone.' I opened the door.

'It's going rusty though, look.'

'It only needs a good clean,' I said. 'I thought you said you weren't here to take sides.'

'I'm not.'

'And what about my rights, eh? What about them?'

'Here's a thought Mr Henry. When you've done what it is you have to do, why don't you have a little sort through all these books? Start with them. Take the ones inside you want to keep and sell off all the rest in a car boot sale.'

'A car boot sale?'

'You sell unwanted items from the back of a car. They have one in the school playing fields every Sunday morning.'

'I know what a car boot sale is. And I haven't got a car.'

'You don't really need a car.'

'And they're not unwanted items.'

'Or a yard sale. Twenty pence each – help yourself.'

He ticked a couple of boxes on his form and thrust a copy of it towards me.

'I don't want it,' I said and folded my arms.

'Have a think about it.'

'No.'

'I'll be back in a week or so,' said the man from Environmental Health and posted the document through the letterbox.

CHAPTER FOUR

They'd let him go. I could hardly believe it when I watched the news that evening. David James Coulson, the father of Tragic Lorna, had been released by the police without charge. I ate my dinner without taking my eyes from the screen, scooping the cold beans and sausages straight from the tin. The forty-three-year-old former father of two stood outside the police station, his arm clasped around the waist of his wife. Mrs Coulson was in tears. It had been a harrowing time for his family, Mr Coulson declared, and none of them would rest until the killer or killers of his daughter had been brought to justice. He declined to answer any questions and the couple stepped into a waiting car, which had the name of a well known tabloid newspaper on the side. A few cameras flashed, but this time there weren't any screams or thumping fists, and no sign of the woman with the woollen hat.

There were some other news stories that didn't hold my attention – a cricket match, a bank in trouble and a royal visit. But the final item most certainly moved me. A terrible tragedy had happened in Scotland. A small boy had been swept out to sea by a freak wave while walking with his parents. The coastguards hadn't yet called off their search but the tone of the report was clear enough. There was no hope of finding little Graham Dawes alive. As I watched the young couple describe the last moments they saw their five-year-old son, I had tears in my eyes. Life can be so unfair.

It was a long way to go to Scotland and it wouldn't be an easy journey at all. But I'd have to go. I couldn't turn my back on little Graham Dawes. I needed to see the place for myself. But more than that, I needed to bring something back, some memento however small, to make sure that the boy was never forgotten.

A trip to Scotland posed all sorts of problems. The travelling arrangements were difficult enough, but that wasn't the only consideration. There was also the video recorder to think about. Even a fresh video tape in long-playing mode only allows for a maximum eight hours recording time. And it isn't possible for a second tape to start automatically when the first one ends, at least not as far as I'm aware. It most probably requires two video recorders. I do own two, but only one of them actually works. Jamal might know how to do it of course, but there wasn't time to call him now. I'd just have to leave things as they are this time. It would make for an agonising journey, made worse by the realisation that back at home, just after five o'clock, the tape would suddenly stop recording and start winding itself backwards. After that there'd be nothing. No recording of the six o'clock news, or the bulletin at seven. So I could end up missing a crucial development. After all, there was a double-murderer on the loose now. A gum-chewing double-murderer. I found myself sweating at the thought of all that unrecorded news. I just had to hope nothing critical would happen in that time, or that if it did they'd repeat it at ten o'clock or even later. I'd be home by then. I consoled myself with the thought that my mission was more important than tapes of the day's news. The news kept changing – what I brought home I'd keep forever.

The tide was out when I reached my destination. The sea looked benign, and the beach was much like any other. How different it must have been yesterday, when the waves had crashed over the salt-rusted barriers. They were selling ice cream on the sea-front now as if nothing had happened, and holiday-makers were laughing. How quickly everything returned to normal. It's often that way though. People don't like to be reminded of the dark things. Especially not in a place where they've come to have fun.

I walked up and down the beach, looking for something appropriate that I could take back in memory of little Graham. It took longer than I'd anticipated but eventually I found a pale blue ball, punctured and sand-worn. Had it belonged to him? I didn't think it very likely. I suspected from its appearance that it had been scuffed by countless tides, not to mention the weather. But it was here, so it had been a witness of sorts, tossed about in the same sea that had claimed the boy's life. I'd label it and put it away for safe-keeping when I got home.

But when I did get back I found that things had gone from bad to worse. The late news, the one I had been able to videotape, was now reporting that another girl had been murdered. What was more, her body had been found in woods just a few miles from my home. As yet, she hadn't been named. The police were so far refusing to link her death with the still unsolved murder of Lorna Coulson. The Coulsons, it was reported, had gone to Barcelona for a break. Anyone who still doubted Mr Coulson's innocence would be reassured by the news that he was in another country when the latest murder took place.

Of course another murder meant another journey, although this time I didn't need a map or a railway timetable. The location was a place called

Parson's Wood, no more than a couple of miles from my house. It was strange seeing it on television, even if only briefly. I hadn't been to Parson's Wood in a long time, not since I was a small boy when I'd gone with my mother and Susan. We'd had a picnic there and eaten jam sandwiches and I'd been frightened of the wasps. And Mother had told me not to move because the wasps didn't really want to hurt me. I just had to sit very still and that way the wasps wouldn't get annoyed. So I'd sat like a statue and before very long the wasps lost interest and flew away. I'd wanted to know why they'd come, but Mother hadn't really been able to say. All I can recall is her telling me that everything had a purpose, even if it wasn't always clear what that purpose was.

The fifty-three bus and then the eight took me there. But even before I'd reached the wood I could see the police presence. Two vans were parked at angles to the road, their blue lights flashing out of synch. Across the road, near the houses, were a couple of unmarked vehicles. Some uniformed policemen stood by the main gates. I crossed the road before I reached them. The police weren't going to allow me into the wood and I wasn't about to ask their permission.

A sizeable crowd had gathered. I only noticed them when I passed the first and larger of the vans so I was quite startled when I saw the two small dogs snapping and whining on their lead. Their elderly owner didn't seem to notice them and she certainly didn't notice me. When I looked further I could see a few more of the characters I'd encountered at Lorna's murder site. There was no sign of the young mother and her pram, but the tea-drinking couple were there – as was the gentleman with the ginger moustache and the man who'd been eating sandwiches. He looked at me briefly as I mounted the kerb and joined the crowd.

'Morning,' he said.

'Morning,' I replied.

The man then unwrapped some sandwiches and began eating. I was glad he did. I wouldn't have known what to say to him if he'd said any more.

I scanned the rest of the crowd for a sign of DI Hillyard or DS Wyatt but I couldn't spot them. It was still early days though. They might not have been put in charge of this case yet, with Lorna's murder still unsolved. It might not be connected anyway. The man standing next to me finished his second sandwich, crumpled up the tin foil and stuffed it in his pocket. And then I heard a voice I recognised.

'You're not being reasonable. Some of us want to lay some flowers near the site.'

It was the woman I'd seen before. The one who'd thrown the white carnations, and who'd fallen to the ground as she'd pummelled her fists on the van.

'Why can't we do that?'

I could see her now. She was wearing the same black woollen hat, and the same anguished expression.

'The poor girl was murdered over there, not here. This is someone's house. We can't leave them here, can we?'

'Shame,' I heard someone call out.

Sandwiches said nothing.

The woman's next words were drowned out by the wail of sirens. Two cars parked by the gate and a couple of plain clothes officers that I didn't recognise got out. They passed through the police cordon and disappeared into the depths of the wood without acknowledging the crowd of people opposite. There'd be a tent in there now, I thought. A big white tent. It might even be near the spot where we'd had our picnic. I remembered that Mother had made me wear a floppy hat and that Susan's pushchair had been angled into the shade to stop her getting burnt. I hadn't thought about that day in years. It was funny how it had taken a murder to bring it all back.

There was no chance of getting close to the spot now, so I turned around and left. I'd seen all I could. If I wanted to collect a souvenir I'd have to come back another day when things had quietened down.

o0o

The morning news report didn't leave any room for doubt. There were striking similarities with the Lorna Coulson case, the police spokeswoman said. She refused to divulge any details but suggested it was unlikely that two murderers had employed such similar methods. I squirmed as I watched and the bulging cardboard box pressed uncomfortably against my hip. I ought to rearrange the contents when I'd got a free moment. Shift that pressure cooker so the handle pointed the other way, and replace the cushion I was sitting on. It was still damp from yesterday's tea.

The victim was named as Tabitha Williams, a seventeen-year-old girl who lived locally. I studied her picture, but it wasn't a face or a name I recognised. But then again, I hardly knew anybody. I only knew the Peakes were the family next door because their post was occasionally delivered to my house by mistake. Perhaps Tabitha's killer was a local man too, I thought. It might have been someone I'd passed in the street, or stood next to at the murder site. Killers often returned to the scene of their crimes, or so they reckoned. It might have been the tall man with the beard who rocked backwards and forwards on his heels, or the dark-skinned youth with the leaflets in his hand. Or maybe it was Ginger Whiskers or Sandwiches. It was possible the old lady had come with her two dogs to taunt the police. She didn't look much like a murderer, but that was the perfect disguise, wasn't it? She was almost the last person anyone would

24

suspect.

'Parson's Wood, a spot popular with local dog walkers, was sealed off as police combed the area for clues.'

I stared in disbelief at the images, which took a few moments to register. But I wasn't mistaken. The strange looking figure in the ten second news-clip, the one staring across the road as the police cars arrived, was me.

There was a knocking at the door. My heart began thumping twice as fast.

'Go away,' I mumbled.

The news item had ended. I stopped the recording and wound back the tape. I had to watch the last part of it again. I scrunched forward on the soggy cushion. It was definitely me, there was no doubt about it. I was standing next to Sandwiches. Sandwiches wasn't actually eating his sandwiches, but it was definitely him as well. The dark-skinned youth was busy giving out sheets of paper. He looked vaguely familiar but I couldn't quite place him. I played the tape again, and then again after that. I'd never seen myself on television before. I made a mental note to try and remember where I kept the sticky labels. The tape deserved to be marked as special.

There was another knock at the door. I jumped.

'Go away,' I shouted. 'Why can't you leave me alone.'

'Henry, it's me.'

'Susan?'

I struggled to my feet. I was at the kitchen door when I realised that the tape was still running, so I went back and stopped it playing. Then I ran the tape along to the end of the news item and resumed recording. The story could move on at any minute and I couldn't afford to miss any new developments.

'Henry!'

'I'm coming.'

When I opened the door she had her phone in one hand. The bag of clothes was at her feet. A few strands of hair were stuck to her cheek.

'What were you doing?' she asked.

'Nothing,' I said.

'Didn't you hear me just now?'

'No.'

'I was knocking for ages.'

'It's hard to hear out at the back.'

'But you were listening out for me? I mean you did know it was Thursday?'

'Of course.'

'And it's not as if I have all the time in the world.'

She fiddled about with her mobile phone.

'I know.'

'Well get a move on then.'

'I'll only be a second.'

'Henry!'

'I just need to check something first,' I said and went back to the kitchen.

'Where's the bag?' she called after me.

I looked at the videotape. I could see from the display it still had a good three and a half hours of recording time left. There was no reason to panic and worry that I'd run out again. With luck I'd be back from Susan's in a couple of hours.

'Henry?'

When I re-emerged Susan was still standing in the doorway.

'What were you doing?' she asked.

'Nothing,' I said.

'And where are your things?'

'Oh – upstairs.'

'You do this on purpose, don't you?' she said as I slipped past and picked my way up the stairs.

At the top I squeezed into the space where my mattress is. I paused for breath then hauled down a half filled laundry bag that lay on top of a cardboard box. I grabbed a couple of items of clothing from the floor, stuffed them into the bag and backed out of the room.

'Is that all?' asked Susan. 'Only it doesn't look like much for a week. Any bedding?'

'It's fine,' I said. I slipped on a loose piece of paper and almost lost my balance.

'It must be filthy. I don't suppose you've changed it since last time. Three weeks it must be now.'

'I said it was fine.'

'Suit yourself.' She walked to the car.

Once I was completely certain the video was still recording and the front door had been properly secured I followed her out. I dumped my laundry basket on the back seat. The catch failed to engage when I shut the door behind me.

'You'll need to give it a good slam,' she said.

'Father used to always say that damaged the doors,' I said.

'Father said a lot of things,' said Susan and started the car.

We didn't talk much for a few minutes. Susan occasionally swore at the traffic, but that was about all. Then I had a sudden panic.

'What's the right time?' I asked.

'Five-to-twelve,' she replied.

'Can we have the radio on?'

'No.'

'Only the news will be on in a minute.'

'It's broken.'

'Oh.'

'We could always talk. You haven't asked me about Christopher.'

'Haven't I?'

'No.'

'How is he?'

'He's fine.'

'Good.'

'He's taken up taekwondo of all things.'

'What's that?' I asked.

'It's a martial art,' said Susan. 'You kick people. I'm tempted to learn it myself.'

'How was his trip to France?' I said.

'He didn't go in the end.'

'Didn't he?'

'No.'

'That's a shame,' I said. 'I'd quite like to go to France. Did he have second thoughts?'

'He didn't. I did. I couldn't afford it.'

'Oh Susan.'

'Don't 'Oh Susan' me, Henry.'

She turned into a narrow suburban street, only to find it was blocked by a supermarket van. Its doors were flung wide open.

'Isn't that just typical?' she said. 'Who gets their groceries delivered at this time of day, anyway?'

She turned and looked at me. The anger was etched into her face.

'What?' she snapped.

'I didn't say anything.'

'Why are you so helpless Henry, eh? Why?'

'I'm not,' I said.

'I can't spend all my time looking after you. God knows I've got enough on my plate.' She drummed her fingers on the steering wheel. 'I haven't got time for this. Not now.' The driver came back a few moments later pushing a pile of empty crates. Susan wound down her window. 'Are you going to be long?' she said. 'Only we can't get past.'

'I'll just be a minute,' said the driver.

'We are in a hurry.'

The driver loaded up his crates, bolted the van doors and drove off. Susan followed closely behind.

'No consideration,' she said.

'So what about Derek?' I said.

'What about him?'

'He could have helped surely.'

Susan said nothing.

'He's working though isn't he?'

'Yes, he's working.'

'Couldn't he have paid then?'

'I suppose so. I didn't ask him.'

'Why not?'

She honked the car horn at an errant driver. 'Did you see that?'

'Susan?'

'What?'

'Why didn't you ask me if you were short of money? You know I'd have helped.'

'I wasn't dropping hints Henry. I don't want your money.'

'It's not my money though is it?' I looked at my sister but her eyes remained fixed on the road. 'It's our money.'

She shook her head. 'It's your money Henry. Father left it to you. If he'd wanted me to have any of it he'd have done something different.'

'I never understood why he did that,' I said.

'There's lots about people we don't understand, isn't there?'

'It doesn't seem fair.'

'Well there you are Henry, life isn't fair. But we'll manage. I'll manage.'

'I know. It's just—'

She held up her hand towards me. 'Let's leave it there, shall we.'

I looked away. We passed a church where the tower clock said twenty-past two and half-past nine.

'What's the time now?' I asked.

'Just gone twelve.'

I felt my skin tingle. I'd forgotten the news. The report would be on now with all the latest developments. Everyone would know all about it except me. I felt uncomfortable at the thought and scratched myself.

'I wish you'd brought the bedding,' said Susan.

'It's fine I told you.'

'You're not sleeping in that kitchen now are you?'

'No.'

'You'd tell me if you were.'

'I'm not.'

'Well make sure you have a proper bath. There's peach shower gel.'

'Can you use that in the bath?'

'I'm sure it won't kill you.'

They'd be analysing the news now in detail. I scratched myself again.

'Have you heard anything?' I asked.

'About what?'

'The murder. Murders.'

'Only what I saw on the news yesterday.'

'Nothing today?'

'No.'

'You know they found her in Parson's Wood,' I said. 'We had a picnic there.'

'A picnic? What, you and me? When?'

'Mother took us.'

'Well how am I supposed to remember that? I'd be what – two?'

'Three.'

'Well then.'

She honked the horn as a car pulled out in front of her.

'You ought to be careful though,' I said. 'I mean he's struck twice now. Assuming it's a he.'

'It's always a 'he' Henry.'

'And here as well.'

'I'm touched by your concern but from what I gather he doesn't seem too interested in middle aged women.'

'He might be.'

'You're meant to say 'You're only thirty-seven Susan, that's not middle aged.''

'Sorry.'

'Forget it.'

o0o

'Keep an eye on the bath Henry,' she said as she came down the stairs. 'Don't let it overflow.'

'I won't,' I said.

'I've put some of the seaweed and birch bath salts in. The one in the coloured bottle.'

'Aren't they Derek's? Won't he mind?'

She smiled at me and picked up her car keys. 'I'll be back in about an hour.'

'Susan?'

'What?'

'Have you got a spare video recorder?'

'A spare one? No, of course not. Why?'

'I just wondered, that's all.'

'Who has a video recorder these days?'

'I do,' I said.

'You would. Has it broken?'

'No no, it's fine.'

She sighed. 'You can't go on like this you know.'

'Like what?'

'Who did you think I was earlier?'

'What do you mean?'

'When you didn't answer the door. You shouted – like you were expecting someone.'

'Did I?'

'Yes.'

'I don't know.'

'Henry?'

'What?'

'Have those kids been messing about again?'

'Yes,' I said.

'And?'

'There was a man from the council.'

Susan raised her eyebrows. 'Environmental health by any chance?'

'How did you know?'

'I'll be back in an hour Henry. Don't use all the hot water, will you?' She gave her arm a gentle scratch. 'Only I'd like to have a shower when I get back.'

CHAPTER FIVE

On the corner where Pangbourne Road meets Somerton Avenue, the water was gushing over a blocked drain. I stepped over it, soaking my feet as I did so. I should have listened to Susan. She was usually right about these things.

'There's something in the air,' she'd said when she dropped me off. 'I can smell it.'

The morning news had been nothing but the weather. Overnight the sticky heat had broken and unleashed a downpour. The rain had hammered on the landing window for most of the night. It had gathered on the sill and forced its way through the cracked pane. From the sound of water, dripping steadily onto plastic, I could tell there was a leak in the bathroom too.

I might not be keen on hot weather, but I like the rain even less. Rain has a way of ruining things. It gets under the polythene sheets and damages my books. It collects in the bottom of storage crates where the slime builds up and in the empty tin cans where the mosquitoes like to lay their eggs. I don't know how many hours I must have spent tipping water away or checking that it can't collect. It's never-ending work.

The only good thing about rain is that it keeps people away. There are no officials or pollsters or people from the gas wanting to sell me electricity. Burglars don't like the rain either. Rain means they get wet and leave footprints behind as evidence. In some ways it's easier to leave the house when it's raining. I don't have to worry so much then about whether I've remembered to lock the front door or if I might be having a break-in. Mind you, this wasn't just rain. This was rain on a biblical scale and didn't only stop burglars in their tracks. When rain was as heavy as this, nobody ventured out at all. It felt like the perfect time to go back to Parson's Wood.

I was soaked to the skin by the time I got there. My raincoat had proved to be useless, and my feet squelched in my shoes. I'd tried waiting for a bus but when the first one went past without stopping and a second one didn't come at all I thought it might be best to walk instead.

This time there weren't any crowds of people. No spectators, no Coloured Flasks, Miss Two Dogs, Sandwiches, cluster of police vehicles or crazy woollen-hatted woman. Even the police officer who'd been standing guard had gone, most likely sheltering somewhere from the rain. The crime-scene tape they'd put all over the railings was torn, and there was none at all on the gate, so I pushed at it and went in.

The wood was nothing like I remembered. It was dark and damp and full of enormous beech trees which shaded out the ground. In my mind's eye I could picture a glorious day with my mother and Susan in her pushchair when there'd been sunshine and grass and wasps. I'd seen the photograph often enough. But this was nothing like that, and it was certainly no place to have a picnic. I began to wonder where we might have been sitting on that day, and whether I'd recognise the spot if I walked past it. Maybe Mother had known what was going to happen, even then. The picnic might have been her way of giving me something to keep forever. I snatched a leaf from a low-hanging branch and immediately got drenched by a shower of drops. I slipped the leaf into my raincoat pocket and told myself I mustn't forget to press it when I got home – along with a little note, just to jog my memory. But leaves make for unsatisfactory souvenirs, because even preserved they decay with time. I thought it would be much better if I could find something more permanent, maybe even an item that had belonged to us. It was highly unlikely after all this time, but it didn't have to be much. People left all manner of traces of themselves behind, without even knowing it. Susan could have dropped a toy from her pushchair that nobody had noticed. Or Mother might have lost a hairgrip. She used to wear hairgrips, I hadn't forgotten that. It was possible anyway. Things could last for ages if they weren't disturbed.

I headed down first one path then another, looking for signs of anything man-made amongst the wispy undergrowth. The lack of landmarks didn't make it easy though. The trees all seemed to have grown considerably in the last three decades. It was only after I'd been walking for some minutes and I caught sight of the white police tent that I remembered the real reason I'd come to Parson's Wood. I abandoned my searching and headed towards it. So that was where Tabitha Williams had been found. I peered at the tent, which had been set up under an enormous beech. The killer couldn't have dragged Tabitha's body here. It was too far from the road. The two of them had either come together, or he'd lain in wait for her.

The blue and white tape brought my journey to a premature end. The tent was some way distant and though I couldn't see inside I sensed it was empty. There was certainly nobody about. Perhaps the tent wasn't waterproof and the forensics team had gone somewhere to find shelter. It seemed the most likely explanation. That would mean there was nobody guarding the murder site. I could have a peek inside a white tent at last and satisfy my curiosity. But going under the tape would mean I was trespassing on a crime scene, wouldn't it? 'Police - Do not cross' – there was no mistaking the message. And the police were the last people I wanted to upset. There was no telling where things might end up if I got on the wrong side of the law.

So instead, I walked alongside the tape, passing around bushes and brambles, keeping my eyes fixed on the white tent. I did wonder where all the police had gone. They couldn't all have been keeping dry somewhere. Of course it was possible they'd packed everything up and gone to a press conference because they were about to announce a major breakthrough. Not that I cared much for that solution. If there was a press conference then I was in the wrong place. I ought to be sitting in front of my television set, watching for every twitch and misplaced sip of water. Instead I was in a wood, getting soaked.

After a few yards, the perimeter took a detour inside a dense clump of holly bushes. I was unable to follow the tape as closely as I'd have liked and I was forced to walk around them. For a few moments I lost sight of the tent, but when I emerged on the other side I saw something else. Sitting on a bench on the far side was the woman, with the same woollen hat pulled tight over her head. I stopped, uncertain about what to do next. Should I continue walking or was it best to turn around and head back in the opposite direction? If I carried on I'd eventually pass her. She'd see me then if she hadn't seen me now. I'd be completely exposed. I noticed that my pulse had quickened and my breathing had become shallow. I tried to control it like Dr Singh had taught me, but it didn't work. This wasn't like sitting in the doctor's surgery. Perhaps it might be best just to head home before anything happened. After all, the woman might speak to me and what would I do then? What would I say? What sort of things did people say to each other?

I stood still for a moment, half hidden by a tree, and stared at her. I wondered what she was doing here in the pouring rain and what made her come to the same places as me. I tried to think logically. If I carried on walking I could try and act casually when I passed the bench and pretend that I'd never seen the woman before. Just because I recognised her didn't mean she had any idea who I was. I could say 'good morning' and walk past. Or better still, I could say nothing at all. And if she did speak to me when I went past I'd just strike up a conversation. That was what people did, they struck up conversations. But the best thing would be if the woman left before I got there. Because I don't really know how to act casually or to pretend something or strike up a conversation.

I was still worrying about what I might say to her when the woman got up from her seat. I watched for a second as she left the path and began walking towards me. And then I panicked. Suddenly I couldn't think about conversations or acting casually. My first and only instinct was to get away. I tried to turn around but my legs went weak and I stumbled and fell to the ground. I scrambled to my feet, desperate to be anywhere but that awful place, and began to walk as briskly as I could manage. Was she gaining on me? I didn't dare turn around to see. I concentrated on the holly bushes just ahead of me. I could bury myself in there and she'd never find me. The leaves might hurt but the suffering would be worth it. So I forced my way into it, wriggled to the floor and waited.

The ground was covered in old leaves and decaying matter and the sharp holly leaves jabbed against my neck. As I crouched down I wondered if I'd been right to run away. It wasn't as if I'd been doing anything wrong. But it would surely seem as though I had done. If the branches parted and the woman stared down at me, well – I'd look like a weirdo, wouldn't I? What would I say? That I'd been enjoying a walk when I'd lost my footing and tripped over? And the more I thought about what I'd done the more foolish I felt, until I realised that the best thing was to stop hiding and stand up and act like an adult. And I was just about to do that when I saw the object on the ground.

It was another piece of chewing gum wrapped in silver paper, almost identical to the one I'd found at the site of Lorna Coulson's murder, and Shannon Armitage's before that. Almost identical – because this one was still soft to the touch, which suggested that not very long ago the gum had been in someone's mouth. I felt light-headed and my skin glistened with sweat. I wanted to scrape the leaf-mould over the thing with my foot, or grind it into the ground. Most of all I wanted to forget that I'd ever seen it. But that was impossible. The realisation that it had been dropped – no, discarded – by the murderer, was terrifying. Even more so was the fact that three young women were dead, three pieces of chewing gum had been thrown alongside them, and somehow I'd found every one.

I wanted to be back at home that second, amongst all my things with the door locked safely behind me. I felt trapped and vulnerable. Instead of sheltering me the bushes now felt like a prison holding me captive.

I knew my life would be in danger if the murderer was aware that I'd picked up the chewing gum. I wouldn't last five minutes. I tried to take a deep breath, but the air seemed thick and I struggled. My chest felt tight, as though my ribs were crushing me. I placed my palm on the wet ground to steady myself. I mustn't faint; not here, not now. I managed a gulp of the damp, musty air and tried to calm myself down. Tabitha Williams had been killed three days ago, hadn't she – the murderer wouldn't still be here. Unless of course the killer was one of those murderers who couldn't resist returning to the scenes of their crimes. Perhaps like Mr and Mrs Flask had done – or Sandwiches or Ginger Whiskers. But then I'd seen the woman too. The woman with the black woollen hat. I shuddered at the realisation.

34

It was her, wasn't it? The gum was fresh, and she was here. All that fuss at tragic Lorna's murder site, and later when she'd banged on the side of the van for the TV cameras. That had just been a diversion. She'd been acting like that to throw everyone off the scent. No wonder the police hadn't worked it out. They'd been thinking rationally. But murderers weren't rational, they didn't behave like normal people.

The killer had used a knife. That was one thing the *Mirror* and the *Telegraph* were both agreed on, though they had kept calling the killer a he. They'd got that wrong, not that it was going to help me now. Because at any second she'd come crashing through the branches, slashing and screaming for all she was worth, and I'd be unable to defend myself. My raincoat hadn't kept out the rain so it wouldn't offer much protection against a kitchen knife. What a fool I'd been. There were no witnesses here, it was perfect. She must have guessed I'd come back so she'd waited for me. And I'd walked straight into her trap. How could I have made such a stupid mistake? Out of everyone – the police, the forensics and all the experts – I was the one who'd managed to solve the murders that were gripping the nation. Me – Henry V. Henry. And now I was going to pay for that knowledge with my life. And when they found my body here, among the mulch, no-one would have the faintest idea what I'd been doing in the bushes. They'd empty out my pockets and look at the leaf and the silver-wrapped chewing gum and throw them away as rubbish. Then they'd put up a white tent and get to work. And the bald detective inspector and the sergeant whose names I couldn't remember would stare at me while the forensics team poked and prodded my skin with their scalpels and things. After that they'd go to the house and throw all my belongings into a skip. I've seen that on TV before so I know it happens. I've got a tape of it somewhere. They'd throw that in the skip as well. And so I tensed myself and prepared for the arrival of the blade.

But the attack never came.

And the longer I waited the more it felt like the woman was toying with me, making me suffer like she had done her other victims. I wanted to cry out 'If you're going to kill me, just get on with it.' But I was too frightened. Just like I'd been when I was locked in the wardrobe. *'Say you're sorry and I'll let you out.'* I'd never forgotten Father's words. And I'd wrapped myself in my scarf and cuddled Mother's jumper. Her scent still clung to it. And I'd cried and hammered on the door and I could hear my little sister crying too. And Father was crying when he opened the door, I remember that. And he said he was sorry. But the very next day the wardrobe had been emptied and Mother's jumper had gone and that had made me cry all over again.

While I was thinking about that time I began to realise that I wasn't frightened any more. Because nothing that might come to pass now could be worse than what had happened back then. So taking as deep a breath as

I could and before I could change my mind, I got to my feet and began pushing my way through the wet branches. If I was going to face a knife-wielding maniac, it was better that I did so out in the open. But when I stepped out of the bushes the woman wasn't there at all. I looked around as much as I dared, but there was no sign of her.

I could see there was some activity around the white forensics tent. A police constable was standing not far from the empty bench, alongside a couple of people in white coats. He looked at me as I walked out of the holly. I felt sure he'd call out to me, but nothing happened. So I walked as briskly as I could to the nearest path, all the while fiddling with the wrapped piece of chewing gum in my pocket. Maybe I should hand it over to the police now and mention the other ones I'd found and explain all about the woman with the hat and everything. But I worried about what they'd say. Most likely they'd ask me all sorts of difficult questions. They'd want to know why I'd been poking around in bushes, for one thing. Hadn't the police sign said 'Do Not Cross'? Or they might suggest that I'd put the chewing gum there myself and was making it all up, that was possible. They might even come round to the house and take away all my mementoes. And I couldn't let that happen. Not after I'd spent so long collecting them and looking after them. I was the only person who understood what they all were.

I headed for the gate on the opposite side of the park. It did mean a longer walk home but I thought that was the best option. If the woman was still looking out for me I might be able to throw her off my scent. In any case it was busier that way and I could get lost amongst all the people.

Beyond the park the street lamps were starting to glow. The streets were filling up too now that the rain had stopped. It was quite a welcome sight. A serial killer would never strike in a busy place, not in the heart of a crowd. No, she'd wait until I was alone somewhere, out of sight. So it was important the killer didn't find out where I lived, I owed that much to the victims. I could worry about what I was going to do next when I was safely back at home.

But I was going to have to do something. Serial killers never stopped until they were caught, I knew that much. And all those mementoes I'd collected would be worth nothing if I kept quiet and she killed again.

Every once in a while I crossed the road and doubled back on myself. Then I'd stop and pretend to examine a shop window or a street sign, checking to see if anyone was close behind me. But whenever I looked there was nobody paying me the slightest attention. The only person I encountered was the dark-skinned youth I'd seen the day before at Parson's Wood. He was carrying a big bunch of papers in his hand just like he had done then, and he smiled at me as he walked past. I watched him as he posted one of his papers through a letterbox and realised that was why he looked familiar. I'd seen him last week doing exactly the same thing. Well, whatever he was selling, I didn't want it.

I was very relieved when I arrived back home. There was a handwritten note on the doormat. I recognised Susan's handwriting and was pleased to read that she had, after all, located an old VHS recorder for me. I felt warmed by this piece of news. It was almost as if Susan had known how stressful my day had been and had managed to find the single thing that would cheer me up the most. That was something to look forward to, I thought. There had to be someone out there who could join two video recorders together, even if it wasn't Jamal. They could do all sorts of things these days.

I was upstairs when I heard the knock at the front door. My heart leaped at the sound. Susan had brought the video round, hadn't she? I smiled. She's too good for words, I thought. She might hide behind a gruff façade, but she meant it all for the best really. From the landing I could see her outline behind the frosted glass. There was a second knock.

'Wait there,' I yelled and stashed the chewing gum away. 'I'm coming.'

I bounded downstairs as fast as I could and flung open the door.

'I hope you've brought all the cables Susan.'

But it wasn't Susan standing on the front door step. It was the woman. The crazy blonde-haired woman with the black woollen hat and carnations who'd banged on the van and who'd murdered three girls with a kitchen knife.

And she looked at me and smiled.

'Well,' she said. 'Aren't you going to invite me in?'

CHAPTER SIX

The woman's name was Rose. She liked very sweet tea. And she didn't have a knife, as it turned out.

But I didn't know any of those things when I opened the door. When I saw her standing in front of me I couldn't think of anything at all. My skin flushed hot and cold and my mind went blank. The first thought that came to me was would any of my neighbours hear if I called out? And if they did, would they come running to help? Or would they ignore my cries completely and find me when it was too late and I was lying in a pool of blood on my own front doorstep?

'You've changed,' she said.

I didn't say anything.

'You were wearing black trousers earlier. And now you've got brown ones on.'

I wanted to shut the door but her foot was planted too close to the threshold.

'I can't wear brown,' she said. 'It doesn't really suit me.'

Someone I didn't recognise walked past the front gate. I didn't know whether I should call out for help.

'Is this where you live?' She put her hand up to her mouth. 'What am I saying? Of course it is. It's nice round here, isn't it? There are some lovely houses. You took ages coming back from the wood. Why did you go the long way round?'

She looked right past me as she spoke. Her eyes were darting this way and that.

'What a lot of things you've got. Can I use your loo?'

'Sorry?'

'Can I use your loo?'

'It's not a good time,' I said in a very quiet voice.

'Beg pardon?'

'It's not a good time right now.'

'I know,' she said. 'It's a terrible time. Terrible. I wish we could do something, don't you?'

I pushed the door a few inches.

'You have got nice hands,' she said. 'Well, I can only see one of them.'

'What do you want?' I said.

'The same as you. You must know that. You have got a lot of books, haven't you?'

'You can take some if you like.'

'I don't want them.'

'Help yourself.'

'I couldn't.'

'It's fine, really.'

I tried to nudge the door a little further, but it came up against the woman's foot. Then as I pushed I caught the strains of some familiar music.

'I've got to go now,' I said. 'Goodbye.'

'Is that the news?'

'Take some books.'

I shoved the door even harder but found it resisting.

'Please,' she said.

'No,' I said.

She pushed back against me.

'I need to see,' she said.

I could hear the newsreader's voice coming from the kitchen. No doubt he was running through the upcoming items. I was going to miss it. And I couldn't remember if I'd pressed the record button.

'Please?'

I wanted to tell the woman I couldn't let her in because she was a serial killer. She didn't look like a murderer, or act like a murderer, but how could I know for sure? I wanted to make her promise that if I let her in that she wouldn't kill me. But that sounded silly. Killers couldn't be trusted to keep their word, could they? No, I'd just have to trust that my instinct was right and that the woman who I'd been convinced was a serial killer a few minutes ago was no such thing. But I'd need to decide quickly, because otherwise I was going to miss the news.

'Please?'

I let go of the door. The woman stepped over the threshold into the hallway.

'Thank you,' she said. 'We can't miss the news, can we?'

I ushered her through the gap into the kitchen.

'I haven't got any chairs,' I said. 'It's still a bit messy.'

'I'll stand,' said the woman.

She found a place against the sink and leaned against it. For a second I thought about offering her a seat between the boxes, but then I realised the cushions might still be damp. I moved to the other side of the room where I could see the television and keep an eye on the woman at the same time.

'My name's Rose,' she said.

I pressed myself against a box which started to sag under my weight.

'What's your name?'

'I'm Henry,' I said.

'Don't you normally sit there?' she said. She pointed to my den with its flattened cushions.

'Not always.'

I was being sucked further into the box, and clunked against some old pots and pans. The news was still mainly about the weather. I wasn't interested in the weather – and neither was she.

'I was hoping there'd be some proper news,' she said. 'Weren't you Henry?'

'Yes,' I said.

She moved along the sink, nearer to the television. I shuffled in the opposite direction, keeping her in my field of vision. Then the cardboard collapsed and I slumped with it.

'Aren't you uncomfortable like that?' she asked.

'No.' I lay there for a moment then pulled myself up.

'It was where they found poor Lorna Coulson, wasn't it?' she said. 'Where I first saw you.'

'You were throwing flowers,' I said.

'Those bloody police though Henry,' she said. 'Giving us all hassle when we hadn't done anything. Like it's our fault. I wouldn't mind but they haven't made a breakthrough have they?'

'No.'

'They haven't got a clue.'

'No.'

'I mean nothing, right?'

'No.'

'Have you got a toilet?' She leaned forward. 'Only I mentioned it earlier and I'm a bit desperate now.'

I blushed. I didn't know what to say.

'So can I use it?'

'Oh. Yes.'

'Thanks.'

She moved towards the kitchen door and I stood to one side.

'Is it this one here?' She pointed to a door in the hall which was partially blocked by bags and boxes.

'No. It's not in a fit state at the minute.'

'Oh you should see mine,' she said and laughed.

'There's one upstairs,' I said.

I led her through my things and up past the magazines and leaflets. When we reached the landing I showed her the door.

'Thank you Henry,' she said.

There wasn't much room but I stood outside. I thought I'd better.

'I'll be fine,' she said. 'You don't need to wait.'

And she shut the door behind her. I didn't really want to leave her up there all on her own. I've never left anyone upstairs in the house, all on their own. But this time I did.

While I waited I busied myself in the kitchen. I rinsed two cups and boiled the kettle. Some minutes later she reappeared.

'I thought I'd make some tea,' I said.

'That would be lovely,' she said. 'Two sugars for me please Henry.'

'I don't have sugar,' I said. 'My father told us it was bad for our teeth.'

'I can't drink tea without sugar.'

'Sorry.'

'It's not your fault. Do you like chocolate?' She took a bar from her pocket and snapped it in half. 'Or is that something else your father feels strongly about?'

'He never liked us having it,' I said.

She held out her hand to me.

'He's not here though now, is he?'

'No, he's not,' I said. I took the piece of chocolate and once she'd started eating hers I put some into my mouth.

'Mmm.' She closed her eyes and tipped back her head. 'There's nothing like it is there? I don't know what I'd do without chocolate.'

'It is nice,' I said.

'See what you've been missing?' She crumpled the chocolate wrapper and squashed the foil into a tiny ball.

'What do you think about chewing gum?' I said.

'Not much,' she said. 'Why do you ask?'

'Oh I just wondered.'

'Well it's kind of you to offer Henry but I can't say I'm that keen on it.'

'OK. Good.'

'Is that what you're going to have?'

'No,' I said. 'I don't really like it that much either.' I felt pleased when I heard her say she didn't like chewing gum. It meant my instinct had been right. She wasn't the serial killer. There was nothing to worry about. 'What do you know about the other people?'

'What other people?'

'The people who go to the sites, like us. Do you know that couple with the flasks or the old lady with the little dogs?'

42

'I've seen them,' she said. 'I haven't talked to them much.'

'How about that man who always brings sandwiches? Do you know the one I mean?'

'Yes.'

'Have you talked to him?'

'Once, I think. His name's Ken something.'

'I've talked to him,' I said.

'Have you?'

'I call him Sandwiches.'

'I don't know what his second name is,' she said. 'He had a daughter who...' She shook her head. 'It was very sad. But he does what he can – like the rest of us.'

The news had finished now. A chat show had come on.

'I couldn't believe it when they let him go, could you?' She looked at me. 'I was sure he'd done it.'

'So was I,' I said.

'I hope they catch the bastard that killed her. Excuse my language.'

'That's all right.'

'I never liked the look of him. He seemed sort of shifty to me. Not someone you can trust. You can usually tell, can't you?'

I nodded. 'I thought he looked nervous,' I said. 'At the press conference.'

'Oh, you noticed that too.'

'He kept taking little sips of water.'

'Yes. He did, didn't he?'

'Nine times altogether.'

'Really?'

'Let me show you,' I said. 'Wait here.'

I left Rose, went into the hallway and clambered up the side of the boxes which blocked the entrance to the front room. As I leaned over it, the cardboard began to give way under my weight and I sank down into a pile of bedding and clothes and other items. I grunted as I struggled to stay afloat, while I stretched across to the recess behind. After a minute or so of fishing about I'd managed to retrieve three unmarked video cassettes. I took them back to the kitchen, pausing for a moment to recover my breath.

'It's on one of these,' I said. I was breathing quite heavily. 'I should have sorted them out properly really and put some labels on them. But there's never any time is there?'

'I know,' she said.

My first guess was wrong. But at the second attempt, and after a few minutes of winding and rewinding, I eventually located the press conference. 'There,' I said. 'Look.'

'One ... two ...' Rose began counting.

'He has nine sips in three minutes,' I said.

'That's not normal is it?'

I shook my head. We watched the rest of the old news report in silence.

'I'm sorry about the sugar,' I said when it had finished.

'It doesn't matter,' she said.

'I'm sure most people would have sugar.'

'Never mind. It's nice just talking, isn't it?'

'Yes.' I took out the old VHS and replaced it with the one I'd just been using then pressed the record button. 'There's a late news bulletin.'

'I know.'

'I mustn't miss it.'

'Of course not,' she said. 'The news is important.'

'Yes.'

'I try not to miss the news. Only I don't tape it. Not like you.'

I nodded. 'Is this a conversation?' I said.

'I don't understand,' she said.

'Are we having a conversation right now?'

'Yes, I suppose so. Why?'

'Sorry?'

'What made you say that?'

'Nothing,' I said. 'It doesn't matter.'

'You are funny Henry.' She gave a gentle laugh.

'Am I?'

'Yes. All these questions.'

I blushed again. She began to move from her place at the sink.

'I ought to go,' said Rose. 'It's been lovely talking but the time's getting on, isn't it?'

'You'll miss the next news,' I said.

'I'll miss my train if I stay. Anyway, you'll tape the news, won't you?'

'It's recording now.' I pointed at the light on the VHS player. 'It'll be on in ten minutes.'

'Henry, have you ever heard of Timothy Weyland?'

'I'm not sure,' I said. 'Should I have?'

'He killed his family about twelve years ago. Shot his wife and three children. His business was failing and he was about to go bankrupt and lose their big house. So he torched his property and tried to make out it was an accident.'

'Oh yes, I remember.'

'The youngest was only eighteen months.'

'That's terrible.'

'They said it was clinical depression. But that doesn't mean you have to go around killing people does it? What had the little ones done to deserve being murdered like that?'

'I don't know,' I said.

'He's being transferred next week,' said Rose. 'To a prison with what they call a more relaxed regime.'

'How do you know all that?'

'I think it's important to know about these things Henry. Do you understand?'

I nodded.

'I'm going up there when he's being moved. Would you like to come with me? It's easy to get close to the van because they have to drive slowly when they come through the prison gates. And there's a public right of way so you can rush across and bang on the sides before anyone can stop you.'

I watched her closely while she spoke. There was a sparkle in her eyes.

'I've done it there before,' she said. 'And other places.'

I nodded.

'I can't tell you how good it feels,' she said. 'I think it's important we let them know we haven't forgotten, don't you?'

'Yes,' I said. 'We mustn't forget.'

'So how about it Henry? You could meet me there – or somewhere else if you'd prefer. What do you say? Would you like that?'

'Yes,' I said. 'I would.'

'Yes I would Rose,' she said.

'Yes I would Rose,' I said.

'Good.' She made her way to the kitchen door before stopping. 'Now you can show me out,' she said.

'It's just there.' I pointed down the hall.

She held out her hand. 'I'd like you to walk me there Henry.'

I felt uncomfortable as I wriggled my way past her in the narrow passage. Her body pressed against mine and I could smell her and feel her breath on my cheek. It took a little to-ing and fro-ing before I managed to open the front door. Outside it had started raining again.

'Summer, eh?' She turned up her collar.

I shrugged.

'Tuesday then, 10 am, you know which station,' she said.

I nodded.

'See you soon. Bye Henry.' She kissed me on the cheek.

'Bye,' I said and closed the door.

CHAPTER SEVEN

On Tuesday I forgot to buy the *Radio Times*. That wasn't like me at all. Each week at around nine o'clock I double lock the front door and walk to the local newsagents. Tuesday is when the new *Radio Times* comes out and I like to get to the shop early to pick up a copy. Because sometimes they sell out when there's a royal wedding or when it's Christmas. *'Why don't you have it delivered Mr Henry and save yourself the walk?'* the newsagent said to me once. But I decided against it. Dr Singh advised me that regular exercise would be good for my heart. And so once a week I walk to and from the shops. Only on this particular Tuesday it completely slipped my mind. And I was half way to the prison before I remembered that I'd forgotten. I must have been too busy thinking about pieces of chewing gum and if there was anything I should do, knowing what I did. Then something jogged my memory and I panicked. And while the countryside sped past the carriage window I tried to reassure myself that I'd shut the door and pressed the record button and that there wasn't any royal event this particular week. I could buy the *Radio Times* at my destination.

Rose was there to meet me at the station. I saw her waving before I was half-way down the platform. As I passed through the gate she rushed over and pecked me on the cheek.

'I wasn't sure you'd come,' she said. 'I wanted to phone and check but I haven't got your number.'

'My phone's not working at the moment,' I said.

'It's lovely to see you,' she said.

I looked at her. She was standing quite still and her hands were clasped at her waist.

'I said it's lovely to see you Henry,' she said again.

'It's lovely to see you too,' I said.

She smiled. 'I like your scarf. Were you cold?'

'No,' I said.

'I suppose I should ask about your journey. How was it?'

It hadn't been too good really, what with all the worrying, but I didn't really feel I could tell her that. 'Fine,' I said.

'Mine was pretty good once I'd got away.' She led me across the station concourse. 'Mum didn't want me to leave of course – she never does – but she can hardly complain about me doing this, can she?'

'No.'

'Not that she doesn't try. She has this way of making me feel guilty about anything I want to do. Treats me like – well, I don't really want to use the word Henry – but she does, half of the time. So I said to her 'I might not always be here, you know. For you to boss me about."

I fumbled for my ticket and showed it to the man at the gate.

'I said 'What would happen if I met a nice man and wanted to get married?' Well she didn't like that at all. I love her of course Henry, otherwise I wouldn't still be there. But – well, mums, eh? I don't suppose yours is like that is she?'

'No,' I said.

We walked outside onto a busy street.

'We've got a little while before they move him,' said Rose. 'And we don't have to be there straightaway. So I was thinking we could have a wander about or go and have a coffee somewhere. I say coffee, but we could have tea if you prefer. I know you like tea. What do you want to do Henry?'

'I'd like to buy a *Radio Times*,' I said.

I'd never been to a prison before, so Rose filled the time with a run-down of what the day would hold. We'd get there with time to spare and then find a place where she could approach the van as it came through the prison gates. There'd be a considerable police presence who'd try and stop any protestors, but that was only to be expected.

When we arrived a small group of people were already gathered on the grass beyond the thick concrete walls. Rose explained to me that some of the people in the crowd were frequent prison visitors and that she'd made friends with a few of them. She suggested that I might like to be introduced to them, but I said that I'd prefer not to. So instead she pointed out a few of the characters. There was a man called Nick who had a placard. He had a friend called Charles who'd suffered a broken foot when a van had driven over it. Christine was a large lady who'd once managed to hit the small window of a prison van with an egg.

I thought I might see someone I recognised, but there was nobody – no Sandwiches, Two Dogs, Cloth Cap, Mr and Mrs Flask or any of the others. One young man busied himself with a rolled-up banner but the majority just shuffled about or stood chatting in little groups. It seemed like people had come for a good day-out and everyone was determined to enjoy themselves. It was a far cry from some of the gatherings I've been to, near burnt-out buildings and lay-bys where children have perished.

After we'd been waiting for an hour or so I noticed the atmosphere change and the crowd began to get a little more agitated. Moments later a group of uniformed police jumped out of some vans and lined the route.

'What's happening?' I said.

'Watch,' said Rose.

As soon as the police were in place, the gates opened and a prison transfer vehicle emerged. That was the signal for a few dozen people to rush forwards howling obscenities. I stayed where I was and watched as Rose and the others pushed at the police cordon. She was right at the front, almost snarling as she battered against them. It was just like I'd seen on TV, only a lot more impressive to witness in real life. People were thrusting against one another and screaming and shouting. Then in just a matter of seconds it was all over. The van made its escape, and after a few cat calls the crowd quietly broke up.

On Wednesday Rose and me went out to the countryside, to a small town an hour or so outside London. A few days earlier a local man in his twenties had come to the same spot and parked his car on the level crossing. A high speed train had driven straight through it, killing the young man and injuring several passengers when it derailed. By the time we got there the car had been taken away and the line re-opened. A few tiny pieces of splintered plastic and a long stretch of flattened undergrowth on either side of the track were all that remained of the accident. A few bunches of flowers had been tied to the level crossing gates. Rose muttered something to herself and threw some flower petals.

I knelt down and picked up some of the plastic fragments from the road. There were coloured pieces and clear ones, mostly very small in size, with all manner of marks and patterns on them. I don't know much about cars but I could tell that the plastic had come from a number of different car lights. Were they the remains of the young man's suicide, or just some debris left behind by careless drivers? It was impossible to tell. I decided to take some anyway, as a memento of the unfortunate young driver, and began to stuff some pieces into my pocket.

'What are you doing?' asked Rose.

'Just taking some things,' I said.

'Are they from the car? His car?'

'I don't know. Some, maybe.'

'But you can't be sure.'

'No.'

A sliver of plastic caught my eye. I stooped down and gathered it up.

'In a few week's time this will all be changed,' I said. 'The flowers will have gone and no-one will know anything about what happened here when they pass through.'

'But you will,' she said.

'I'll have these,' I said. I showed her some plastic fragments.

'Do you collect things wherever you go?'

'I try to.'

'Poor man,' she said.

'Yes,' I said.

As we walked back we talked about whether there'd been any developments regarding the murder enquiries. Rose didn't think it was likely, because there'd been no news the day before.

'They'll get him in the end though,' she said. 'He'll make a mistake and they'll catch him.'

'Or her,' I said.

'It's always a him Henry,' she said.

I waited for a few moments before I spoke again.

'Actually, I think I might have found something. No, I'll rephrase that. I've definitely found something.'

'What?' she said. 'Can I see?' She looked down at my hands.

'No,' I said. 'It's not here.'

'Oh.'

'Well it's more like three things really.'

'You are being mysterious,' she said.

'They're pieces of chewing gum.'

'Chewing gum?'

'They're neatly wrapped in silver paper. I found one in the grass that first day I saw you. It was just like one I found near Shannon Armitage. You remember Shannon Armitage.'

'Of course.'

'And then I found another one – identical – in the bushes close to where they found Tabitha Williams.'

'You asked me if I liked chewing gum, didn't you?'

'Yes.'

'Is that why you ran away when I came over to you in the wood?'

'I didn't,' I said.

'You did.'

'I can't run.'

'I saw you. Henry?'

I didn't say anything.

'Look at me.'

I looked at her.

'What happened?' she said.

'I was scared,' I said.

'Scared?'

'Yes.'

'What were you scared of?'

'You'll laugh if I tell you.'

'I won't.'

'Do you promise?'

'Yes.'

'Say "I promise",' I said.

'I promise,' she said.

'I promise I won't laugh.'

'I promise I won't laugh. Go on.'

'I thought you might be the murderer,' I said.

'Me?' she squealed. 'You think I'm a killer?'

'Thought.'

'Really?'

'Yes. But not for long.'

'Oh Henry.'

I looked down.

'I did wonder why you wouldn't let me in.'

I didn't say anything.

'There,' she said. 'You see? I didn't laugh, did I?'

'No,' I said.

'Maybe you should take your chewing gum to the police, Henry.'

'I'm not sure,' I said.

'Are you worried they might ask too many questions?'

'They will though, won't they?'

'Perhaps it doesn't need the police,' she said.

'What do you mean?'

'Well...'

'You think I can find the killer?'

'Not on your own.' She shrugged her shoulders.

'Maybe it's something we could do together.'

I looked at Rose and she smiled at me.

'Why not?' she said.

'Like Hillyard and Wyatt?'

'No.' She wrinkled her nose. 'They've been useless. They didn't find the chewing gum, did they? That was you.'

'What should we do then?'

'We find out everything we can. Gather evidence.'

'We've got evidence,' I said.

'I was thinking of people,' said Rose. 'We should investigate them and find out about them. What did you call him? Ginger features. Who's he?'

'Whiskers. Ginger Whiskers.'

'And that lady with the dogs.'

'Miss Two Dogs.'

'There you go. She might be married. We don't know.'

'Which of your friends should we start with?'

'They're not my friends. Friends talk to each other Henry. And I don't think you could be friends with someone who had a secret like that, do you?'

'No,' I said.

We hadn't gone much further when Rose spotted something lying in a ditch. She slid down the bank after it. Half buried in the mud and long grass was a concrete figure of a cat, licking its paw. We came to the conclusion that it was probably a garden ornament, although how it had come to rest at the bottom of a ditch in a quiet country lane left us both puzzled.

'We ought to take it,' she said.

'You should,' I said. 'You saw it.'

'No,' she said. 'I think you should put it in your garden. Once it's been cleaned up it'll look fine. There's only a bit broken from its tail.'

I fished a plastic carrier bag from my pocket and put the concrete cat in it.

'What will you call it?' she asked.

'I don't know,' I said. 'I hadn't really thought.'

'I'll call it Henry then.'

'That might be confusing,' I said. 'It would make for too many Henrys.'

'Well, it looks like a Henry to me,' said Rose.

I didn't say anything.

'I think he proves what good detectives we are.' And she slipped her arm into mine and kept it there all the way back to the bus station.

CHAPTER EIGHT

When I got home on Thursday I saw that Susan had called round while I'd been out with Rose. She'd let herself in and dumped last week's sack of clean washing at the bottom of the stairs. I was disappointed to see that she hadn't left the video recorder. I guessed she'd forgotten it. There was no point checking whether she'd gone upstairs and collected my dirty things. Susan never went upstairs.

We'd been to Parson's Wood. It had partially reopened to the public although the police barrier remained in place. The forensics tent was still there too. We sat on the same bench Rose had used before and watched people come and go for half an hour. A young girl passed by and left a small bunch of flowers near a fence-post. An elderly couple carefully placed a card next to the bouquets. But mostly people just came, looked, and left. We were on the verge of leaving ourselves when I saw a familiar figure.

'Look.' I gave Rose a nudge. 'It's that detective sergeant. Wyatt.'

'I know,' she said. 'They've been put in charge of the case.'

'Have they?'

'It said so this morning on the news.'

'I didn't see that,' I said.

'It was BBC online,' she said. 'On the computer.'

'Oh.'

I wanted to deny it and tell her that you couldn't trust what computers said, but I kept quiet. We watched Wyatt go into the white tent.

'I think she's nicer than that other one,' I said under my breath. 'The bald one.'

'I don't think so,' said Rose. 'She's a bit too full of herself. I thought it might be her at first.'

'What – the killer?' I found it hard to say the word.

'She was very rude to me.'

'Yes.' I remembered their confrontation.

'And it's the perfect cover if you want to murder people. No-one ever suspects the police, do they? I know we reckon it's never a woman but there's always a first time.'

'Yes. But it isn't her,' I said.

'You can't know that for sure.'

I shook my head. 'I found the gum before Wyatt joined the case. It can't be her.'

'I wonder what she's doing here now.'

'Checking for clues I suppose. Seeing if the murderer left any evidence behind.'

'Or covering her own tracks. There wouldn't be any here now though, would there? Not after more than a week of searching.'

'Some things can last for years,' I said. 'That was where I found the chewing gum.' I indicated the holly bushes.

'And it was in there?'

'On the ground.'

'The bastard.'

I blushed.

'He might have killed again you know,' she said.

'Someone else? They didn't say anything. Was it on the computer?'

'No. You read the papers, don't you? You might remember reading about a murder that happened at Bradnam Common. Two years ago it was – last June.' She paused for a moment then cleared her throat. 'My sister Jacqueline was the victim. It was a senseless killing – brutal. You can imagine how my mother felt.'

I didn't say anything.

'I... They never caught the man that did it. So he's still out there. And the police soon lose interest, don't they? But I haven't. And I've followed just about every murder case since then – looking for patterns and clues – anything that might give me a lead. Trying to keep going, trying to make sure it doesn't happen again. So I look at every face I see and I ask myself 'Is it you?' Is that a killer staring back at me?'

She grabbed my wrist and her fingernails dug into my flesh. 'Supposing there's one of your pieces of chewing gum at Bradnam Common.'

'It's not very likely,' I said.

'Even so, we have to go and check, don't we? It would be proof the murder had been done by the same person.'

'Yes it would.'

'So we have to make sure. Oh Henry, imagine. I could be getting close to solving this. We could.' Her eyes flashed. 'It's your turn to promise me now, like I promised you. So, do you promise to go to Bradnam Common with me? Henry?'

'Yes,' I said.

'No, say 'I promise."
'I promise.'
'To go to Bradnam Common and look with me.'
'I promise to go and look with you.'
And she gave me a squeeze that hurt my arm.

oOo

We arrived at Bradnam Common shortly after eleven o'clock the following morning. The weather had turned from overcast to a persistent drizzle. It was far from ideal, but at least it was preferable to a downpour. Heavy rain would have meant big fat raindrops and restricted visibility and glistening water on the ground.

I'd expected a more open place, but the common turned out to be an area of Forestry Commission land, largely filled with row upon row of conifers. The sign near the car park boasted that lizards and Speckled Wood butterflies could be seen at the right time of year, and requested that visitors take their litter home with them. I said to Rose that I hoped at least one person had ignored that advice.

We studied the map and decided to follow one of the marked walking routes that started from the car park. Rose had been there once before and recalled that it led to a clearing where her sister Jacqueline's body had been found. I didn't think that sounded very promising at all. If the chewing gum murderer had killed her in an open space then the silver foil would have been cleared away or perhaps carried off by a magpie or something. Two years was a long time. But I didn't say anything. I could tell how much it meant to her and it was nice spending time together.

'We haven't picked the best day for it,' she said.

'No,' I said. My raincoat was still damp from my visit to Parson's Wood.

'The sun dips behind those trees in the late afternoon.' She indicated some giant firs. 'It gets dark very quickly then. I'd say we've got about four hours.'

The clearing was a scrubby area with a few felled trees and the remains of a fire.

'That's where she was found,' said Rose. Her eyes were looking down, but I knew she hadn't seen anything.

'We don't have to do this if you don't want to,' I said. I tried to imagine how I would have felt if it had been my sister.

'No,' she said. 'That's why we've come.'

She walked over to the blackened patch of ground. I could see we had a daunting task ahead of us.

'I wonder how the police would do it,' I said.

'I don't know,' she said. 'Why do you ask me? You're the expert.'

'I'm not a policeman.'

'At finding chewing gum. You've got keen eyes Henry.'

'Have I?'

'You know you have. So where would you start?'

'It's no use looking here,' I said. 'The killer wouldn't have discarded his chewing gum next to his victim's body. He didn't in Parson's Wood. The problem we've got is that he'd most likely have thrown it into the undergrowth on his way back to the car park.'

'The bracken's waist high,' she said.

'It's had two years to grow over it. I don't think we'd ever find it, even if it was there.'

'So we shouldn't start there.'

'We don't even know that he chewed gum back then,' I said. 'Or he might not have had any gum with him. Or he might have been careful for once and taken it home or left it in his car. Or perhaps in those days he didn't bother wrapping his chewing gum.'

Rose shook her head. 'People don't just pick up habits like that.'

'No,' I said. I walked across the burnt area, just so I could be satisfied there was nothing there. 'We'd better start then.'

I found a point not far from the charred grass and began walking in a tight circle, my eyes fixed to the ground.

'What are you doing?' she asked.

'I remembered what it is the police do,' I said. 'They get down on their hands and knees and crawl in a straight line.'

'That's not what you're doing.'

'There's only one of me. Two of us. So we can't do a fingertip search.' I continued walking my circle, moving further away from my starting point with each turn.

'What do you want me to do?' she said.

'I don't know,' I said. 'Maybe you could start looking around the edge.'

'Which edge?'

'By the logs.' I kept my head bowed. I didn't want to look up and lose my place.

It was easy to begin with, and my circles took me through puddles, brambles and a small pile of timber that was stacked ready for collection. I knew there was another obstacle to negotiate though, a fact of which Rose reminded me.

'Henry, there's a bog,' she called out.

'Yes,' I said.

'You'd better stop or you're going to walk straight into it.'

'I know,' I said, but I continued walking.

'Henry! You can't go in there.'

'I've got to. Otherwise I won't be walking in a circle.'

A moment later and my feet were squelching in it. The water smelled horrible, and was deeper than I'd anticipated, and my second step almost brought it up to my waist. My black and yellow scarf trailed in the murky water behind me. I was cold and uncomfortable and knew only too well that in a few minutes time I'd be wading through it again. Maybe there was a piece of gum at the bottom, I thought, as my feet sank in the soft mud, and I stuck my arm into the stagnant water. It only took one plunge for me to realise that I would never find any chewing gum that way.

'Are you having any luck?' she called out.

'No,' I shouted. 'You?'

'No.'

I noticed that the rain was steadily getting worse. That wouldn't help with the light. But it had kept almost everyone away. I'd never have felt free to search for the chewing gum if there'd been crowds of people about, enjoying the sunshine and the countryside and watching what I was up to.

Every man-made item that I came across I examined carefully: crisp packets, cans, straws, a plastic spoon, cigarette butts, a hub cap. Each one was then dropped into a polythene bag. Even if I couldn't find what I was looking for, the very least I could do was show Jacqueline some respect and tidy away the rubbish. By the time I'd walked twenty three circles I'd lost my bearings completely and forgotten where Rose was. At almost the exact moment I realised this, she asked me how I was doing, just as if she was reading my mind. I was cheered up by that and assured her that I was fine. As the circle widened and took me under the trees, I became aware that the sun was disappearing. But I couldn't stop now, I told myself. I had to keep going until I couldn't see the ground any more.

I was half-way through my thirty-first circuit and thinking that I'd have nothing to show for my trip besides a carrier bag full of other people's litter, when I struck gold. Lying at the foot of a stack of fir timbers, so insignificant as to be almost invisible, was a miniscule grey-coloured parcel. I knew what it was straightaway and pounced on it, scarcely able to believe my luck. I crouched down and dropped it into the palm of my shaking hand. The paper was badly damaged, and the silver lamination had almost rotted away completely, but there was still enough to show whose handiwork it was. Chewing Gum had been here and left his mark – casually throwing away his calling card where he thought no-one would find it. How wrong he was.

Two years it had lain there, sheltered from the elements by a pile of decaying timbers – waiting for that moment when someone who understood its significance would find it.

'Rose,' I called out. 'Rose.' I had a lump in my throat.

She didn't say anything but I could hear her running towards me.

'I've found it,' I said. 'I've got it for you.'

I held out my hand. She looked at it for a moment, gave a whimper, and then folded my fingers over it. Then she threw her arms around me and cried.

Night had fallen by the time we got back. It hadn't been a pleasant journey on the train. We sat with a group of commuters to begin with, until someone commented on the smell, at which point Rose thought it best to move. But there weren't any more seats so we stood for an hour in the corridor, and my trousers dripped water onto the floor.

It was another hour until her train and Rose was feeling hungry so we went to the shopping arcade for some fish and chips. I suggested we eat them there but Rose had other ideas.

'It's not too far to your house, is it?' she said.

It wasn't, so we walked back. As we went through my front gate I was surprised to see a figure on my doorstep, crouching by the letterbox. My heart skipped a beat. What was going on? I wondered if he was doing something to the house.

'Hello,' I said in the loudest voice I could manage.

The figure stood up sharply and turned round. It was a boy in his late teens, lean, dark-skinned and dressed in baggy clothing. Even in the gloom I could see it was the same youth I'd spotted near Parson's Wood, and passed in my street.

'What are you doing?' I said.

'Nothing,' said the youth. He had a bundle of something in his hand.

'Go on – clear off.' I waved my arm as though I were brandishing a stick. For a second we looked at one another, then the boy said something.

'You're nuts man,' he said, and walked quickly past us.

'And don't come back,' I shouted. I fumbled for my keys, wondering if I might have foiled a crime before it had happened.

As soon as I opened the front door I knew at once who I'd disturbed. There, wedged in the letterbox, was another leaflet advertising the services of Jamal. Jamal the computer expert; Jamal who might be able to connect my two video recorders. Clutching the leaflet in my hand, I rushed into the street.

'Wait a minute,' I called out and stood by the gate, hoping I might catch sight of Jamal. But if he could hear me he chose not to reply.

CHAPTER NINE

Rose and me ended up eating our fish and chips standing up in my kitchen, resting our food on cardboard boxes. The recording light was still glowing on the video.

'Shall we watch the news?' I said.

She looked at me. 'Do you always leave the telly on?'

'I don't like to switch it off.'

'Only I'm getting a bit of a headache Henry. Would you mind turning it off for me?'

I scratched my arm. 'It's not very good for the set.'

'I'm sure it'll be fine just this once.' Rose screwed up her chip paper. 'Who's Susan?' she said.

I was a bit startled by the question. 'Why?'

'I'm curious,' she said. 'Who is she?'

'How do you know about Susan?'

'You mentioned her.'

'Did I?'

'When I came here last week I knocked on the door and you were upstairs and you shouted something like 'Is that you Susan?' And then you came rushing down the stairs and it was me.'

'Yes.'

'So who is she Henry? Is she your girlfriend?'

I nearly choked on the last of my fish.

'Is she?'

I hung my head. I could feel myself blushing and I could sense that Rose was looking at me.

'Henry?'

'No,' I said.

'You don't sound sure.'

My skin was tingling and felt prickly. I scratched at it with a wooden chip fork.

'She's a friend though. I'm right about that, aren't I?'

'She's my sister,' I said.

'Oh. I see.' Rose rinsed her fingers under the tap then looked around for something to wipe them on.

'Susan washes my clothes for me,' I said. 'My machine doesn't work at the moment.'

She nodded. I finished off the last of my chips.

'What's Susan's house like?' she said.

'Why do you ask?'

'I just wondered, that's all. Is it nice?'

I had to think for a second. 'Yes,' I said. 'It's all right I suppose.'

I rummaged through some carrier bags and eventually found what I was looking for. 'Would you like a cup of tea?' I said. 'I bought some sugar.' I showed her the bag.

'It's a bit late for tea,' she said.

'I always get thirsty after fish and chips,' I said. 'It's the salt that does that.'

I squeezed past the boxes near the sink, pushed aside the dirty pans and held the kettle under the cold tap.

'Is it like this?' she said.

'Is what like this?'

'Her house.'

'Whose house?'

'Susan's.'

'What about it?'

'Is it like this?'

'She lives on an estate,' I said. 'It's a new house.'

'Is she married?'

'What do you want to know that for?'

'Nothing really,' she said. 'Is she though?'

'Why are you asking me so many questions?' I began scratching my leg.

'I'm not,' she said.

'Yes you are.'

'Well if I am it's only because I want to know more about you,' she said.

'A minute ago you wanted to know all about Susan.'

'I don't really want to know about Susan.'

'I'm confused,' I said.

The kettle shuddered and shook then switched itself off.

'Tea?' I said and poured some water over a teabag.

Rose shook her head.

'Where's the spoon? There's never a spoon.'

I found one at the bottom of the sink and prodded the tea bag with it.

'I'm sorry,' said Rose.

'It's OK,' I said. 'You don't have to have tea.'

'No, I'm sorry if I upset you.'

I could feel myself blushing again so I tried not to look at her as I slipped past.

'You know I've been thinking about your collection,' she said. 'It would be ever so nice if you showed it to me.'

I could feel my skin starting to tingle so I began to rub my arm.

'Henry?'

'I don't think that's a good idea,' I said.

'Really? Why not?'

'It just isn't.'

'Oh go on,' she said. 'Please.'

I shook my head.

'I'll be ever so careful with them.'

'No,' I said.

'Why?'

'Because I never have done.'

'What, never?'

'No.'

'Never ever ever?'

'No.'

'There's always a first time,' she said.

'I'd feel odd about showing them to anyone,' I said.

'I'm not just anyone though Henry am I?' She touched my sleeve. 'I mean, I hope I'm a bit special to you.'

Rose reached out her hand to me. I held out my own in response.

'No, give me the cup,' she said.

I passed it to her and without looking back she placed it on the draining board. The cup toppled over, spilling my tea into the sink.

'I was drinking that,' I said.

She put a finger up to her lips.

'But I hadn't finished my tea,' I said quietly.

'Don't say anything,' she said.

'Why? What's going on?'

'Nothing.' She took a step towards me, put her hand on my shirt and began smoothing the collar between her finger and thumb.

'What's the worst that could happen if you showed them to me?'

'I don't know,' I said. I could feel her breath on my face.

'Well then.'

'I'd be worried I suppose. Embarrassed.'

'What is there to be embarrassed about?'

'Well, it's personal isn't it? Not everybody would understand.'

'It doesn't need to be everybody Henry.' She took off her woollen hat and dropped it on a cardboard box. 'Just you and me. I understand. I do.'

'Do you?' I said.

'Oh yes.' She ran her fingertips along the seam of my shirt. 'I did say I wouldn't laugh, didn't I?'

'That was about something else,' I said.

'But I didn't though, did I?'

'No.'

'And I'm sure you'd like to really.'

I wanted to turn away but all I could do was look directly into Rose's eyes. 'I'm just a bit scared,' I said in a soft voice.

'There's nothing to be scared about,' she said. 'Trust me.'

She moved another step closer and she was right up against me. I tried to go backwards, but found myself trapped between big cardboard boxes on either side and the television behind. Rose kept coming forward.

'And if you did,' she said, 'You could have something of mine.'

'Have you been collecting things as well?' I said.

'Not exactly.'

She began fingering the top button of my shirt. First one then a second button popped open.

'What are you doing?' I said.

'What does it feel like I'm doing?' she said.

'I don't know,' I said.

'I'm sure you do.'

I shook my head.

'Well if you looked down you'd be able to see,' she said.

A third button came free.

'I can't,' I said.

'Of course you can.'

I made a strange sort of noise that didn't sound like me at all.

'Shush,' she said.

And then suddenly she pressed her lips against mine. I was caught by surprise and jerked my head back. My shirt flapped open.

'I'm not sure this is such a good idea,' I said.

'Let's not worry about that now, shall we?' she said. I felt her hands on my wet trousers. 'You aren't worried are you?'

I didn't have time for a reply. Her mouth latched onto mine and I stumbled, falling back onto the cushions which were still damp from tea. She was pawing at me and tearing at my clothes, making a sort of growling noise as she did so. And I noticed I was doing the same thing myself, grabbing at Rose as we fell. And then we were writhing on the kitchen floor, the two of us, our arms and legs going this way and that. She pulled at my buttons and I tugged at some straps as we rolled about. My foot smashed onto a box and I heard a cake stand clatter against a stack of soup bowls. Rose's elbow banged against the giant carton that my new fridge had come in. My head thumped against another box and something fell out of it. And all the time I could hear myself grunting. Then Rose cried out as an object dug into her back.

'God, what's that?' she yelled.

I didn't say anything.

'Feel that,' she said and guided my hand.

'It's a pressure cooker.' I was a bit out of breath so I was panting.

Rose shuffled slightly on the cushions trying to free herself, but she just got more tangled up amongst all the discarded clothes and what not.

'I can't move my arm,' she said.

I rolled out of the way and clattered into another cardboard box.

'We can stop if you like,' she said.

'Is that what you want?' I said.

'I'm asking you.'

'Uh huh.'

'Is that a yes?'

'What?'

'Henry? Yes we should stop?'

'Do you want to?'

'Just tell me what you want Henry.'

'I don't know,' I said.

'Don't you?' she said. 'Because I know what I want.' And then she pulled my hand towards her. I jumped a bit as she tugged at me.

'Can't you feel?' she said.

I could feel all right and made a sort of groaning noise.

'That's good isn't it?' she said. She was a bit out of breath as well. 'And it feels to me like you want me too.'

I tried to clear my throat, but I couldn't speak.

'Don't ask me what I'm doing because you know exactly what I'm doing,' she said.

And before I could do anything she was on top of me, her naked body pressed against mine, grinding up and down. I was pinned to the cushions and flapped about underneath. I was wet with perspiration, cold tea and pond water. And then, just at that moment, I heard a click and a clunk and a whirring sound and I realised the video tape had reached its end and was now winding back to the start. I tried to wriggle myself free.

'Ignore it,' she said.

'We'll miss the news,' I said.

'Forget the news. Concentrate on me instead. Touch me there Henry.'

She tugged my hand towards her breast. 'Gently now,' she said. 'Don't be too rough. You see – I like that. Just like you do. You can kiss them as well if you like.'

I swallowed hard. My skin was wet but my mouth was dry.

'Have you done this before?' I said.

'Not like this,' she said.

'But—'

'Shush. Don't talk. Just try and relax.'

'I can't relax.'

'Course you can.'

'I can't,' I said. 'If I relax I won't...'

She covered my mouth. 'Yes you will,' she said and started grinding again. 'Trust me.'

And before I could say another word she was guiding me towards her. My heart was thumping but I tried not to think about things too much. Then I was grinding and thrusting myself, and a few minutes later I was all spent and collapsed on the kitchen floor.

I could hear the fridge humming as I lay still in the darkness. I felt awkward and uncomfortable. And I'd missed the news. I started to yawn and then managed to stop myself. I heard Rose sniffing beside me. I looked towards her, saw her fingers brush her cheeks and then I heard her sniff again. 'Are you OK?' I asked.

There was the tiniest of snuffles.

'I'm sorry,' I said. 'Did I hurt you?'

'No.' She sighed. 'No you didn't hurt me.'

'Good.' I lay still and didn't say any more. I couldn't think of any conversation.

'Now you know for sure don't you,' she said after a few minutes had passed.

'What's that?' I said.

'You know that I'm not a serial killer. A serial killer would have picked up a knife off the draining board.' She was turned away from me, facing the big cardboard box. 'Anyway serial killers are all men, and I'm a woman.'

I didn't say anything.

'I'm cold,' she said. 'Aren't you cold?'

'A little bit,' I said.

'Have you got any blankets? I'd like a blanket.'

I raised myself from the floor and felt quite self conscious. Apart from one sock I was naked and for a moment I wondered what had happened to the other one. I'd never been like this in my kitchen before, and I was thankful it was dark. So I ignored the light switch and began groping my way around all the obstacles. After a couple of false starts I finally found something in a box by the door and pulled out some folded material. I shook it free and with my face turned away I spread it out over Rose's naked body. She cried out as the material made contact.

'That's freezing,' she said. 'What is it?'

'A curtain,' I said.

'Some of the hooks are still on.'

'I'm sorry, it's all I've got down here. Should I look for something else?'

'No, don't worry. It's fine.'

I stood beside her on the damp cushion.

'You too,' she said. She rustled the fabric and the curtain rings clinked together. 'Don't just abandon me now you've had your wicked way.'

I could feel myself blushing. 'I wasn't wicked was I?'

'I'm pulling your leg Henry.'

'Oh.'

The sweat on my back had started to cool and I shivered a little bit. I could hear an electrical item buzzing away. Apart from that it was very quiet.

'Say something,' she said.

'Would you like some tea?' I said.

'Not now. I'd like you under here with me.' She reached out and her fingers closed round my ankle. 'Come on.'

I shuffled about on the spot.

'Don't be embarrassed,' she said. 'You're not embarrassed are you?'

'No,' I said.

'Good. Well then.' She patted the damp cushion.

I lifted up the curtain and squirmed underneath.

'So is this where you sleep at night?' she asked.

'No, my bed's upstairs,' I said.

She rolled over towards me and leaned on her elbow. 'Henry?'

'Yes?'

'Have you ever..?' she began asking me a question, then stopped. 'No, I don't suppose you have.'

'Don't suppose I have what?' I said.

'Nothing,' she said.

'Tell me.'

'It's not important. Talk to me Henry.'

'What about?'

'Anything,' she said.

'Anything?'

'Within reason.'

'What time is it?' I said.

'I don't know. Late. Does it matter? Talk about something else.'

'Isn't your mother going to be wondering where you are?'

She shuffled closer to me. 'I guess,' she said. 'But you know what mums are like.'

'Not really,' I said.

'Don't be like that. Course you do. Always fussing about something or other.' I wriggled free of her touch. 'Henry?'

'What?'

'What's the matter?'

'Nothing,' I said.

'There is something the matter. You are embarrassed, aren't you?' I drew my knees up to my chest. 'Please say something.'

'I should put another tape on,' I said. 'I'll miss the late news.'

'Leave it till the morning,' she said. 'There won't be any more news now. Is that all you're upset about?'

I felt very cold beneath the curtain. My arms were covered in goose pimples.

'Henry?'

I noticed my heartbeat, and the sound of my breathing. 'He locked me in,' I said.

'Who did? What are you talking about?'

She reached out and stroked my skin, which made me shudder. 'When Mother died,' I said.

'Oh.'

'I was away at school,' I said. 'Boarding school. Father came to pick me up at the end of term and Susan was strapped into the back seat of the car. We didn't have a child safety seat or anything like that.'

'Sure.'

'They didn't have them back then. Not like they do now.'

'Of course,' she said. 'Go on.'

'Father took my luggage and told me to get in the car. So I said 'What's Susan doing here? Shouldn't she be at home?' But he didn't say anything. And we drove off and I had a bundle of things with me and I said 'I've done some pictures Father, would you like to see?' And he said 'Don't be ridiculous Henry.' Because he was driving. And then I said 'I can't wait to show Mother my pictures.' I was very pleased with them, you see. And Father just stopped the car. I can still hear the screech. And he sat still for I don't know how long – he didn't look round or anything – and then he said 'Your mother's dead.' Nothing else. 'Your mother's dead.' And then we drove off. He never mentioned her again. Not in front of me anyway. And when we got home, all of Mother's things had gone. It was almost like she'd never existed at all. I went around looking for any little trace of her, you know – and I found a few of her things in the wardrobe. There was a jumper. And a scarf. And Father shut me in there. Locked the door. I can't remember how long for but it felt like ages. You don't have a sense of time or anything when you're eight, do you?'

'You poor thing.'

'I didn't dare look at first but next time I checked the jumper had gone.'

'What had happened to your mum? Did you ever find out?'

'Breast cancer. My aunt told me. My father wanted to keep it quiet so it wouldn't upset us – well, me really. Susan was barely three, she didn't understand anything.'

'So what happened to your dad?' she said. 'Is he..?'

'He died when I was about twenty,' I said. 'Left me all his money and a big house. Susan got nothing. I've never understood why.'

'People can be like that,' said Rose. 'Sometimes they do things for reasons we just can't make sense of.'

'I've never told anybody about that.'

'I'm glad you told me.'

I breathed a big sigh and she wrapped her arms around me.

'Do you believe in God, Henry?' she said.

'I don't know,' I said.

'Everyone knows if they believe or not.'

'I don't.'

'You must.'

'Must I? Well when I needed God he didn't seem very interested.'

'God cares about all of us,' she said.

'He didn't seem to care about me,' I said.

'God always does things for a reason Henry.'

'Does he? Even if we can't make sense of it?'

'Now you're turning my words against me,' she said. Her breath was warm on the back of my neck.

'I'm sorry.'

She sighed. 'So could I see those things of yours Henry? Your mementoes.'

'They're upstairs,' I said.

'That's not a problem is it? You have still got them haven't you?'

'Of course I have. It's just...' My voice trailed away.

'You can show me,' she said and kissed me on the shoulder. 'And then we can watch the news.'

It took me a few minutes of struggling before I managed to pull out the box. I put on some clothes and then went back to the kitchen. The light was on. It was very bright and made my eyes blink.

'I wondered what you'd been up to,' she said and pointed at my trousers. She'd draped the curtain around herself and was propped up against one of the big boxes. 'Are they all in there?'

'Most of them,' I said. I sat on the floor and put the container next to me. It was a medium-sized cardboard box that had once contained jaffa cakes. Rose craned her neck, trying to look inside.

'Let me see.'

'In a minute,' I said.

'It's just like Christmas, isn't it?'

'I expect so,' I said.

'Sorry.'

I took out an old discoloured Polaroid. 'That's my mother,' I said and handed it to her.

'And is that you?'

'Yes. And Susan. You can just see her. The colour's faded a bit.'

'So did your father take the picture?'

'No. He wasn't there. Mother took it on a timer.'

'Right.'

'It's Parson's Wood,' I said.

'Is it?'

'I hadn't been back there until - well, you know.'

I put the photograph back in the box and brought out a clear plastic slip case. There was a faded blue ball in it and a small square of neatly trimmed card. 'That's from Scotland,' I said. 'The card's got all the details. I can't be sure it belonged to Graham Dawes, but I never look at it without thinking of him. You remember Graham Dawes, don't you?'

'Of course,' said Rose. 'It's beautiful.'

'It's priceless,' I said.

And then I showed her some of the other things I've collected: the doll's hand, the scrap of torn muddied cloth, the plastic tulip. She studied each one for a moment or two then handed it back. I gave her another slip case, smaller than the others. 'This is the piece of chewing gum I found near where you'd been standing. Right where Lorna Coulson was murdered. Look at how it's been folded.'

She stared at it through the clear plastic. 'It's an odd thing to do, isn't it?'

I took out the other two pieces of gum and showed them to her. 'This was the first one I found, near the spot where Shannon Armitage was killed. And this is the one I found last week in the holly bush at Parson's Wood.'

'Oh my God,' she said. 'It's true, isn't it?'

'And yours makes four.'

'Four,' she repeated.

'That makes him a proper serial killer. So the next thing we've got to do is find him.'

'Yes.' She peered into the box. 'What's that?'

'It's a brooch.' I gave it to her. She turned it over in her hand.

'It came from outside Siobhan Douglas's house,' I said.

'From where?' she asked.

'Siobhan Douglas's house. She hung herself, you might remember. You wouldn't think they'd throw something like that away, would you? Not when their daughter had taken her own life. But there it was, in the rubbish. It's not rubbish though, is it? It's an important reminder. Would you think that was rubbish?'

'What?'

'You wouldn't, would you?'

'Wouldn't what?'

I took the last item from the box. 'This belonged to that poor boy who was killed in the hotel fire,' I said. 'Asif Khadari. Do you remember?' I held out a blue plastic figure for her, but she didn't take it from me so I put it back.

'The rest of them are in another box,' I said. 'I'll just be a minute.'

I'd forgotten how precariously balanced it was, wedged on a couple of bulging suitcases further into my bedroom. With all the other items shielding it, I had to be careful not to over-extend my reach and topple over. So, it took me quite a bit of effort before I managed to retrieve it. There weren't quite as many objects in the box, but some of them – like the top – were quite large and not as easy to handle. And there was the button, too, the object that had started it all. That had been quite a thing to find on my first trip. I guessed it hadn't come off Pauline Furber's coat. Girls didn't wear coats that had fancy wooden buttons with inlaid silver bands as a rule. I wondered what Rose would make of it.

'I think this is all of them,' I said as I negotiated the landing. Then about half-way down the stairs I stopped. I could feel a rush of cold air on my bare feet and I knew at once that something wasn't quite right. I lowered the box and saw what was unsettling me. The front door was open. Under normal circumstances I'd have panicked and assumed that someone had broken into the house – but this was no normal situation. I could feel a gnawing sensation welling up in the pit of my stomach as I squeezed my way through the hallway. Something awful had happened. I half suspected what it was, and hoped that I was wrong, but when I got to the kitchen, I could see that my gut reaction had been right. Rose had gone.

CHAPTER TEN

It was about ten-past eleven when I heard the letterbox flap and I jumped up. I tensed, hoping there'd be a knock on the door and a voice calling 'Henry', but neither thing happened. Instead all there was, a moment or two later, was the sound of letters landing on the mat. I told a lie last night. When Rose asked me if I ever slept downstairs I'd said no. But after she'd gone I didn't want to go upstairs so I just kept waiting in the kitchen for hours and in the end I must have fallen asleep.

I switched on the television. It was soon chattering away like it always does. The colours seemed very bright, but I didn't pay any attention to what anyone was saying. I sat huddled under the curtains, my mind somewhere else. Then a programme about railway journeys came on and it occurred to me I'd forgotten to press the record button on the video. Not that it mattered by then, of course – the news had finished. But I suppose what really surprised me was that it didn't seem to bother me at all. Sometimes I've been beside myself with worry, fretting that I might have missed something important. Only on this particular morning the news didn't seem to matter. I wouldn't have been able to concentrate on it in any case, what with all the things on my mind. What on earth had happened last night anyway? Had I done something to upset Rose, was that it? There didn't seem to be any other explanation. Why else would she have left like that without saying goodbye? Maybe I just didn't understand women, perhaps that was the problem. I could only think that her disappearance must have been in some way related to our having been... intimate last night. Because I knew that I hadn't dreamed that up. I could still smell her scent on the curtains. But she'd gone just like that, without saying goodbye. It couldn't have been a coincidence that she'd waited till I'd left the room before getting up and going. She must have regretted what we'd done, that was it. I felt myself shivering a bit at the thought.

I tried to piece together everything that had happened and work out if there might not be some other explanation for Rose's sudden departure. She might have been upset by something she'd seen on the television. Then I remembered that the television had been switched off all evening. I could recall the silence. Or perhaps her leaving was connected to the mementoes. Had she taken any? She'd certainly been interested in them. She could have been waiting for me to turn my back before she took one of them. But when I checked I could see that nothing had been taken – not so much as a single item, nor a solitary scrap of card. It was all too baffling for words.

I made some tea. A wasp was crawling around by the rancid milk, its antennae twitching with pleasure. There was another one lying dead on the window sill. Summer was coming to an end, I thought. That's what wasps signified. Endings.

It was while the tea was stewing that I noticed Rose's hat. It was lying on the box where she'd left it the previous evening. I picked it up and held it in my hands. It made me feel a lot better. She'd come back for her hat, wouldn't she? I realised now I'd been worrying that I wouldn't see her again. That she'd vanished from my life as quickly as she'd arrived. But the hat said otherwise.

Of course it would be nice if I could somehow get in contact with Rose directly, not least to tell her I'd got her hat and was looking after it. There was still a working telephone box not too far from the house. I could go there and call her and we could have another one of our conversations. But I'd no sooner thought of that than I realised I'd never asked Rose for her phone number, and I couldn't recall her giving it to me. I wondered if she might have written it down on a piece of paper before she left. I looked high and low around the kitchen – I even balanced on top of the fridge-box to try and get a better view, but I couldn't find anything. All I could think was that she'd been very keen to get away and hadn't wanted to say why. There was no note and no number. Apart from her hat, I had nothing.

Perhaps she might write me a letter. She knew I didn't have a phone, so it was a possibility. But a letter wouldn't get to me before Monday at the earliest. Tomorrow was Sunday, so there wouldn't be any post then. I began to think the most likely thing she'd do was surprise me with a visit. She'd done it before, so she might do it again. In which case it would be best not to leave the house in case she dropped by. I'd just have to make do with whatever supplies of food I'd got. But as Saturday turned into Sunday, Rose didn't come back and time passed very slowly indeed.

It was only when the late news on Sunday mentioned Tabitha Williams that it dawned on me that I'd neglected to keep abreast of the latest developments in the case. Seeing DI Hillyard and DS Wyatt was a stark reminder of what I'd been missing.

There had been significant developments, the DI explained. He wouldn't elaborate on what those developments were but said he hoped they'd soon be in a position to make an arrest. Wyatt thanked the public for their help, especially those who'd contacted the police with information. I felt a pang of guilt when she said that and wondered if I should have taken the chewing gum packages to the police. The chewing gum probably contained DNA, which they might be able to match in their laboratories. But if I did give the chewing gum to the police they'd want to know why I'd kept them for so long and what exactly I was concealing.

The chewing gum was the clue though, of that I had no doubt. The killer was obsessive and left a trail behind him, almost as if he wanted to be caught. Yet it was strange that no-one but me could see that.

All I got in Monday morning's post was a letter from a dog charity. I decided that I wouldn't be donating any money to Gruff Justice, and dropped the letter straight into the rubbish bin. I consoled myself that the deadline for a message from Rose had not yet expired. If she'd written me a letter when she got home but missed the Saturday post then it wouldn't have been collected before Monday morning in any case. It might, even now, be lying in a sorting office somewhere.

Later that day I found myself in the phone box. I wasn't altogether certain why. Nor, as I stood there fumbling about for change could I recall even leaving the front door, let alone locking it. I remembered the number well enough though, even if it had been a while since I'd called it.

'Hello?' came the voice.

'Hello.'

'Who is this please?'

'It's me, Henry,' I said.

'Henry!'

'Didn't you recognise my voice?'

'Of course. You don't usually phone, that's all.'

'I wanted to say thanks Susan. For last Thursday.'

'Well there's a first,' she said. 'I did wonder where you'd got to. Was it anywhere nice?'

'Yes,' I said. 'It was.'

'Good. You might have thought to tell me.'

'Sorry.'

'It's lucky I remembered my key. So is everything all right? Is that the reason for this?'

'I was just thinking about you, that's all.'

'On Monday evening?'

'Why not?'

'I don't know, you tell me.'

'I am allowed to think about you aren't I?'

'Yes. What's this about Henry?'

I thought for a moment. 'Nothing really,' I said.

'Good. Good. Look, I'd love to talk but I'm a bit busy right now.'

'I can call back later.'

'It's just that I'm in the middle of making dinner and when I'm finished I've got to help Christopher with his homework. He's got to write five hundred words on the Black Death before tomorrow. Two weeks he's had to do it and he leaves it till the last minute.'

'I could help,' I said.

'I'll be OK.'

'I've got a book somewhere. I could bring it over.'

'It's a bit late now.'

'It's no trouble.'

'Look Henry.' She paused. 'I'm sure we can find something on the internet.'

'Of course.'

'But you should come over soon. Spend some time with Christopher. Maybe next weekend. No, on second thoughts not next weekend. The one after. I'll have to check.'

'Sure.'

'Great.'

'Susan.'

'Yes?'

'Nothing.'

Tuesday brought only more junk mail and I began to reconcile myself to the idea that I might not see Rose again – unless of course there was another murder. But the thought of standing at another murder site was too awful to think about, so I tried to put it out of my mind.

The cushions had dried, so I settled down and watched the television with half-closed eyes. Four days after the event, I noted, the smell had gone from the curtains. I tried instead to remember Rose's scent, but found that I couldn't. Even her hat smelled unfamiliar.

Hillyard's breakthrough failed to make Tuesday's news. In fact there was no mention of Tabitha Williams or Lorna Coulson at all. The newspapers had started to lose interest too. The front page of the *Mirror* had a celebrity gossip story, while the *Telegraph* featured a cabinet reshuffle. I noticed that I'd stopped counting the time until the next news report. It just made the hours pass more slowly. I'd often complained that there wasn't enough time to do anything. Now there seemed to be too much.

I was gazing at a television programme about moving into the perfect house when I was disturbed by a knock at the door. I sprang to my feet at once. Without bothering to slip on any shoes I picked up the woollen hat, squeezed through the doorway and shouted out that I was on my way. But it wasn't Rose who was standing on the doorstep. It was Mr Shields, the Environmental Health officer, with a clipboard and a bundle of papers wedged under his arm.

'Mr Henry.' He grinned at me. 'And how are you this morning?'

'Would you like to come in?' I said.

'Me?'

'Yes.' I pulled back the door as much as the stuff behind it would allow.

'I'd better lock my car,' said Mr Shields.

'I'll put the kettle on,' I said. 'Do you like tea? I've got sugar.'

I shifted some bags from the kitchen chairs so we could sit down.

'I was hoping you might have made some progress since I saw you last,' said Shields. 'I can quite see the extent of your problems if this is any indication of the rest of your house. Is it much the same upstairs?'

'There's no kitchen up there, so it isn't the same,' I said.

'Is it full of things?'

'Not full exactly.'

'But I can infer that space is at a premium. Otherwise I'm sure all those things wouldn't be cluttering up the stairs.'

'I can manage the stairs,' I said.

Shields unfolded one of his leaflets. 'As I said before Mr Henry, lifestyle choices are not an issue until they start to impact on other people. That applies to loud music, dangerous dogs, unauthorised use of premises for business purposes and of course the accumulation of... assorted items. No-one wants to look out over an eyesore every day, do they? So have you given any thought to what I said last time?'

'Yes,' I said.

'Good,' said Mr Shields. 'As I mentioned before we've got people who can help.' He handed over a sheaf of leaflets. 'Because admitting that you've got a problem means you're half-way to solving it.'

I gazed at the leaflets then looked around for somewhere to put them.

'Just remember they're for reading, not storing away,' he said. 'You're not the only person I work with who lives this sort of lifestyle you know.'

'No.'

'Tell me Mr Henry, do you work?'

'Yes,' I said.

'That's interesting,' said Shields. 'I hadn't expected... so what sort of job do you do?'

'Oh, all sorts of things.'

'Really? Whereabouts?'

'Here and there,' I said. 'But mostly here.'

'That's something I'd like to do, become self employed. It's no picnic being a wage slave.'

'Do you need to make money to be self employed?' I asked.

'It's usually seen as ideal, yes.'

'Hmm.'

Shields gave a sigh. 'Shall I mark you down as unemployed Mr Henry?'

'I don't claim benefits,' I said.

'Was that a yes?'

'Yes.'

The Environmental Health officer began ticking some boxes on his form, and scribbling notes on another.

'Is this a conversation we're having?' I said.

Shields shrugged his shoulders. 'I suppose so. Why?'

'Nothing.'

I watched as Shields began fiddling in his coat pocket. He took out a small box, and shook something into his mouth.

'It's something I have to do,' he said between chews. 'They said to me, Stephen, if you carry on like that you'll be dead by the time you're forty.'

His jaws continued grinding up and down. I didn't say anything.

'Dead.' The Environmental Health officer said the word again and drew a line across his throat with his finger. 'Who wants to hear that, eh?' He raised his eyebrows and looked at me. 'But the trouble is...' Shields struggled for the words. 'The trouble is nicotine gums are not a patch on cigarettes, if you'll excuse the pun. You kick the smoking habit and become hooked on chewing gum instead. You're not a smoker, are you Mr Henry?'

I felt my skin prickling and there was a buzzing sound in my ears. Was it something medical, or another of the late summer's wasps?

'Do you smoke Mr Henry?'

'What?'

'Cigarettes.'

'Do I smoke?'

'Yes.'

'No.'

'You're best not starting. It's a dangerous business to be sure.'

'Yes.'

Shields looked straight at me. 'Sometimes I could kill for one,' he said. 'Just for old time's sake.'

I swallowed. And how did the man from Environmental Health dispose of the gum when he'd finished chewing, I wondered. Did he drop it on the pavement or wrap it up in a silver coloured parcel? Had he been all the way up to Lorna Coulson's murder site? Perhaps the serial killer was in my kitchen right now, drinking my tea and making veiled threats.

'Have you been to Parson's Wood?' I said.

'Of course,' he said.

Before he could elaborate further there was a sharp knock at the front door. I stood up and without a word to Shields I headed towards it. I was still hoping it might be Rose, but it was a man's voice that was calling me – my next door neighbour. Almost anyone would have been preferable to him, I thought, until I reminded myself I could have a suspected murderer sitting in my kitchen.

'Wasps,' said the tattooed man angrily.

I didn't say anything. It was hard to know what to say.

'There's wasps now.' He was chewing very aggressively, and every so often the gum was visible. 'So what are you gonna do about it?'

'I don't know,' I said.

Tattoos then proceeded to tell me, and anyone else who might be passing by, that he'd seen a number of wasps flying from one of my upstairs windows. They'd promptly flown straight towards his house, and was that fair? First it had been the rats and now it was the wasps. He counted out the pests on his ink marked fingers.

I was just wondering if I ought to invite Tattoos in, as a safeguard, when Mr Shields squeezed past and excused himself. He said he couldn't stay any longer as he had another appointment. No sooner had he spotted him than Tattoos asked Shields what he was planning to do about me. He accused me of lowering the tone of the neighbourhood, and said he'd had just about as much of it as he could stand and what did anyone expect from a man who had more books in his front garden than most people had in their house? Mr Shields told him it was important that the law took its course and that everybody acted sensibly and that due processes were taking place with regard to the matter of Mr Henry. And what about the wasps, asked Tattoos. Shields told him that regrettably he had no information regarding wasps.

It was with some relief that I shut the door on both men and went back to the kitchen. I realised I'd got a little carried away. The chances of Shields or even my gum-chewing neighbour being the killer was a bit far-fetched. But the encounter had given me an idea. So I went upstairs and collected as many of my video tapes as I could and stacked them all in a pile. It was time to do some serious research.

One by one I began going through each of the videos, fast-forwarding through all the entertainment shows and documentaries, and then poring over every detail of the news. The chewing gum was the clue. I remembered Rose and me wondering if anyone we knew chewed gum. I could have a look and see if any of them were chewing on a news-clip. Or if anybody else was, come to that. Perhaps one of the videos might reveal another suspect, one we hadn't thought about before. It was painstaking work, not least because there were dozens of unlabelled tapes, and the news itself constituted only a small part of each one, so I had to watch every single minute slowly and deliberately and then watch it all over again. I was determined that I wouldn't miss a thing.

It took me several hours before I chanced upon the first clip. There was Mr Coulson and his wife talking to the press. Neither of them was chewing gum. Nor, as far as I could see were any of the photographers. It was the same when I found footage of Hillyard and Wyatt. That was when I realised the problem I faced, because of course people didn't tend to chew on TV. If they did chew gum they saved it for when they were off-duty or when the cameras weren't rolling. I wondered if I might not be wasting my time, but on the ninth tape I had a shock when I caught my first glimpse of Rose. There she was, pummelling her fists on the side of the police van that was carrying Mr Coulson. I felt a bit strange watching the tape and I had a lump in my throat. How many things had happened since I'd first seen Rose battering the van on the evening news? I'd thought she was the killer to begin with. Then she'd been to the house and we'd become friends and gone travelling together. And then we'd made love on my kitchen floor. Was it making love, or had we been having sex? I wasn't sure if there was a difference. I hadn't seen Rose since. I took a short break to collect my thoughts.

The next few hours didn't reveal much more. But just when I was about to give up, I rediscovered the footage from outside Parson's Wood. It was the news item where I'd been on camera for three seconds of a ten-second clip. I ignored myself and looked at the others. There was that dark-skinned youth with the leaflets, who I now knew was Jamal. And not far from me was Sandwiches. I paused the tape before rewinding it and watching Sandwiches closely. Was he chewing gum or eating one of his sandwiches? It wasn't really possible to tell in just a few seconds of video tape. I thought watching it repeatedly would help me, so I wound back the tape and kept replaying it, hoping to find an answer. By the fifth, or possibly the sixth time of watching, however, I'd stopped looking at Sandwiches, because something else had grabbed my attention. The figure at the back of the crowd, standing anonymously amongst the onlookers – and chewing away to his heart's content – well, wasn't that the same Mr Shields I'd just invited into my house? The picture was a bit fuzzy, but each repeated viewing only confirmed my suspicions. Shields had been quite open about it when I'd asked him if he'd ever been to Parson's Wood. And there he was, as large as life. It was funny what you could see when you looked closely. I felt my chest. My heart was beating faster than usual. I knew I'd stumbled upon something really crucial.

The sharp knocking on the front door almost made me jump out of my skin. I shrank for a moment into the cushions. It was the Environmental Health officer, wasn't it? He must have suspected that I was on to him, and now that it was quiet he'd come back to kill me. There was another knock. I thought perhaps if I lay low for a few minutes he might go away. The house was quite dark so he might think there was no-one at home. Of course if Shields had been watching the house he'd know that I was still there. He'd said something about rushing off to a meeting but that could have been a bluff, designed to put me off my guard. He might have just been sitting outside waiting all day. I wondered if I should try and clear some of the boxes around the back door and make my escape that way. I could probably scramble my way over the garden wall into Tattoos' garden. Unless that was him at the front door now – and I'd got the wrong chewing gum killer. In which case I'd be going from the frying pan straight into the fire. My heart was thumping now. None of this was what Dr Singh had ordered.

I decided, on balance, that Tattoos was the less likely murderer of the two, and was trying to make my way towards the back door when I heard a voice coming from the front. It seemed vaguely familiar, although it didn't belong to either Mr Shields or my tattooed neighbour.

'Mr Henry?'

It would come to me in a minute. There was another knock.

'Mr Henry, could you open the door please?'

I peered round the kitchen door frame. In the darkness it was difficult to see who was standing on the other side of the frosted glass, but I was confident it wasn't Shields or Tattoos, so I wriggled through the hallway.

'I'm coming,' I said and seconds later opened the door to two familiar figures. They were both smartly dressed, the elder one a balding man, the younger one a woman with neatly trimmed black hair.

'Mr Henry Henry?'

'Yes,' I said. 'I'm so glad you've come.'

The two of them looked at each other before speaking to me.

'I'm Detective Inspector Hillyard,' said the bald man directly in front of me. 'And this is my colleague Detective Sergeant Wyatt.'

'I know,' I said.

Both police officers showed me their identification but I barely glanced at it. I'd seen both of them on my television set every day for the past few weeks. But even though I knew what they looked like, nothing could prepare me for what the police officers were about to say.

'Mr Henry, I'm placing you under arrest on suspicion of murder,' said Hillyard.

I choked for a second. 'No,' I said. It was half a statement, half a question.

'In connection with the death of Rosamund Grace Bowyer.'

'No, no, no, no. That can't be right.'

'Otherwise known as Rose Bowyer.'

I made a noise which sounded like a strangulated cry. My ears began ringing and there was a whistling sound in my head. The detective inspector continued talking but I couldn't hear a word. Nor was I listening when Hillyard explained what was happening and where we were going.

I walked out to the waiting car through the crates of books under their plastic sheets, past the crowd of local people who'd come to stare, but I scarcely noticed a thing. And as the car door slammed behind me, the fact that I'd failed to properly lock up the house or press the record button on my video never once crossed my mind.

CHAPTER ELEVEN

The room was just like the kind I'd seen on television a hundred times before. The decor was bland and featureless and a neon strip-light on the ceiling buzzed continuously. I found the noise irritating and before long it began to clash with the whistling sound in my ears. It was far too hot as well. It felt like everything was designed to cause me discomfort, and I found myself sweating and light-headed. I knew only too well that perspiring would make me look even more guilty. But the more I thought about it, the stickier I became. The duty solicitor next to me said nothing. Behind him a uniformed policeman stood motionless in the corner, no doubt ready to pounce if I should try and run away. That just showed how little they knew about me. I'd been given a cup of tea but I decided against drinking it. It would probably taste like dishwater, but that would be the least of it. For my own well-being I knew I'd better not drink the tea.

The police knew how to unsettle people in these sorts of situations, how to make them say and do things they didn't want to. I wasn't going to fall for that. No comment. That was what I was supposed to say, wasn't it? So I didn't incriminate myself. No comment to this, no comment to that. The only trouble was that in every drama I'd seen it was always the guilty ones who said 'No comment'. The people who had something to hide. No comment was no good.

'I haven't done anything you know,' I said in a quiet voice without looking at anybody. 'There's been some terrible mistake.'

They should have understood my position by now. I'd repeated the same two phrases over and over in the car. But neither Hillyard nor Wyatt had said a word. So I had to be careful. Police officers who don't wear uniforms are clever. They were just waiting for me to make the slightest mistake and incriminate myself. So that meant I had to be clever as well, but not too clever. The police never liked it when a suspect acted too clever. That was something else I remembered from television. I heard the door being shut and the chairs scraping along the floor. And I could see that the recorder had been switched on and the interview was about to begin.

The first question was relatively straightforward. Could I confirm that I was Henry Vespasian Henry?

Yes, I told them. I could confirm that was who I was.

'Where's that then?' asked Wyatt.

I looked at her, puzzled.

'Not where, DS Wyatt, who,' Hillyard explained. 'Vespasian was a Roman emperor. Isn't that correct Mr Henry?'

'Yes,' I said.

'Though anyone less like a Roman emperor I don't think I've ever seen.'

The solicitor coughed.

'Any idea how you came by that name?'

'No.'

'Did your dad have a thing for ancient Rome, was that it? Were you conceived in the eternal city?'

'I don't know.' I wanted to ask them if my name was relevant, but I thought it best to keep quiet. They were probably just having a joke at my expense. I'd heard plenty of those before.

'Let's start at the beginning shall we? How long have you known Miss Rosamund Grace Bowyer?'

'Not very long. I'm not sure exactly.'

'How long is not very long? A month? A year?'

'I didn't know she was called Rosamund,' I said.

'Did you kill her Mr Henry?'

'No I didn't.'

'You didn't kill her.'

'No.' Hadn't I just said that, I thought to myself? I couldn't have been much clearer. And how was I supposed to have killed her anyway, when I hadn't even got her address? They wouldn't believe that though. Still, I had to stay calm. This was all part of it.

'We have photographs of the two of you going back several weeks.'

Wyatt peeled off a selection of pictures and laid them on the table in front of me like playing cards. 'Do you recognise them?'

I'd never seen the pictures before, but I guessed that wasn't what she meant. 'Yes, I suppose I do,' I said.

'They were taken at the site where we found Lorna Coulson's body.'

'Yes.'

There was Rose in her black woollen hat about to throw her flowers. And there were the others – Pram Girl, Ginger Whiskers, Sandwiches, Mr and Mrs Flask, Two Dogs, Cloth Cap, plus some others I couldn't remember. And me.

'I didn't know we were being photographed,' I said.

'What were you doing there Henry Vespasian?'

I flinched. 'What do you mean?' I said.

'Why were you there? I mean it's rather a long way from your house, isn't it? Two hours by train. It's not exactly just round the corner.'

'No.'

'So – explain.'

No comment. That's what my head was telling me. No comment.

'I wanted to see for myself,' I said.

'See what exactly?'

'Where she was found.'

'And why would that be, eh?'

No comment, no comment. 'I...'

'Yes?'

'Do you think I killed her, is that it?'

'Why did you go?'

'I just said.' I could hear my voice echoing round the room.

'Were you curious?'

'Curious?'

'You know what curious means. Would you describe yourself as a macabre individual Henry Vespasian?' The detective inspector drummed his fingers on the table.

I rubbed my temple. They were trying to make me say things I didn't want to. Rose wasn't really dead. It was all part of a plan to unsettle me.

'Mr Henry?'

'What?'

'The Detective Inspector asked whether you have any sort of fixation with death,' said Wyatt.

'No I don't,' I said.

'No? I was under the impression you rather enjoyed a good killing.'

The detective sergeant stared at me. There was no expression on her face. She looked nothing like the well-mannered policewoman I'd seen at the press conferences. I wondered how I could have misjudged her so badly.

'Henry?'

'No of course I don't,' I said. I looked at each of them in turn. 'Who could be like that?'

'And yet there you were at the murder site.'

'Yes, but...'

'But what?'

'That doesn't mean – well it doesn't. There were lots of people at the murder site, weren't there?' I started counting the individuals in the picture.

'It's not something any of my officers would have been looking forward to,' said Hillyard.

'It's a long way to go,' said Wyatt.

'Eleven,' I said.

'Isn't it?'

'I counted eleven.'

'And yet you didn't even know Lorna. Or had you met her somewhere on your travels?'

'No.'

'A pretty girl like that – you must have been tempted, eh?' Hillyard frowned. 'Did she spurn your advances, was that it? She wouldn't look twice at a pathetic specimen like you. So you wanted her to pay for that Henry, didn't you?'

'No.' I tried to stop myself shaking. 'I'd seen her on TV, that was all. In the news report. And the press conference.'

'And you thought 'They must think it's the dad. He's going down for murder.''

No comment.

'Isn't that what you thought Henry Vespasian? Those stupid coppers don't know anything?'

No comment. 'No comment.'

'No comment?'

There, I'd said it. The buzzing light had started to flicker. They probably made it buzz to distract the suspects. I rubbed my forehead. Was it hot? I couldn't tell.

'You've got the wrong man you know.' I looked at the duty solicitor. 'Tell them.'

'What would your mother think Henry Vespasian? About what you've been up to. I don't think she'd like it much, would she?'

'You mustn't talk about my mother,' I said.

'No? Why's that then?'

I pressed my fingers against the table and watched the tips go white. I turned to the duty solicitor once again. 'Tell them they can't,' I said.

The duty solicitor cleared his throat, but apart from that said nothing.

'Let's go back to Miss Bowyer again,' said Wyatt. 'Rosamund Bowyer. You met up with her after Tabitha Williams was killed, didn't you? At the murder site.'

'No.' I almost squealed when I said it. 'No, that isn't true.'

'Not too far from your house, is it? No need for a train to get there, was there? Very handy.'

'I didn't meet her there.'

'But you were both at the wood, we know that.'

'Yes but I didn't speak to her. Not there.'

'Later though.'

I didn't say anything.

'You spoke to her later though Henry, didn't you?'

'Yes.' When she'd come to my house and I'd thought she was the serial killer. Before we'd been on our trips together. And before we'd been intimate on my kitchen floor.

'We've got pictures.'

'Pictures?' My heart started racing. Pictures of what? I didn't want to see any more pictures.

A few more photographs were pushed across the desk. There we were, Rose and me. By the railway line; near the prison; on a CCTV picture; her arm through mine.

'Proper sweethearts, eh?' said Wyatt. 'The regular loving couple.'

'Would your mother have liked her Henry?' said Hillyard. 'Only I'm not so sure she'd have approved would she?'

'Stop saying things about my mother.'

'You and her together. Did she make you feel dirty Henry, was that it? Unclean?'

'No, you've got it all wrong,' I said.

'Have we? DNA is pretty conclusive.'

'It wasn't me.'

'Another girl killed not far from your house. Just like Lorna.'

'I wasn't the only person there you know.'

'It's your mother I feel sorry for,' said Hillyard.

'Stop saying that.' I banged my fist on the table. Some lukewarm tea slopped out of the cup.

'Do you think she'd be happy about how you'd turned out? Her Henry Vespasian in his house full of junk.'

No comment, no comment.

'Of course there's no law against being a weirdo. This great country of ours wouldn't be half the place without its oddballs and eccentrics, would it?'

No comment.

'Would it?'

'I suppose.'

'You see Mr Henry, all my experience tells me that people who live messy disorganised lives don't make for good murderers, if you'll excuse my language. There's too much left to chance, too many loose ends for us to find. But you Mr Henry – now what are we to make of you, eh? Are you what we'd call organised? Or is all that stuff in your house just a smokescreen?'

There was Chewing Gum, wasn't there? Chewing Gum had been there before me – when each one of the girls had been killed. And Shields liked his gum, didn't he? I ought to tell them about the Environmental Health officer. He'd been to the wood as well.

'Do you work Mr Henry?'

'I do things yes,' I said. 'I keep very busy.'

'Doing things is not the same as working,' said Hillyard. 'DS Wyatt and I work. We hold down responsible positions in the community. Mr Piggott here is an upstanding member of the legal profession.'

The duty solicitor gave another cough.

'But not you Mr Henry. So on top of everything you're not even contributing to society, are you? We work our fingers to the bone in here, the DS and me, trying to keep the streets safe from murdering scum, paying our taxes, bringing up our families, doing our little bit. And what is it that you do exactly, Mr Henry? This keeping busy of yours; this doing things.'

No comment.

'Was she onto you Henry, was that it?'

'On to me?'

'She'd figured you out, hadn't she? Your Miss Bowyer.'

'No.'

'Pegged you for the murderer.'

Wyatt leaned towards me. 'What's on all those videos Henry?'

I looked at her and then at Hillyard. 'What do you mean?'

'Is it pornography Henry? Hardcore?'

'No. No of course it's not.'

'We can check you know.'

'Is it girls? Little girls?'

'You don't like women do you Henry Vespasian?'

'You mustn't say that – it isn't true.'

'Did your mother warn you about them?'

'No.' I rubbed my face. My eyes were hurting.

'What's on the tapes Henry?'

'Nothing.'

'There must be something.'

'Tell us what's on them.'

'News. It's just the news.'

'You tape the news.'

'Yes.'

'So why do you tape the news Henry?'

'I'm not doing anything wrong.'

'Can't you just watch it? Why do you have to record it?'

'I don't know. I just like to.'

'Especially when there's a murder, eh?'

'You're making a mistake,' I said. 'I'm not the murderer. The real killer is still out there.'

The door opened. A young policewoman came in and whispered something in Hillyard's ear. He got up and left with the WPC.

'DI Hillyard has just left the interview room,' said Wyatt. 'I'm pausing the tape at 17.19.'

'So is that it then?' I said. 'Does that mean I can go?'

Wyatt shook her head. 'We're not finished yet.'

'Is there any chance of a cup of tea?' said the duty solicitor. Wyatt nodded her head towards the constable, who left the room.

The buzzing noise seemed to be getting louder but I tried my best to ignore it. It was important I kept a clear head. Before long they'd all come to their senses and admit that they'd made a terrible mistake. Maybe Hillyard had been called away because someone had realised they'd picked up the wrong man. I wondered whether I ought to try and engage Wyatt in conversation. I'd become quite practised at that recently. Perhaps I should mention the evidence that clearly pointed to the real culprit – the neatly wrapped chewing gum.

Hillyard came back before I had a chance. He went over to Wyatt and whispered something in her ear before sitting down. Then he took some photographs from a folder and fanned them in his hand.

'I'd like you to look at these photographs, Mr Henry.'

'I've seen them,' I said. They were going to say some more things about my mother, weren't they? They thought they'd found a weakness they could exploit. I felt quite sure they enjoyed upsetting me.

'You haven't seen these,' said Hillyard. 'Look at them.'

He laid the pictures out on the table very deliberately.

'Rosamund Grace Bowyer. It's not a pretty sight.'

It was hard to make out the first picture but I could recognise Rose's top. It was the one she'd worn – the one whose buttons I'd undone. But it was badly torn and caked with blood. And then I saw, to my horror, that Rose was still wearing it. I could hear a sound rattling in my throat. They hadn't been lying. It was Rose. She'd been subjected to what must have been a savage attack. I felt sick to the pit of my stomach, which was tightening like a knot. The next picture was worse. By the fourth photo, I couldn't stop shaking.

'What did she keep in her rucksack Mr Henry? You can just make out the strap in the corner of this photograph if you look closely.'

'I don't know.'

'You're not looking at it.' Hillyard thrust the picture directly under my drooping head.

'I don't know,' I said. 'I don't know.' I was weeping now. A tear ran down my cheek and splashed onto the photograph.

'It was empty when we found it,' said Wyatt.

'I don't know,' I said again. I sniffed and wiped my nose on my sleeve.

A moment later I jumped when Hillyard placed a polythene bag on the table. Even with the glare of the buzzing light I could see quite clearly what was inside it.

'Do you recognise this knife Mr Henry?' Hillyard's voice was calm and measured.

'No,' I said and gave another sniff. 'No I don't.'

'And can you explain how it came to be in your kitchen?'

I could feel the duty solicitor looking at me. I could feel everyone looking at me. I wanted to speak, and tell them once again that it was all a ghastly mistake, but I couldn't think of any words.

'Mr Henry?'

Hillyard tapped his finger on the table then slid the knife across it. I was desperate to turn away – to do anything rather than look at the hideous thing in front of me, but I found that I couldn't.

'We found it stashed in a bag of clothes,' said Hillyard. 'Wiped clean, but not completely. There are one or two traces of blood at the base of the handle. That's always a difficult area.' He touched it through the polythene. 'I dare say we'll make a positive match with Miss Bowyer.'

'Of course we have to ask ourselves why Mr Henry would keep the knife in his possession when its discovery would incriminate him.'

Wyatt was staring at me.

'We have Mr Henry's personal habits to account for that stroke of good fortune DS Wyatt. Our Mr Henry is an inveterate hoarder, you see. He can't bear to let anything go. Objects, at any rate. People are another matter.'

'No!' I jerked forward, my body shaking. This had gone far enough. 'I've never seen this knife before. It isn't one of mine.'

'How would you know Mr Henry? Your house is crammed full of things.'

'I just know,' I said. 'You must have put it there.'

Hillyard's expression became a snarl. 'The police are not in the habit of fabricating evidence Mr Henry. But no doubt that will soon be established in a court of law.'

'It isn't mine,' I said. 'You've got to believe me. You do believe me, don't you? Someone must have put it there. It's the only explanation.'

Hillyard leaned back in his chair. 'There is a more logical explanation Mr Henry. Which is that you killed Miss Bowyer.'

'No, no I didn't.'

'You killed her because she'd found out what you'd done to those other girls. Lorna Coulson, Tabitha Williams.'

'And Pauline Furber,' said Wyatt.

'You've got it wrong.' I heard my voice crack.

'I don't think we have got it wrong Mr Henry. As a matter of fact I think we've got it very much right.' Hillyard pushed back his chair and stood up. 'We'll leave it there for now,' he said.

And after a few formalities I was led away to a small cell.

CHAPTER TWELVE

The interview room might have been unpleasant, but the cell in which I found myself was a stark reminder that I was in serious trouble. It dawned on me that my future could consist of blank, painted walls and floors that reeked of disinfectant. They'd cart me off to prison. They'd shove me into a van and people would shout and scream 'murderer' at me and try and beat their fists on the side. There'd be Nick with his placard, Charles with his broken foot and Christine with her eggs. But that wouldn't be anything like as bad as the treatment I could expect from other prisoners. I'd be singled out for special punishment while the wardens looked the other way. They'd put broken glass into my food and razor blades in my soap. I'd seen that in a drama on television. And it would never end, would it? One assault would follow on from another. And nobody would care that I'd been the victim of a miscarriage of justice.

I tried not to dwell too much on my own misfortunes. Rose was dead. However awful I might feel about what had happened to me her fate had been far worse. I'd been so busy answering questions and feeling anxious I'd barely had time to think about that. We'd solved the riddle about what had happened at Bradnam Common together and then she'd had it all snatched away. Rose's death must be linked to it somehow, I felt sure of it. The chewing gum killer had struck again. They'd have found a small pellet of silver wrapped chewing gum near her body, if anyone had been bothering to look. I'd go there and find it myself if I could just get out of here. No – when I got out of here.

After a couple of hours I was given some water and hot food. It was shepherd's pie. As hungry as I was though, I wouldn't allow myself to eat it. Most likely someone had spat into it – or perhaps done something worse. The gravy could have been concealing anything. It wasn't easy though, because it smelled nice and I was hungry. But I ignored my stomach rumbles. I knew I had to stay strong.

It didn't seem fair what had happened, especially as all I'd been trying to do was help. Yet I was the one who was now under suspicion. Guilty as charged, according to Hillyard and Wyatt. Perhaps my big mistake had been trying to help in the first place. I must have ruffled the wrong feathers somewhere. If I'd just stayed at home and watched it all on the news, instead of going to see things for myself, then I'd have been fine. I felt like yelling with frustration – but what would have been the point? Now more than ever I needed to keep a clear head and not let my emotions get the better of me. There was something that was missing somehow, a detail I'd overlooked – I just needed to discover what it was. I wondered if I'd been the only person singled out for questioning. Had Ginger Whiskers, Cloth Cap, Sandwiches, Mr and Mrs Flask, Miss Two Dogs and all the others each been brought in to their local police stations? It was possible – but the murder weapon had been found in my house, and nobody else's.

They'd take the house to pieces, brick by brick, looking for anything else that would tie me to the murders. And then the rest of my things would be thrown into a skip. All my valuables, my precious objects and every single memento I'd ever collected. Every scrap of my research would be disposed of as well – and all the clues that pointed to the real murderer. The souvenir hunters would take care of the rest. They'd have a field day. Ghouls would come to the house and try and get their hands on any bits and pieces. It pained me to think that they were probably there now. 'Look, I've got an egg cup from the murderer's house.' 'I've got some of the killer's books.' The only way the authorities could stop that would be to incinerate everything and reduce it all to ash and smoke. And when it was a notorious case – when the perpetrator was seen as the embodiment of evil, they knocked the house down as well. That way it didn't become a shrine for weirdos, making their pilgrimages and picking up trophies.

I'd been set up, I was certain of that. Despite what Hillyard had said there wasn't really any other explanation. As I told him, I was familiar with all of my things, and I'd never have forgotten something like that knife. Chewing Gum must have been watching the house and keeping an eye on my movements – and when I'd gone out he'd broken into the house and left the knife behind. He'd killed Rose and come into my house. He'd seen the two of us together somewhere. In Parson's Wood? It could have been one of the police. For all Hillyard's denial they have been known to plant evidence. It must have happened some time when I was out. But which particular time? If only I could remember all my movements. I looked at the empty polystyrene cup and cursed myself for being so weak. They'd failed to get me with the tea but they'd succeeded with the water, hadn't they? That was all part of the plan. No wonder it tasted a bit funny. They put stuff into it that affects the mind, some sort of chemical that stopped people remembering things. That's why it was vital I kept my wits about me. My wits were all I had now.

I thought it might be an idea to call Susan before it was too late. I was allowed to make a phone call, and she was my next of kin when all said and done. Susan would believe me, even if no-one else did. She'd been looking for a lawyer recently too, I hadn't forgotten that. Perhaps there was someone she could recommend. It was just a shame she couldn't provide me with an alibi, but I'd spoken to her on the Monday, the 13th, and the murder hadn't happened till the morning of the following day. I hadn't told Susan about Rose, but she was going to find out soon enough, if she didn't know already. I'd most likely be in the papers – papers I wasn't going to be able to read, and papers that were still being delivered. I ought to tell her not to go round to the house next Thursday. There wouldn't be much need for any washing to be done. The house would be swarming with police, anyway, taking things away to be examined or burnt. They'd want to know who she was and what she was doing and whether she was related to the accused. And people would take pictures of her and then she'd be in the papers as well. No, Susan needed to be spared that sort of treatment. I shuddered to think that the real killer – Rose's murderer – would probably be there as well, watching it all. He'd be laughing to himself most likely. Because it was a man. It was always a man.

Poor Susan. She'd never had it easy. She could barely remember Mother, and for some reason Father had never really cared for her. But if she was resentful she'd never let it show. Not to me at any rate. She just carried on, doing her best. I realised I'd never told her before how much she meant to me, and all of a sudden that seemed important. I'd tell her when she came to visit me – discreetly of course. She's never been one for a fuss. In any case, I wouldn't want the guard to overhear a private conversation.

It occurred to me that I'd probably be on the news that evening. I wondered how I might have reacted to seeing myself featured in the news, after having taped it for so long. As it was, I'd only be able to imagine it.

I wouldn't just be on the television either. My face would be staring out from the newsstands, most likely on the front page. 'Murders – Man Quizzed.' That would be the headline. Or would they refer to me as a monster? That was a popular description. I'd seen that once or twice over the years. 'There's Henry V Henry' my newsagent would tell each customer as they came in the shop. 'Did you know he was a serial killer? He takes the Telegraph and the Mirror.' That was something else Susan was going to have to do for me. She'd have to cancel the papers and settle my account. The newsagent needn't bother putting aside the Radio Times for me either. The new edition would be out soon, and I hadn't even managed to pick up the last one. I could forget all that in prison. Each day was much like the last in there. In prison there weren't any special days when special things happened – no royal weddings, no anniversaries, and definitely no walks to the shops. And it was that realisation, as I contemplated a future without the *Radio Times*, when it suddenly dawned on me that although I might not have my videos or my papers or my collection of mementoes any more, I did have something even more precious. I had an alibi.

oOo

'I'm not sure I should be doing this really.'

I had to find out what had really happened to Rose. Whoever had killed Rose was behind all this. The break in at the house, and the deaths of the other girls – Lorna, Tabitha, Pauline – and now Rose.

'A murderer for heaven's sake.'

It was the man I called Chewing Gum, for want of a better name. Chewing Gum must have worked out we'd been close to figuring out his identity. That's why he'd tried to frame me for murder.

'For all I know it's not even safe for me to be in the car with you.'

In a way I'd been lucky. There'd been a witness.

'Well is it? Is it safe?'

If it was possible to use the word luck when someone had been brutally murdered.

'Henry?'

'Go,' I said and pointed a finger at the traffic lights. Susan drove off.

'Getting into trouble is one thing,' she said. 'I mean, we all know you're a little bit... You wouldn't deny that, would you? But to be accused of murder. I just don't know what to say, I really don't. I've not told Christopher of course. Well what would I say to him Henry? Eh?'

But that someone wasn't just anyone. That someone was Rose – someone I'd known and ... Someone I'd known.

'I cancelled the papers for you, before you ask. I didn't know where to look – headlines everywhere. I bought one myself. Well, I don't suppose you were going to tell me.'

It just so happened that Rose was being murdered at the very moment that Mr Shields had called, on Tuesday, around eleven in the morning. And I could account for my whereabouts.

'There was talk that he'd killed his girlfriend. I say him, but it was you Henry. Not that they mentioned you by name, but it was definitely you. Seriously though – a girlfriend. Hah!'

Shields had been in my kitchen, talking endlessly about environmental health and public safety and what a potential fire trap the house was.

'I thought – well, I've heard everything now, I really have.'

And how the neighbours were being inconvenienced. I'd been desperate to send him packing. I could see the man was on edge.

'A relationship requires talking, and that's not your cup of tea at all, is it?

94

You don't even talk to your neighbours, do you? Eh?'

And I'd suddenly remembered that it had been a Tuesday morning when the Environmental Health officer had called round and started chewing his gum. I'd been all set to go to the shops for the *Radio Times* when Shields had turned up and after that the magazine had completely slipped my mind.

'So if you had a girlfriend Henry, then what have I been doing waiting on you hand and foot?'

The same thing had happened at the police station. I'd gone to pieces under pressure and forgotten things. It was stress that had caused that. Plus all the stuff they put in the water. I owed Chewing Gum for that. I owed Chewing Gum for a lot of things.

'Chewing gum?'

'What?' I almost jumped from my seat.

'Would you like a piece of chewing gum Henry?'

'No. Since when have you eaten chewing gum?'

'I don't know. Ages. Who cares?'

'I didn't know.'

'You don't have to tell people. It's not like being gay or something, is it? It's only chewing gum for heaven's sake. I don't always have time to brush my teeth and it freshens my breath. You should try it.'

I suddenly noticed two blobs of discarded gum in the dashboard recess.

'I don't like chewing gum at all,' I said.

'Suit yourself,' she said. 'Nothing to do with Father I don't suppose?'

'Well he wouldn't have approved, would he?'

'Let's not get into that, eh?'

'You brought it up Susan.'

We drove a little further without talking before Susan broke the silence.

'You see the thing is Henry, and I don't want to keep going on about it, but they must have thought that something wasn't right, mustn't they? The police, I mean.'

'Unless it was one of the police,' I said.

'Oh come on, that sort of thing doesn't happen, does it?'

'Why not?'

'I'm not going to argue. But they'll have had their suspicions. You don't need to be a genius to work that out. You've only got to see your house anyway to realise that.'

The house. 'What's happened to the house?'

'And it won't be just the police either. Anyone – I know you're not going to like me saying this, but I'll say it anyway – anyone normal would think the same.'

'Susan?'

'That doesn't mean I'm saying you're a serial killer Henry, OK?'

What had happened to the house? My heart began to flutter as we got nearer and familiar streets came into view. I kept thinking 'Please don't let anything have changed,' and repeated the words over in my head. And at first sight things did seem much the same as they had done when I'd last seen them. There was no sign of a baying mob ready to scream for my blood as soon as they clapped eyes on me. Not yet, anyway. But it could still happen. I might not have been charged but the police hadn't exactly given me a clean bill of health. 'We'll be in touch Mr Henry.' That's what they'd said to me. 'Make sure you don't do anything foolish.' They didn't say what they considered foolish.

There was the house.

I couldn't see any police presence outside – at least, nothing obvious. I felt pleased about that until it dawned on me that I hadn't noticed I was being watched before. Yet someone had been doing just that. They could have been hiding behind a net curtain or in a discreetly parked car or just walking past the front gate. So perhaps it might be better if the police were keeping a closer eye on the house. Unless, that is, one of them was the murderer. But I'd be on my guard from now on. Nothing would escape my attention.

'Well?' said Susan.

'Well what?'

'Have you been listening to anything I've been saying?'

'Of course,' I said.

'So what did I say?'

'Could you just repeat it again?'

'I bet you've been fretting about that bloody house, haven't you? It's nothing but junk, the lot of it.'

'It's not junk.'

'I don't know why you kept all that old stuff of theirs – the bed, the chairs, that ugly wardrobe. It can't mean anything to you. Nothing good, anyway.'

'Thank you for the lift,' I said and opened the door.

'And they seriously thought that you could be a murderer.'

'No Susan.' I leaned across towards her and whispered. 'But he's probably watching us right now.'

'Oh stop it.'

I got out of the car. 'So will I see you on Thursday?'

She sighed. 'I expect you will.'

'Thanks,' I said.

'Wonders never cease,' she said. 'Prison seems to have done you some good.'

'I beg your pardon.'

She checked the mirrors. 'First time I can ever remember you saying thanks for anything Henry. The world really is changing.'

And before I could contradict her, Susan was gone.

It came as a pleasant surprise to see that the bookcases in the front garden had remained largely intact. I peeked under the plastic sheets and saw that the neighbours had left well alone. Most likely the police had warned them off, or nobody had thought my books worthy of investigation.

At first glance it looked like it was much the same inside. The hallway was full of bags and boxes, and the magazines and cards were still piled on the stairs. There was the sash window brochure and the computer leaflet from Jamal. They hadn't been touched. It was a different story in the kitchen, though. Before I'd even got through the doorway I could see that the room had been turned upside down. Boxes had been emptied and bags ripped open. There were old tablecloths, curtains, cookery books and all sorts of kitchen utensils scattered across the room. The television set, which had been quite central, was facing the back wall. But at least it looked like it might still work. The video recorder was another thing altogether. It lay upended against a cardboard box with its covering plate removed and all its wires exposed. Nor could I see a single one of my tapes anywhere.

My precious boxes of mementoes, I'm glad to say, appeared to have been overlooked. At least, they were still roughly where I recalled having seen them last, wedged behind a couple of bin-bags full of old coats. If the police had come across them they mustn't have thought them worth the trouble. Or perhaps they were more fascinated by the piles of unlabelled video tapes, and what they might contain. I felt angry at losing them, but vindicated at the same time. Hadn't I told the police the tapes were full of news?

I went back to the kitchen and surveyed the mess. It would take a long time to get it all sorted out again. I'd need some new bags and replacement boxes. The TV and video would require the most attention. I took a dirty cup from the sink, wiped it clean with my finger and made some tea. As the kettle boiled, my mind drifted back to the time I'd spent with Rose. It never occurred to me it would all end so suddenly, and so finally. I looked at the spot on the floor where the two of us had lain together and heaved a sigh. There was nothing to mark it out as anything special – only what was still there in my mind. But Rose wouldn't be forgotten. I'd see to that.
I righted a plastic chair and sat down, cradling the tea in my hands. I was going to find out exactly who'd killed Rose – and the other girls. I was going to unmask Chewing Gum and bring him to justice. It was the very least she – and they – deserved.

CHAPTER THIRTEEN

The kitchen was a mess. Nothing seemed to be where it should, and it upset me to look at it. I knew I wouldn't be able to think properly until everything was back in its proper place, so I began repairing and then refilling damaged boxes. It took me most of the day, and even then it was hard to see any significant improvement.

I couldn't bear to switch the television on. They'd most probably be talking about me, and I didn't want to hear anything like that. So apart from the humming of the fridge, the buzzing of a couple of wasps, and my grunts and groans, I worked in silence. Boxes I could fix, but the video recorder, unfortunately, was beyond my abilities. It was propped up against the back wall, its workings exposed for all to see. I consoled myself with the fact that I could get it repaired once the kitchen was finished.

The problem I had was space, or lack of it. The solution, I realised, probably lay outside. There was still some room in the back garden. The bulkier boxes might be better off there, while I sorted out the kitchen.

Unfortunately, when I tried to open the door, I discovered that it was locked and the key was missing. It wasn't in the lock, nor was it dangling on its designated hook. I guessed it must be somewhere on the floor, in which case it would eventually turn up when I'd cleared everything away, though that might not be for a while. Of course it was possible that one of the policemen who'd searched the kitchen might have dropped it somewhere. They had no respect for my other possessions, so why would they have cared about a back door key?

I wished that Rose was there so I could talk to her – about the white tents, about travelling here and there when I didn't really like to, about Henry the concrete cat, about the case, about Chewing Gum, about everything. There was so much we'd never have a chance to talk about, so many conversations. If only I hadn't gone upstairs when I had done and left her on her own. I should have taken Rose upstairs with me. But what had made her run off in such a hurry? Was it seeing all the pieces of chewing gum? It wasn't long after I'd shown them to her. Maybe she'd recognised them, or suddenly realised who it was who'd dropped them. So why hadn't she told me then, if she knew something? Didn't she think I could help? We were supposed to be working together.

Rose had talked about her sister. But she hadn't said very much about her, even after we'd found the gum at Bradnam Common. Perhaps it had been too painful to talk about. Yet now she'd become the victim herself, which made two women from the same family. That had to be more than just a terrible coincidence. The police hadn't seen fit to mention that when they'd questioned me, but they couldn't have been ignorant, surely. The mess in the kitchen was going to have to wait. I dropped the bag I was stuffing with old tea towels and pushed my way into the hallway.

It was time I did some research of my own. Rose said the murder had been a little over two years ago. Well, I happened to have a reference library going back that far – a spare bedroom and a loft full of newspapers. It might be a problem accessing them, but the end result would be worth it. That was why it was so important not to throw things away.

It was only when I approached the box room that I began to appreciate just how difficult my task was going to be. It was jam-packed right to the top of the doorway. I'd started off storing old office equipment in there, cupboards, units and so on, and filled each of them up with newspapers. In time the papers had taken over, until first the units and then the room itself disappeared completely. It would be a mammoth undertaking to empty the room, but in all likelihood the ones in there were probably too old. There were more newspapers stored in the large back bedroom, but those were quite recent. So I decided to begin my search in the loft.

Above the landing there was a hatch, and inside it a collapsible ladder that pulled down. There was scarcely enough clearance room so it proved a tight squeeze for me to clamber to the top. I was out of breath as well when I stepped off the ladder.

The light still worked, but the papers were so tightly packed that it made little difference. I tried to remember if I'd put them in order, but judging by the first pile it looked as though there was no plan at all. The papers had just been heaped any old how, toppling against one another and falling into any gaps that still remained. I heaved a sigh and closed the loft hatch behind me.

It took me a few minutes to devise a system to cope with such a daunting task. I found that the best method was to sit on the only area of free space, the hatch itself, and work methodically from left to right, examining the front page of every newspaper. Once each stack was completely scrutinised, I moved onto the next one, moving several piles to get to the newspapers at the back. It was sweaty work and involved all manner of discomfort, but it was necessary. I'd made the mistake once before of covering the loft hatch in papers before realising that I'd blocked my only means of getting out.

I didn't learn much in the first hour apart from the fact that some of the newspapers had sustained damage. I couldn't be certain, but it looked as though something had been eating them. Most probably it was mice, I told myself, although there was no sign of any droppings. Quite why they'd gone up to the loft when all the food was in the kitchen was something I couldn't fathom. I just hoped that the mystery chewer didn't turn out to be a rat. The thought of coming face to face with one in the cramped confines of the loft was not a prospect that appealed to me. But each pile I shifted failed to reveal any mice or rats.

I was just coming to terms with the possibility that the killing hadn't been front page news when a headline caught my eye. *'Bradnam Common Murder'* it said. *'Man released'*. A short paragraph revealed that an unnamed man who'd been questioned about the killing had not been charged. I felt a tingle, not least because a similar thing had happened to me. But the more I read, the more one particular aspect of the case troubled me. It was the victim's name. She was Jacqueline Treacy – 'Jackie to her friends' – not Jacqueline Bowyer. Was the name significant? They could still have been sisters. Or Bowyer might have been Rose's married name. I recalled her saying something to do with getting married, but she might just have been making conversation. Neither Hillyard nor Wyatt had said anything about Rose being a married woman. But there was something else. Jacqueline Treacy had been a girl of seventeen. Rose hadn't told me her age but I guessed she was no more than a couple of years older than Susan. That was a difference of twenty years or more. But perhaps the two of them had another relationship. 'You know what mothers are like?' I could remember Rose saying that. Well she'd have known if she'd been one herself, wouldn't she?

As I went down through the pile I also went back through time, and the murder case began to unfold in reverse. First a suspect was released, then a DS Johnson gave a statement. After that the trail went cold and the media took the police to task for the way they'd handled the case.

And then suddenly, there she was.

The face was slightly unfamiliar, so it took a second or two to register. Her hair was neater, for one thing. But it was the headline underneath the photograph that leaped out at me. *'Bungling Cop Axed'* it said. And then in the caption underneath were the words 'Detective Inspector Rosamund Bowyer'.

I scrambled, confused, from one paper to the other. Rose hadn't been a policewoman, she'd have told me if she had been. Friends told each other things like that, they had conversations. I tore at the pages of the next paper, desperate to see more. *'Murder Case Ma'am Gets The Chop'* declared the *Mirror*'s front page. Rose was pictured with her head bowed. I began to read more quickly, until the words blurred in front of my eyes. She'd lied to me, hadn't she? All that stuff she'd said about trying to get justice for her sister – that was just talk. She was a police officer. And she'd befriended me – no, more than that – she'd seduced me. There was a phrase for something like that, I'd seen it on television. A honey trap, they called it. Members of the police would go undercover and pretend they weren't the police and try and obtain confessions using sex as bait. Undercover, or under curtains. My hands shook as I turned the pages.

I read on through burning eyes. It seemed that DI Bowyer had been charged with failing to properly secure a crime scene and for allowing vital evidence to become either lost or contaminated. She'd let people trample all over the murder site, the Bungling Cop.

'When were you going to tell me?' I mumbled. 'Did you think I wasn't going to find out, or didn't you care?'

I went through the next lot of newspapers. There she was telling the nation's collected media she was confident they were making progress. A few days earlier and she was fresh to the case – a high flying young police officer determined to catch the killer. The day before, there was nothing. Jacqueline – *Jackie to her friends'* – had still been alive and was not yet news.

Rose couldn't still have been working for the police when we were together. Surely not after all that time. Or had it all been make believe? Was she just pretending to be an agitator, searching for justice, while she was trying to get close to someone she thought was the murderer? Well she'd found him all right, hadn't she? She'd got what she wanted. And what had it cost her? Only her life, that's all. The stupid, stupid...

I stared at Rose's photo for a moment then roared at the top of my voice, a sound like no other I'd ever made. Then the roar turned into a growl and I began thrashing at the newspaper, crumpling it and tearing at it with my hands. I tried pulling it in half, but found my arms weren't strong enough. In frustration I compressed the paper into a ball and flung it to one side. But there wasn't really room to throw it anywhere, and the bundle rebounded off a stack of papers and landed at my knees, where it began to unfurl and resume its former shape. I snarled at it and shoved it away and then I saw Rose's face on the next newspaper and I did the same to that. And she was pictured on the one below, as well. There was just no escaping Detective Inspector Rosamund Bowyer; Rose Bowyer; Rose; my Rose; dead Rose.

With my heart pounding I leaned on the pile of newspapers for support, and with another cry, smaller this time, I smoothed the newspaper as flat as I could and rested my head on Rose's crumpled face. And in the loft, in my den of newspapers, I wept and wept.

CHAPTER FOURTEEN

I thought the television would distract me, but it proved to be a frustrating experience. I couldn't tape anything, so I was compelled to sit and watch every moment. The news made no reference to my recent questioning, but the murder case, significantly, was no longer the lead item. The police spokesman acknowledged that they'd failed to make a breakthrough and instead he issued a warning. A dangerous individual or individuals were still on the loose and unaccompanied females needed to exercise caution, he said.

At eleven-thirty-five, confident there'd be no further news bulletins for the next twenty-five minutes, I plucked up the courage and left the house. I felt as though Chewing Gum might be watching my every move as I made my way to the local phone box. I didn't really want to call the electrical repair shop, not after the way they'd treated me last time, but I didn't think that I had much choice. But three attempts, each time accompanied by the discontinued tone, told me that the only remaining electrical repair shop had closed. There was just one course of action left. I took a second scrap of paper from my pocket and began dialling the number. It was answered immediately.

'Hello?' I said.

'Hello?' came the reply.

'Hello,' I said again.

And then the line went dead. I tried again. It rang several times before it was answered.

'Hello,' I said.

There was silence. Then somebody said: 'Who is it?'

'My name's Henry,' I said. 'Is that Jamal?' It went quiet again. 'Hello?'

'Who are you?' came the voice.

'I said my name is Henry.' I shouted this time. 'Hello?'

'Yeah, this is Jamal.'

'Good. I'm calling about your leaflet,' I said.

'Uh huh.' More silence. 'Go on.'

'Only I've had some difficulties you see and I thought you might be able to help.'

'Whoa whoa, hold on,' said Jamal. 'You're that guy, right?'

'What guy?' I said.

'That guy, man. You know. I came by your house and you shouted at me. I ain't helping you man, you're nuts.'

'I didn't mean to shout at you,' I said.

'Yeah, but you did though, didn't you?'

'I'm sorry about that.'

'You should have thought of that first man.'

'Yes. Wait a second.' I fumbled in my pocket.

'Are you in a call box?' asked Jamal.

'Yes.'

'Wild.'

'Only I really need some help.' There was silence. 'What?'

'I didn't say nothing,' said Jamal.

'Well?' I said. 'What do you say?'

'Forget it man. Try someone else.'

'Please,' I said. But I was already talking to myself.

oOo

I knelt down on the floor, turned the case on its back and picked up the screwdriver. There was nothing else for it. If no-one else was prepared to help me mend the video recorder then the very least I could do was try and repair it myself. I did have an instruction manual somewhere, but it would take ages to find, so I'd just have to use my initiative instead. I felt quietly confident. After all it was initiative that had led me to that piece of chewing gum on Bradnam Common.

After half an hour of utter frustration, I put down the screwdriver to watch the news. The murder weapon, a knife, had yielded negative test results. The blood, it turned out, didn't match any of the known victims. I was just trying to absorb this information when to my surprise DI Hillyard made an appearance. The detective inspector was responding to the criticism that the enquiry had become bogged down and was getting nowhere. He said that he understood the public's dissatisfaction at the lack of progress but that it was important everyone kept faith in the police force. They were doing everything in their power to catch the culprit and no stone was being left unturned. Then, as if to emphasise his point, Hillyard looked directly down the camera lens. There were people out there who could help the police solve these terrible crimes, he said, and his eyes caught mine. It was important that nothing was overlooked, he went on, no matter how small or insignificant it might seem. The DI finished by imploring anyone with information to come forward and speak to the police in confidence. He looked tired, I thought, and no doubt feeling the pressure. Was Hillyard about to become the next bungling cop?

I tried to suppress my feeling of pleasure at the detective inspector's discomfort. Hillyard was right – catching the murderer was the most important thing. Perhaps I should go to my nearest police station and tell them I had some important information. I'd been a murder suspect before, so they ought to listen to me. I'd request a meeting with Wyatt, rather than Hillyard. She seemed to be the less aggressive of the two. I wouldn't take my chewing gum with me though, not the first time anyway. It was crucial they stayed in safe keeping – until I could show them to the DS in person. It would be a gamble of course, I was well aware of that. The police were getting desperate now, and I couldn't be sure they wouldn't accuse me of being the chewing gum killer myself and trump up some evidence to make it stick. The public wanted closure and someone brought to justice – even if that someone was the wrong person.

There was a knock at the front door and I squealed. It was the police, come back to arrest me. Or worse than that – it was Chewing Gum. He'd come to do me in and make it look like an accident. He'd be in some sort of disguise, most likely. He'd just seem ordinary, before he came in and murdered me and made off with the evidence.

Rat-a-tat went the door knocker again.

I checked the clock and immediately felt a bit more relaxed. The postman usually called around this time. I told myself it was only the postman with an extra large package that wouldn't fit through the box, or maybe a registered letter. Not that I was expecting anything like that. Still, it helped me convince myself I was probably panicking for no good reason. 'Coming,' I called out.

As I squirmed through the bags that blocked the hallway I saw an outline through the frosted glass window. It was a well built man by the look of things – and certainly not the postman. Where was his distinctively-coloured jacket? Terrified, I opened the front door.

'Those wasps.'

It was the man from next door. I couldn't see his tattoos but I knew they were there – fearsome looking knives under his shirt.

'Janice got stung last night,' he said.

'I'm sorry to hear that,' I said. Janice was Mrs Tattoos, I recalled.

'It's come up like a golf ball.' His jaw moved from side to side, pounding away at a piece of chewing gum.

'Oh dear,' I said.

'They're coming from your house,' he said. 'Upstairs.'

'Yes,' I said.

'So what are you going to do about it?' Tattoos folded his arms across his prominent chest.

I didn't say anything. I was too transfixed by his grinding mouth. Was Tattoos really Chewing Gum? I might be living next door to a serial killer. In many ways it made perfect sense.

'Well?'

'Come again?' I said.

'If she was allergic a wasp sting might kill her.'

'Yes.'

'So what are you going to do about it?'

I should go to the police, that was what I ought to do. I should tell them everything I knew.

'I said what are you gonna do?'

'I ought to go to the police,' I said.

'And who do you think they'll listen to, you or me?'

I watched as his chewing became more pronounced.

'So instead of threatening me get someone in to sort the problem out – or I'll do it myself and send you the bill.' And having said his piece Tattoos left without waiting for my response.

I found it hard to concentrate on my repair work after that. The thought that my next-door neighbour might be a serial killer began to take root in my head. It was a far-fetched idea, admittedly, but he did always seem to be chewing gum, and his tattoos matched the murder weapons. I tried to recall some previous encounters I'd had with him. We'd had an argument out in the street once, about a mirrored bathroom cabinet I'd put in the front garden. Tattoos had taken it and I'd asked for it back and Tattoos had said it didn't really belong to me because I'd taken it from his skip in the first place. I assumed he'd thrown it away and told him it was a perfectly good cabinet. And Tattoos had said normal people didn't have bathroom cabinets in their front gardens and jabbed his finger at me. And another neighbour had come along and calmed things down. And when I gave Tattoos the bathroom cabinet back, he threw it straight into the skip, smashing the mirrors as well. Then he'd spat his chewing gum out on the street for good measure. It wasn't very nice behaviour, but having seen him spit out his gum rather than wrap it up in silver paper, I felt more positive that Tattoos wasn't Chewing Gum. I was probably worrying about nothing.

There was another knock at the door.

For heaven's sake, I thought as I squeezed past the kitchen door-frame. I hadn't had a chance to do anything yet. I felt quite indignant when I opened the door.

'What is it now?' I said.

The dark-skinned youth stared at me, slack jawed. 'I knew you was nuts,' he said and turned on his heels.

'Wait, wait,' I said.

'Later.'

'Jamal.' The boy walked past the gate and onto the street. 'Jamal!'

I dashed out after him. 'What?' he said, but carried on walking.

'I thought you were someone else, that's all,' I said. 'I've had a lot of trouble, you see.'

'No kidding.'

'It's true. Do you mind if we stop a moment.'

He stopped. 'Are you always rude with people? Even my mum's not this bad.'

'Sorry.'

'I don't even know why I came back.'

'It's very good of you to do that,' I said. 'I mean I didn't think you would. You did tell me you wouldn't.'

He shrugged his shoulders. 'The man said he needed help.'

'Which man?' I said. 'Oh.'

He adjusted the rucksack that was slung across his shoulder.

'Do you mean that?' I said. 'Would you help me?'

'I had been thinking about it,' he said.

'So that's yes, is it?'

'Yeah.'

'Great, thank you,' I said and waved my arms about to show him the way. 'It's this way.' And we walked back to the front door.

'Wow.' Jamal stepped through, had a look around and sniffed. 'What's that smell man?'

'What smell?'

'That smell that smells like shit.'

'Oh, that must be my trousers,' I said.

'What is wrong with you?' He muttered under his breath. I pretended I hadn't heard him.

'Careful here, it's a bit of a squeeze,' I said as I led him through to the kitchen. 'More for me than you I should say.'

'Jesus,' said Jamal.

'I'm sorry about the mess, only I haven't had time to clear things up.'

'You're one of them hoarders ain't you?'

'A what?'

'A hoarder.'

I looked around the room. 'Yes,' I said. 'I suppose I am.'

'People who keep all their old junk.'

'I don't know that it's junk,' I said.

'You've got two microwaves man.'

'They both need fixing, I'm afraid.'

'And it's all out there in your yard,' He wiped the kitchen window and peered through.

'It's a garden really, not a yard,' I said.

'Looks like a yard' he said. 'You've been on the telly, ain't you?'

'Me?' I flinched.

'I don't know if it was you, but there was these other people. An old hoarder guy.'

'I'm not really old.'

'He had all kinds of crap, man.'

'I remember seeing something like that,' I said. 'They were bullying an old age pensioner and trying to make him throw his things away. I think I've got a tape of it somewhere.'

Jamal laughed.

'What's so funny?' I said.

He shook his head.

'But of course I can't tape anything now.' I gazed down at the broken video recorder.

'So what's up with your computer then?' said Jamal.

'My computer?'

'Yeah man.'

'Nothing,' I said. 'I don't have a computer.'

'You're joking me.'

I shook my head.

'So why did you call me?' He frowned and drew himself up straight. 'Are you a comedian, is that it?'

'I was hoping you might be able to help me out with that.' I pointed at the remains of my dismantled video recorder.

'What is that?'

'It's a video recorder,' I said.

He walked over to it and bent down. 'My mum had one of these when I was a kid,' he said.

'Had?'

'Threw it away.'

'Oh.'

'Have you been messing with it?'

'I tried to repair it myself,' I said. 'I think I've just made it worse.'

Jamal shook his head. 'You can't fix this shit man, it's ancient technology.'

'It was working last week.'

'Not working now though, is it?'

'No,' I said.

He shuffled his rucksack. 'Tough break.'

'It's just that I'm lost without it,' I said. 'I can't keep on top of things.'

'So you ain't got a computer.'

'No.'

'Ever had one?'

'No.'

'Jesus.' He shook his head. 'I don't know anyone like you.'

I shrugged my shoulders and tried to smile.

Jamal dropped his bag onto his hip and took a black object from it which was about the size of a book. He came over next to me and I could see then that it wasn't a book at all, but a small, flat computer, which was starting to come to life.

'I've seen you with that before, haven't I?' I said.

'I dunno,' he said. 'Have you?'

'At Parson's Wood.'

'Check this out,' he said and stroked the surface of the screen. A parade of colourful images flashed by, which Jamal touched with his finger and made larger, one after the other.

'So what are you into?' he said.

'What do I like you mean?'

'Yes.'

'I like to follow the news,' I said, not taking my eyes off the screen. 'Current affairs. Things like that.'

It only took a couple of movements for Jamal to locate some news. He pressed here and there and item after item whizzed past at dizzying speed. I think I must have grunted.

'Was that a good noise?' he said.

'I should say,' I said. There was a slight giggle in my voice. 'This is fantastic. Wonderful.'

Jamal settled on something, pressed the screen and another picture appeared. 'What do they call you then?' he said.

'Henry,' I said.

'I'm Jamal,' he said and held out his hand across the screen. 'Nice meeting you Henry.'

'Yes,' I said as I clasped his hand. 'It is nice.'

I tried to make sense of the words in front of me but Jamal's fingers moved too quickly and before I could read anything the screen was showing something else. 'And this is a computer, isn't it?' I said.

'Yeah.'

'Only it doesn't look much like a computer. To me, anyway.'

'It's what they call a tablet,' he said. 'You've got all the functions of a computer, only in this shape.'

'I see,' I said. 'So does it keep things then? Like a video recorder.'

'Nah man, it's nothing like that. This thing will make your video look like a... Well, it's just nothing next to it, is it? Let me tell you – Henry –

you've got the world in here. Everything.'

'Everything?'

'Whatever you want. More junk than you'll ever know what to do with –
no disrespect.'

'May I?' I stretched out my hand.

'Go ahead,' said Jamal and handed over the tablet.

I held it firmly in one hand then poked at the screen with my finger.

'Not so rough.'

'Sorry.'

'Just stroke it gently,' said Jamal. 'Be tender. Jesus, I can't believe I'm
saying this.'

'What?'

'Don't worry man. It's nothing.'

I slid more images across the screen, backwards and forwards. 'So if I
wanted to read about the serial killings, the news would be on here would
it?'

'Sure.'

'OK.' I nodded.

'They want to catch him quick. Guys like that they do it again.'

'I know.'

'I've got a sister Henry. She's worried.'

'He killed my girlfriend,' I said.

'Serious?'

'Rosamund Grace Bowyer. Well, I knew her as Rose.'

Jamal looked at me, then began looking around the room. 'You're telling
me you've got a girlfriend.'

'Had. She was killed.'

'I didn't mean it like that.'

'Stabbed. Just like the others.' I handed the tablet back to Jamal.

'You sure you want to tell me this?' he said.

'I want to see him caught,' I said. 'Whoever did it. Otherwise your sister
won't be safe.'

'I'm telling you man she's petrified.'

'So I'm looking for clues.' I looked into Jamal's eyes. 'Anything.'

'Ain't that what the police are doing?'

'They're not doing it very well are they?' I said. 'So how far do the
stories go back on your computer, can you check for me?'

Jamal pulled back his sleeve and examined his watch. 'Look Henry, I've
got work I should be doing.'

'Please. I'd like you to show me.'

'If you bought one of these I could give you some lessons,' he said.
'Take you through the basics. I'd have to charge of course. I mean, I'm an
entrepreneur, you understand.'

'Yes.'

'I've got a business to run.'

'But if you could show me now,' I said. 'It's very important. Please.'

Jamal sighed. 'She was your girlfriend, right?'

'She was.'

'That's serious, man.' Moments later familiar images were flashing before my eyes – Hillyard, Wyatt, Rose, Tabitha Williams, Lorna Coulson, Parson's Wood, and last of all a picture of myself. It was quite a shock to think that I had an existence inside the computer. And then I saw the group of us gathered at Lorna Coulson's murder site. Cloth Cap, Ginger Whiskers, Two Dogs, Sandwiches, Mr and Mrs Flask, Pram Girl, Rose, Wyatt, Hillyard and me – we were all there.

'Stop,' I said. Jamal lifted his finger from the screen. 'I was there. That's me, look. And there's Rose. Rosamund Bowyer.'

'Did you know this girl too then?' he said.

'Not exactly.'

Jamal did something that made the picture stretch, and the figures grew on the screen.

'I just wish I knew who all these other people were.' I pointed at the remaining people in the photograph. 'I'm sure they've got some answers.'

'The cops must have spoke to them. And you, right?'

I didn't say anything.

'Henry?'

I nodded. 'So how would I find out who they were?'

'Well you can't from just a photo. It would take years matching one face to another. Don't you know anything about them?'

'No.'

'That's that then.'

'They all had cars, I remember that,' I said. 'Except for Rose and the girl with the pram.'

'I don't suppose you wrote their numbers down did you?'

I shook my head. 'I wasn't really paying attention.'

Jamal's phone rang. He answered it sharply.

'I'll be there in five minutes,' he said, then slipped his phone in his pocket.

I showed him to the door. Jamal began adjusting the straps of his rucksack. 'So Henry, like I said, if you ever change your mind about getting a computer...' He crooked his fingers into a shape.

'What?' I said.

'Give me a call,' he said.

'Oh. Yes. Of course.'

And as I closed the door I suddenly noticed there was a sound coming from the kitchen. It was only when I got there that I realised the television had been chattering away the whole time.

CHAPTER FIFTEEN

I went out very early the following morning. I needed to stock up with a few ready-meals. Cooking has never been one of my strong points. But I was more excited by the idea of looking at some computers. The possibilities of a computer had begun to intrigue me. The metal and plastic scattered on the kitchen floor which used to be my video recorder looked more pathetic every time I looked at it. Jamal was right – it was redundant technology.

I put on my scarf and shut the front door, but by the time I was half-way down the front path I'd forgotten why I was there. Because lying on the ground, next to a plastic tray full of paperback books, was a neatly-folded silver parcel. There couldn't be any doubt about it now, even if there had been before. Chewing Gum knew where I lived.

I could feel my heart thumping in my chest. When had it been dropped? I'd walked the path the day before when I'd chased after Jamal and I was sure it hadn't been there then. It felt soft in my fingers which meant it was fresh. That terrified me even more. Perhaps Chewing Gum was nearby, waiting for me. I dropped my shoulders, crept to the front gate and peered up and down the road. There were people who seemed to be going about their business, but who could tell what that was? I wondered if I should run towards someone and ask them if they'd seen anybody. But which person should I run to, and more importantly how did I know which one I should avoid? I stood for a moment weighing up the options and noticed I was wearing my coat and scarf. I'd clearly been planning to go out somewhere, but I couldn't remember where, or what for.

Instead of going back indoors I began walking. I had to find a phone box. There was one near the junction, not far from the house, but I knew I had to avoid going there. It was too quiet and I needed to be seen. Chewing Gum would never attack me out in the open. So I made my way towards the shopping centre.

When I got there I saw that the phone box I had in mind, the one in the precinct by the litter-filled concrete flower troughs, was no longer working. It had been stripped of its phone and now served as a urinal. There was another one though, more a hood than an actual phone box, not far from the multi-storey car park. I headed towards it, turning to look back every now and then to check that I wasn't being followed and this time I was in luck. The phone worked.

I stood beneath the hood and dialled, bending my knees occasionally to check the people around me. Everything seemed ordinary and nobody paid me the least bit of attention, although that didn't stop me feeling vulnerable. After all I could be attacked at any moment. Nobody ever noticed the best assassins, I knew that from watching television. The ring tone seemed to go on forever before the phone was finally picked up.

'Hello?'

'Susan, thank God you're there.'

'Henry?' There was a pause. 'Is that you?'

'Of course it's me, yes. Yes,' I said.

'What's going on?'

'Nothing right now – I don't know for sure.' There was another pause. 'Susan?'

'What?'

'I thought you'd gone.'

'No.'

'Oh.'

'There's a lot of noise,' she said. 'Where are you?'

'Not far away.'

'Henry, stop being so cryptic.'

'By the car park. Near the shops. Let's leave it at that.'

'Are you in trouble again?'

'I don't want to say over the phone.' I bent down and looked in each direction. 'Can I come around Susan? I need to see you.'

'It's not a good time Henry.'

'I'll be half-an-hour.'

'No.'

'Susan!'

'Didn't you hear me?'

'It won't take long.'

'Are the police after you? Is that it?'

'The police?'

I took another look. An old woman was pushing a basket. A young couple were sitting on a bench, talking, focused on each other. A girl stood outside an office, smoking. None of them looked like they were police or assassins, but how could I tell?

'Henry?'

'What?'

'I said, is it the police?'

'No. I'm not sure. Look, I'll be right round,' I said and cradled the phone before Susan could tell me otherwise.

It was too far to walk to Susan's house, but I went a good way on foot – making sure I took as winding a route as possible. Only once I'd caught the bus did I congratulate myself that I'd managed to avoid being seen by Chewing Gum. No-one else had boarded the bus with me and I felt satisfied that no cars or bicycles had followed me either. A jogger had run alongside for a while, but he soon turned down a side-street and disappeared from sight. Then I remembered how I'd done the same thing when I'd left Parson's Wood and Rose had still managed to track my every move without my knowing it. That must have been something she'd learned to do in the police.

I was relieved when I finally arrived at Susan's house, but surprised to see that the curtains were drawn. It was obvious she hadn't wanted me to visit, but closing the curtains seemed a bit extreme. So I was pleasantly surprised when the landing light came on, though I got quite a shock when Susan opened the door. She was still wearing her night clothes, and a dressing gown was thrown over her shoulders. Her eyes looked dark and her hair hadn't been given its usual care and attention. I noticed she had bare feet.

'I didn't know you were ill,' I said. 'I am sorry.'

'I'm not and you aren't,' she said. She trudged ahead of me into the kitchen. I covered my mouth with my hand.

'What are you doing that for?' She scowled at me.

'I don't want to catch anything.'

She gave a snort.

'I won't keep you long, really I won't,' I said.

'It doesn't matter now, does it? You're here.'

She tried to fill the kettle but somehow managed to soak herself in the process. 'You do it,' she said and thrust the kettle at me. 'You might as well make yourself useful for once.'

She sat down at the kitchen table and took a cigarette from an open packet. She lit it at the third or fourth attempt, and I could see the lighter shaking in her hand. The ashtray was half-filled with cigarette butts.

'If you say one thing about Father.' She jabbed a finger at me. 'I swear to God I'll kill you.'

'I wasn't going to say a word,' I said. I filled the kettle.

'Why are you here?' She sighed.

I walked around the kitchen table and stood opposite her. 'Someone's trying to kill me,' I said.

'Kill you?'

'Yes.'

She laughed. 'You're priceless Henry, you really are.'

'It's true Susan.' I sat down. 'I'm not making it up.'

'Oh no, of course you're not.'

'I've got proof.'

'Always about you, isn't it?' she snapped. 'It's always me, me, me in Henry's little world. You never stop to think for a second that you're not important, do you? That the universe doesn't revolve around you. God almighty Henry, the universe doesn't even notice you exist.'

I tried to interject but Susan blew smoke towards me, making me cough.

'Does it ever occur to you that there are other people in this life Henry, eh?'

'I'm sorry,' I said. 'How is Christopher?'

'Oh to hell with bloody Christopher.' She stubbed out the half-smoked cigarette with angry movements. 'The kettle's boiled.'

I stood up. 'I know who the serial killer is,' I said, dropping tea bags into two cups.

'You?'

'Yes. Well I don't know his precise identity but I know how he works.'

'He kills young women, Henry. Even I know that.'

'Susan—'

'No no, go ahead. Don't let me stop you.' She lit another cigarette. 'You've solved the biggest crime in the country. Well done Hercule Poirot.'

'You're not being serious.'

'Of course I'm not being serious. Is this why you're here?'

'You remember I was arrested for Rose's murder. Rosamund Bowyer.'

'How could I forget?'

'She was a police officer working on the Jacqueline Treacy case. Anyway I think she was killed because she found out who the serial killer was. And now I know – well I sort of know.'

'Henry, you're not making any sense at all.'

'Susan, it's true.'

I sat down at the table with the cups of tea. 'He leaves chewing gum at the scene of the crime.'

'Chewing gum.'

'Yes.'

She laughed.

'Why's that funny?'

Susan shook her head.

'He wraps the gum in little silver paper parcels. He knows I know Susan, which is why he's after me.'

'The serial killer?'

'Yes.'

'Have you listened to yourself Henry? What's the matter with you? As if I needed to ask.'

'I found one this morning. On my front path. It wasn't there yesterday, I swear.'

There was a noise at the front door. I jerked in my seat. 'What was that?' I hissed the words.

'The letterbox. For God's sake Henry, grow up. It's a kid delivering pizza leaflets or some rubbish.'

'Are you sure?'

'You can check if you want.'

I rested my elbow on the table and cupped my forehead in my hand. 'I'd like you to do something for me,' I said.

'Extra washing is it? I could always do with that. I notice you didn't bother to bring any with you. That could have saved me a trip.'

'It's not washing.' I took a deep breath. 'I need to bring some things over Susan. For safe-keeping.'

'Oh no.' She thrust up her hands.

'It would only be a couple of boxes.'

'That's how it starts with a couple of boxes. You've ruined your place Henry – well I'm not going to let you do the same to mine. This house is all I've got.'

'Please, I'm not going to ruin anything.'

'You're damned right you're not.'

'It would just be a few things that I've collected Susan. It wouldn't be for long.'

She closed her eyes and shook her head.

'They need to be kept safe,' I said. 'For a little while. Not long, I promise. They're special things.'

'Stop. Just stop there.'

'Two boxes. You know I wouldn't ask if it wasn't important.'

'Can't you hear Henry? Are you deaf as well as... I said no and that's the end of it.'

'You're not being fair.'

'Well tough. Life's hard, in case you hadn't noticed.'

'Susan–'

'I mean it, I do. I never say no to you Henry, ever. Well I'm saying it now.' She stood up. 'I've got to go,' she said.

I looked up at her.

'That means you have to go as well,' said Susan.

I dragged myself to my feet and we walked to the front door in silence. She sighed. 'I'll see you on Thursday,' she said. 'As usual.'

I nodded and looked down at the doormat. 'So where's that pizza leaflet

Susan? Where is it?'

CHAPTER SIXTEEN

'Henry!'

I was shocked to hear someone shouting my name.

'Henry!'

I didn't much care to be shouted at in the street. It made me feel vulnerable, and it wasn't a good time to feel vulnerable.

'Henry!'

I saw who it was and wished I could call back, if only to say 'Don't shout', but I thought that would just draw more attention to me.

'Henry man, are you deaf or something?'

It didn't seem to bother Jamal though. He was standing by my front gate, his arms folded across his chest.

'I've been waiting for you,' he said.

'Yes.' I went past him as quickly as I could.

'You need to get a phone or something. Where you been?'

'Can't talk here,' I said. I opened the front door and went in. Jamal followed.

'Aw – you want to get a washing machine as well, man. That's proper rank that is.'

'Have you been there long?'

'Not long,' he said.

'How long is not long?'

'I dunno. Five minutes maybe. I thought you was doing something out back. Your bell's not working.'

'I know. Did you see anyone? Was there anyone watching the place?'

'Are your neighbours giving you grief?

'Have a think.'

'What you done that's bad Henry?'

'Was there?'

'There was people walking up and down the street. A few cars.'

'Nothing unusual?'

'Only you, man.'

I frowned.

'I didn't see no-one, no,' he said.

'No, that's just it. You wouldn't.'

'What's that mean?'

'It means he's clever.'

'You're saying I'm not, yeah?'

'No. I'm saying he is.' I turned to the front door, half expecting to see a face pressed against the frosted glass.

'Henry?'

Then I made my way through to the kitchen and tried to look up at the houses in the back, though it wasn't easy. I hadn't noticed before how dirty the windows were.

'Is this dangerous shit you're in?' said Jamal.

I took a deep breath. 'Yes it is.'

'This serial killing, yeah?'

'Yes.' I stopped for a moment, distracted by the sound of a wasp beating itself against the glass. 'Right.'

'Just so there's no confusion here Henry – we ain't talking about you, are we?'

'Good God, no,' I said. 'No. Absolutely not.'

'Cool.'

'If you've come back to ask me if I've decided on a computer, I'm afraid I haven't had time,' I said. 'I've been a bit caught up with other things.'

'Good,' he said.

'Good?'

'Well I was worried you might rush out and get yourself something. And someone like you – what I mean is, if you've never had a computer before you gotta be careful you don't make the wrong choice. Only there's this new place opened up and I know the guy there, Hassan, and he reckons he can get me some special deals. Not that I'm on a commission or nothing, don't get me wrong. But who doesn't want to save money Henry, eh?'

'Of course.'

'I just know you can get carried away when you see all the bargains – twenty-percent off this, forty-percent off that. It's like being a kid in a sweet shop with his pocket money. You get what I'm saying?'

'I think so.'

'And they're doing all these offers on the Shensu P50 right now.'

Jamal took the black tablet from his rucksack.

'Is that one?' I said.

'This?' He pointed at the discreet yellow lettering. 'The Shensu is a skanky bit of kit man. I wouldn't go near one.'

'So not good then.'

'Not good at all Henry.'

'I see.'

The tablet began to pulse into life.

'Perhaps I'd be better off with one like yours then,' I said.

'Perhaps,' he said. 'But I see you as more of a PC guy.'

'PC?'

'Personal computer.'

'Is that the one with the big box?'

'We call that a hard drive.'

'Yes. And the Shensu doesn't have a good one, right?'

Jamal smiled. 'You're learning Henry.'

I smiled back. 'I should make some tea,' I said. 'Do you like tea? You can have it with sugar.'

'In a second.' He skimmed and tapped his fingers across the screen.

'I'm not sure I could learn to do what you're doing,' I said. 'It looks very difficult.'

'It's child's play,' said Jamal. 'I've got a cousin – he's twelve. He knows more about computers than I do. Kids eh?'

'Yes,' I said. I watched the images flash by. 'We didn't have anything like that when I was at school.'

'Course not. These things are only new, man.'

'I mean any sort of computer.'

'I'm sure they've all got them now. It's the law, right?'

'I expect so.'

'You weren't at school round here then?'

'No,' I said. 'I went to a boarding school.'

'What, one of them schools where you sleep there?'

'Yes.'

'I don't know how folks can do that to their kids,' said Jamal. 'They have 'em and then it's like they want to get rid of 'em.' He held up his hands. 'Don't get me wrong Henry, I'm not disrespecting your parents or nothing. I'm just saying, that's all. You get me?'

I nodded.

'What's that?' I said. The screen had stopped moving. 'I've seen that before.'

'That's called your browser,' said Jamal.

'You mean like you can browse in a book-shop?'

'Yeah, I suppose. They call it a browsing page as well so you might be on to something.'

I smiled. Jamal looked around the room. I felt very conscious about how messy it must look.

'You don't get out much, do you?' he said.

'I go out when I have to,' I said. 'I went to Scotland a couple of weeks ago.'

'Scotland? What, you got family up there?'

I shook my head. 'I had things I had to do.'

'I never been to Scotland,' said Jamal. 'But they reckon the weather's bad up there. Like it ain't bad here, you know?'

'It was nice when I went,' I said. 'But – well, it hadn't been.'

'So Henry.' Jamal clapped his hands together. 'The world is your oyster. Where would you go if you had a wish?'

'What, anywhere?'

'Yeah, in the world. Anywhere.'

'I think I'd like to go to France,' I said.

'France?' His voice was a squeal. 'You've got the whole world to pick from, man. France is nothing. That's like going next door.'

'We were supposed to go on holiday to France when I was a boy.'

'OK, it's your choice.' He typed the word in a box on the screen.

'But my mother died and we didn't go and it was never mentioned again.'

'Aw, that's hard to bear man.'

'We never had a proper holiday after that,' I said. 'Staying with your aunt isn't really a proper holiday, is it?'

A patchwork of multi-coloured pictures melted onto the screen. Jamal pressed his finger on one after the other. 'Check that out,' he said.

'Is that France?' I said.

'It don't look like the France I went to, but yeah, it is. Look at that sky. And those colours. Good definition, eh?'

'Amazing.'

'It ain't always that sunny though, I'm telling you. We went on a school trip when I was like ten or something. It pissed down the whole time. We couldn't wait to come home.'

'It's always nice to come home,' I said.

'You been in this place a long time then?'

'All my life.'

'Wow.' He gazed around the kitchen again then wrote another word on the computer. 'Check this out,' he said.

Several tropical images replaced France on the page.

'That's the Seychelles,' said Jamal. 'Look at that, man. You ever seen sand as white as that?'

'No,' I said.

He enlarged another picture. A palm tree was bent over the sea.

'I'd love to go there.'

'Maybe you will one day.'

'Yeah, like that's gonna happen,' he said. 'Don't you want to just dive into that water?'

'I can't swim,' I said.

'Come on Henry. Everyone can swim.'

'I never learned.'

'We all did it in Year Four,' said Jamal. 'Even Terry Sousby and you should have seen him.' He laughed.

'What was he like?'

Jamal blew out his cheeks. 'Proper big, you know? For an eight year old.'

I chuckled at his impression.

'So how about that tea then Henry?'

'I'll put the kettle on,' I said. Then I realised there might be a problem. 'It'll have to be powdered milk, I'm afraid.'

'No it won't,' said Jamal. He produced a plastic carrier bag from his rucksack and brought out a carton of milk. 'I saw you had that stuff last time. I don't know how you can drink it like that man.'

'I know. It does taste pretty horrible, doesn't it?'

'Ain't it the truth.' We both laughed. 'You got anything to have with the tea?' he asked.

'Like biscuits? No,' I said.

'Good job I brought this then, isn't it?'

Jamal took out a long stick of bread and some slices of meat in a plastic packet.

'Is that French bread?' I said.

'Yeah, that's what they call it. Spooky eh? Do you eat chicken?'

'Yes I do,' I said.

'Cool.' He tore a piece from the end of the bread and handed me the rest together with the meat.

'Thanks,' I said and took a bite from the fresh bread. It tasted wonderful.

'I've got some grapes as well,' he said and shook the carrier bag.

'I should give you some money for all this Jamal.'

'No,' he said. 'Don't worry. You're all right.'

'Am I?' I said.

'Yeah.' He laughed again. And we ate our bread and chicken and grapes and drank our tea. 'You gotta say Henry, this is a funny place for a picnic, eh?'

'Parson's Wood.' I blurted out the words.

'What about it?'

'Are there any pictures on the computer?'

'Of Parson's Wood? Are you kidding me?' Jamal put down his bread and typed the words. An incredible mosaic of images, some familiar some not, appeared before my eyes. There were colour photographs, old photographs, people, buildings, maps, charts, everything. The list went on and on.

'What's that one?' I said.

Jamal enlarged the picture.

'That's the old fountain,' he said.

'It's not there now,' I said. 'And look at that.' My voice was trembling.

'They're trees man.'

'No, they aren't just any trees. We sat there ourselves – Mother, Susan and me. Under that exact tree – I'm sure of it. I've got a photograph. Can you make the picture bigger?'

'Sure.'

'There's something carved on the tree.'

'Someone's initials,' said Jamal.

'That means I can find it,' I said. 'I can find the tree.'

'Click on that link Henry.'

'How do I do that?'

'Move the cursor down – that arrow.' He demonstrated what I should do. 'Now click.'

'I press here, do I?'

'That's it.'

Another page suddenly opened up. It was the history of Parson's Wood. My eyes read the words in a blur. 'I never knew that,' I said.

'What's that?'

'Apparently there used to be a building right in the middle of the wood. A faux temple.'

'A what?'

'A faux temple,' I said. 'They pulled it down.'

'What's faux then?' said Jamal.

'It means fake or pretend.'

'Like a pretend church.'

'Something like that, yes.'

'What did they build that for?'

'They used to do things like that in the old days,' I said.

'Weird,' said Jamal. 'Did you learn that at school?'

'I remember reading about them in an encyclopaedia. Follies they were called. I used to have a lovely set of encyclopaedias. Some of them are outside now, I think.'

'I ain't got many books Henry but they're all indoors. The front garden man, that's no place for books.'

'Where do all these pictures come from?' I said.

'People like to share things with each other,' said Jamal. 'There's a community going on, you know.'

'Could I share my photograph as well?'

'Why not?'

I continued reading. 'It says there's a group called the Friends of Parson's Wood.'

Jamal laughed.

'What's so funny?' I said.

'That is. How can a wood have friends?'

'They want volunteers to help clear away the brambles. And then they're hoping to replace the fountain.'

'When you've got an email address Henry, you can get in touch with them.'

'It says 'You can follow us on Facebook'. I've heard of that.'

'It's like one of them social media things,' said Jamal.

'Could I do that then, follow them?' I said.

'Follow trees?'

'The friends of trees.'

'If that's what you want Henry. You can do anything.' Jamal picked up his rucksack and heaved it onto his back. 'I've gotta go,' he said. 'Places to be, people to see. You know?'

I nodded. He made his way to the door, then paused and leaned against a box. 'I've had an idea,' he said. 'Only I've got this computer at home.'

'Yes,' I said.

'It's a laptop rather than a PC and it's nothing too special. Not compared with what you can get nowadays. Two-fifty-gig hard-drive, four-gigs of memory.'

'Right.'

'But it's not doing anything just sitting in my bedroom. So how would you fancy having it? Not for keeps, you understand – I can't afford to give stuff away. It'd just be a loan until we got you sorted out.'

'Of course,' I said.

'You have to remember it's an old model and they don't make them exactly like that no more so you wouldn't be able to get it in the shops. And it ain't going to be as fast as this bad boy.' He patted his bag. 'So you'd have to be prepared for it being slow.'

'Yes.' I nodded.

'I mean crawling, you know what I'm saying?'

'I think so.'

'But it would be like hands-on experience, you know? Like taking a car for a test drive.'

'I can't drive a car,' I said.

'All right, like learning all the functions of your TV, or...' Jamal gazed around the kitchen. 'Getting used to a new fridge. Nothing to be frightened of, right?'

'Right.'

'So are you good with that?'

'Yes.'

'Cool. Just so long as you promise me you'll use it. I mean I don't want you just storing it away Henry, you know?'

'No, of course I won't.'

Jamal held up his fist towards me and grinned.

'Are you going to punch me?' I said.

'Nah man, you just bounce your fist against mine.'

'Do I?'

'Yeah.'

I made my right hand into a fist and placed it against Jamal's.

'It's a bit like a handshake, isn't it?'

'Kind of.'

Two wasps were now battering themselves against separate windows. 'You need to do something about them things man.' Jamal took another sniff. 'But wash them trousers first.'

CHAPTER SEVENTEEN

By the time I came down to the kitchen I noticed that my heart was beating a little bit faster than normal. I knew perfectly well that Jamal's laptop had caused it, but that didn't make it any less stressful. As I squeezed through the doorway I caught sight of the thing for a split second and averted my eyes, but by then it was too late. The damage was done. Even when I sat behind the biggest box, I knew that the laptop was still there.

I made myself a cup of tea and used up the last of Jamal's milk. Then I sat down on my cushion to drink it, but without any enjoyment. All I could think about was the laptop on the other side of the room.

My routine had gone out of the window. I'd missed one news report completely, and when I finally settled down to watch the next bulletin I was too distracted by the slim silver object to pay any attention to what anybody was saying. It had only been in my house for a couple of hours but in that time the laptop had already managed to take over. This was what it would be like if I owned one, I told myself. Perhaps I just wasn't cut out for a computer.

I'd felt so positive a few hours ago when Jamal had suggested lending it to me. But once it arrived things soon became very different. The main difference was that Jamal had gone. I'd expected him to stay and give me a demonstration of how it worked, but it quickly became obvious that wasn't his intention. 'You'll soon get the hang of it,' he said. I wasn't so sure. I'd grown used to the comfort of Jamal demonstrating everything to me. I would stand and watch, mesmerised by his speed of movement and his familiarity with the technology.

'It's a different colour,' I said when he first revealed the laptop.

'The colour don't make no difference Henry.'

'And it's got buttons.'

'They aren't buttons – that's a keyboard. You must know what a keyboard is, even if you didn't have computers at school.'

I did know what a keyboard was, although I didn't call it that. There was an old typewriter in one of the boxes upstairs. I used to type letters on it until two of the keys got locked together. I managed to bend the keys pulling them apart but the typewriter didn't work properly after that so I put it aside for safe-keeping until I could get it repaired, even though there didn't seem to be anybody who mended typewriters any more. The man in the electrical shop had been very dismissive. 'Good luck getting that fixed,' he'd said, though I don't think he meant it. I felt glad that his shop was gone and that he'd never get a chance to repair my video recorder.

It was when I noticed that Jamal was preparing to leave that I started to get anxious. 'Is there a manual?' I asked him.

'A manual?'

'A handbook. To tell you how it all works. I like to look through all the instructions.'

He pulled a face. 'You just learn on screen,' he said. 'Trial and error.'

'Supposing I make a bad error?'

'You won't.'

'But supposing.'

'Like what?'

'I don't know, you're the expert. I might break it, or make something go wrong.'

'Stop being so negative Henry. If the worst happens and you get into trouble, just turn it off and then turn it on again.'

'Is that all?'

'Yes.'

'You sure?'

'Yeah. It's what everybody does.'

'Do they?'

'Just remember who's the boss Henry and don't be frightened of it. It's just a computer. It's not like it can hurt you, is it?'

'No.'

'It's gonna change your life man, just think about that.'

I put down my empty cup, walked over to the laptop and opened the lid. The screen was dull and dark and gave back no reflection. The buttons – the keyboard – was worn in places from Jamal's fingers. I closed the lid again.

I sat down behind the box facing away from the laptop. It was somewhere I could sit and not worry about seeing the thing. It was all very well Jamal telling me not to be frightened of it, but I was. Of course, I didn't have to use the computer if I didn't want to. No-one could make me. I could just leave it lying there, safely switched off. And when Jamal came back I'd tell him that I'd had a go but that I hadn't really taken to it. The computer and I weren't really suited. I wouldn't be able to look Jamal in the eye when I told him. He'd be disappointed, I knew that much. I could imagine some of the things he'd say. It wouldn't be any good telling him I might be ready for a computer in six months time. He'd wash his hands of me, wouldn't he? He'd have other clients who'd be only too happy to use a computer by themselves. Three months then. No, the time factor wasn't really the issue. I was.

I felt my chest tighten. It's a terrible thing to be frightened. Frightened of the things you know, frightened of the things you don't know. I don't suppose Jamal had ever felt like that. He wouldn't understand what it had been like to go to the railway station. But it was the most terrifying thing I'd ever chosen to do. I'd prepared for hours before I could finally leave the house and I felt sick as I walked to the station. I don't know how many times I nearly turned round and went home. But I somehow managed to join the queue and I stood there, quaking, behind a few men and women. Then all of a sudden it was my turn to talk to the person behind the ticket office window. And I knew where I wanted to go but I didn't know there were so many choices and it was all so confusing and I got flustered and somebody in the queue went 'tut' because they were in a hurry and knew exactly what to do. And the easiest thing would have been to run away and go back home without buying my ticket. I could have told myself I'd never be able to cope with a railway station or a crowded train, and it was probably best to just watch the news on television. But I didn't do the easy thing. I stayed at the window and I bought my ticket. And that meant I could catch the train and stand near the spot where Pauline Furber was murdered and pay my respects. So without that I would never have found the first piece of chewing gum, and it was important not to forget that. And each time I bought a ticket after that or travelled on a train it got a little bit easier.

I stood up. It was only a computer, I reminded myself. Jamal was right, it couldn't hurt me. I had the power in my own hands, just like I'd done when I stood by the ticket office window and didn't go home. It was up to me. So I took a deep breath, opened up the laptop and pressed the 'on' button.

The machine made a little noise in acknowledgement, the screen flashed and then the computer went dark again. 'I've broken it already,' I whispered. I listened while it made a few more sounds. Jamal's tablet didn't make noises like that. His computer made a sort of whooshing sound when he slid his finger across it and this one made a grinding noise that wasn't very nice at all. Perhaps it did that because it was old and not because I'd done something wrong. Lots of old things made different noises. Noisier noises. Maybe newer computers had had the noise taken away.

A name flashed onto the screen – the manufacturer I think – and that was quickly followed by a string of words and numbers that must have meant something but I didn't understand and then it went black again for a few seconds. And I thought to myself: it's supposed to do that. And sure enough, a moment or two later, a picture of the countryside popped up and an egg timer was spinning round.

'I was right,' I said. 'It knows what it's doing.'

I waited until the computer had finished making its noises and all the little pictures had appeared before I touched it again. The little images were called icons, I remembered Jamal saying. I felt pleased that I knew the word. Every icon signified something different but I had no idea what most of them meant. I was only familiar with one or two of them.

'Don't worry about most of that stuff,' Jamal had said. So I did what he said and tried my best not to worry.

One of the icons I did recognise was the symbol for the internet. It had a funny looking letter 'E' on it.

'Why doesn't it have an 'I' for internet?' I'd asked.

'It's 'E' for explorer,' Jamal had said.

'But why?'

'I dunno man, it just is. I don't make the rules.'

'An 'I' would be more helpful though, wouldn't it?' Jamal had just shrugged and said it was one of those things. Everyone knew what the symbol meant and that was all that mattered. 'You just click on it and see where it takes you.'

I was just about to do that when a small box appeared on the screen which took me by surprise. Updates were available, a message in the box said. Would I permit the computer to reconfigure, yes or no? I don't know, I thought. Jamal hadn't said anything about updates. He'd told me it was an old computer, but he hadn't mentioned that it needed updating. I wanted to make the message go away, because I didn't want to have to make the choice, but there didn't seem to be any way to do that. The red square with an 'X' in it, the one that I could recall seeing Jamal use to make things disappear, wasn't there.

I felt as though I was being tested by the computer. It was asking me to make a decision – a right one, or a wrong one. I wondered if the computer would want to be updated. It probably did, I thought. Computers were modern things, they'd prefer to be up-to-date. But I could click on 'yes' and then it might ask me to do something else, like on some of the forms I'd had to fill in, the ones that people always told me weren't going to take up any time. So it might be safest to click 'no'. Then again that could mean that I didn't get the latest news. But that would be no good – because the news needed to be up-to-date. So the computer was probably telling me to click 'yes'. I moved my finger to the 'yes' option, and before I had a chance to talk myself out of it, I clicked the cursor. No sooner had I done so than another message appeared on the screen, informing me that the computer was shutting itself down.

'That's no good,' I said. 'You weren't supposed to do that.' I felt quite cross. But the computer wasn't listening to me. The icons were already disappearing from sight, and no sooner had they gone than so did the landscape. A few moments later I was faced once again with the dark, unhelpful screen.

Ten minutes later I plucked up the courage to try again. I had more luck this time. All the icons came back, much to my relief, and when the message box didn't reappear I felt happier still. By clicking '*yes*' I must have made the right choice. Whatever I'd done hadn't broken the computer, and best of all it was now up-to-date.

I was ready now to search the internet. I pressed the icon with the 'E' symbol and the browsing page popped into view. I was pleased to see that it looked exactly the same as the one Jamal had shown me. There was the name, the box, and the slogan: '*Imagination Without Limits*'. I watched it for a while, and then suddenly realised I was smiling. What was it Jamal had said? That I had the world at my fingertips? But where exactly should I start? I looked at the empty box and I couldn't think what to write. I'd thought before about typing in my own name, but now the moment was upon me I didn't much fancy the idea. I shouldn't want to see what all those people on the internet might be saying about me. So what else could I write in the box? I peered around the kitchen for inspiration, but all that caught my eye were bin-liners and cardboard boxes. They weren't very interesting. Then across the room I noticed the door handle. That will have to do, I thought, and I typed '*door handle*' into the browsing box. A collection of names and contacts popped up on the screen, along with lots of pictures. '*Buy door handles direct,*' said one message. '*Door handles to your door,*' said another, which I thought was quite funny. And there were pictures of more types of door handles than I'd ever seen in my life – old-fashioned ones, modern ones, round ones, long ones, door handles that locked and door handles that didn't and brass ones just like I'd got in a box somewhere. There was almost too much to take in. 'I never knew there were so many door handles,' I said to myself and tried to choose my favourite. After a few minutes I gave up. It occurred to me that it would have been far easier to have gone down to the hardware shop and picked one from the small selection they had there. Then I remembered that the hardware shop wasn't there any longer. I didn't need new door handles anyhow.

The Shensu P50. The name of the computer that Jamal had dismissed suddenly came to me. I typed the name into the box then clicked on one of the contacts to have a look. The picture of it seemed very nice but there were a lot of technical things alongside it that I didn't understand. I clicked another page, then another one after that. The place I'd ended up at didn't seem very helpful and I remembered Jamal's advice for when I wanted to go back to somewhere I'd been previously.

'So if I want to go back I just click on the arrow that points left?'

'Yes.'

'Why is left backwards?'

'I dunno.'

'Because you can turn left and you're not going backwards, are you? And you can turn right somewhere and you might be going backwards.'

'You ask some crazy questions man.'

I clicked on the arrow and went back to the previous page. Further down I could see that there were some comments that people had left about the Shensu. I was quite shocked when I saw the language some of them had used. No wonder most people hadn't left their names. From what I could gather the Shensu had insufficient RAM capacity and a poor bit-speed, whatever that was supposed to mean, plus it had a tendency to overheat. I guessed that was another way of saying it got too hot. That was something I could drop into the conversation the next time Jamal and me discussed computers. 'The Shensu overheats, doesn't it?' I was sure he'd be surprised. I felt the laptop and noticed that it was quite warm. Was this one overheating too? And just how hot was it supposed to be? It was impossible to tell. Electrical things can get warmer when they've been switched on for a while. I remember the vacuum cleaner used to get very hot before it broke and for some reason it gets warm at the back of the fridge. And a kettle gets very hot when it's boiling water, so it was hard to know what to think really. Jamal hadn't mentioned that the laptop might get hot. But perhaps it was nothing to worry about. Maybe a little heat was no bad thing.

I made a few more searches, trying not to get too worried when I misspelt a word and ended up somewhere unexpected. I just had to remember to go backwards, and occasionally forwards, with the arrows. The more I did that, the more I began to wonder what it was I'd been so frightened about. Jamal was right, I did have the world at my fingertips. Of course, when I got my own computer I wouldn't be able to keep it in the kitchen. I'd have a printer too, and I'd need something to put it all on and somewhere to sit as well and that took up space. There was precious little in the kitchen as things stood. I thought perhaps I could clear out an area upstairs to make room for it all. There ought to be a spot in the back bedroom if I could somehow remove the wardrobe. That would be a sacrifice worth making.

As I began to get more familiar with things I noticed several repeated references to a website that sold medicine. The thought occurred to me that I might be able to get hold of my old tablets, the ones that came in glass bottles. But when I clicked on the link I saw straightaway that the references to potency and better performance had nothing to do with medicine. Instead there was a film of a man and a woman repeating the act again and again. I felt my cheeks flushing as I looked at them. I hadn't expected to see that. Or wanted to. Over and over the two of them went through the motions till the noises they made were ringing in my head and my skin was tingling. Had we looked like that, Rose and me? Did we make the same sort of noises? I clicked the arrow to go backwards but nothing happened so I clicked it again and then a wheel started spinning around and the couple were stuck there frozen stiff, right in the middle of their – well, I felt sure it wasn't lovemaking.

When the screen didn't change I started to get a bit light-headed. Jamal had said I could always go backwards but I couldn't go backwards because the computer wouldn't let me. And I thought about all those stories I'd heard about people getting into trouble for looking at things they weren't supposed to on their computers. And that made me panic even more.

I turned around and looked the other way and tried to pretend that none of it was happening but when I peeked over my shoulder the two of them were still there, hard at it. What should I do if they were still there when Jamal came back? What would I say to him? I thought about turning the computer off, but I wasn't sure if that would make them go away or that they'd just come back if I turned it on again. It made me quite agitated, and I remembered what the police had told me about not doing anything foolish. And then, just as suddenly, the wheel stopped spinning and the couple vanished. I was very relieved.

The BBC would be safer, I thought. I couldn't go wrong with the news, now it was all up to date. So I typed their letters into the browsing box and clicked. I could see from their front page that there was nothing new in the murder case. There was a quote from DI Hillyard which was the same one I'd heard on the television a couple of days ago. So this was the latest news then, even with updating. It meant there was no news at all.

It was then that I had an idea. Supposing I hadn't been the only person to have made the connection between the serial killer and his chewing gum? As Jamal had said – and as I'd seen only too clearly – people shared all sorts of experiences on the internet. So I typed the words 'chewing gum' into the browsing box and clicked on the button.

'*Chewing gum. 18,000,000 results,*' it said. I looked at all the noughts just to be certain that I hadn't mistaken the number. I counted six and realised I hadn't. That meant there were somewhere in excess of eighteen million references to chewing gum on the internet. '*Chewing gum is a type of gum made for chewing,*' said the first entry. '*It is at least five thousand years old.*'

'Mine isn't,' I thought. I ignored the website. The reference below said '*Take the chewing gum test.*' I decided not to look at that one either. The next few links all seemed to be concerned with selling chewing gum or its supposed health benefits. '*Chewing gum helps the brain,*' said one link. '*Chewing gum can give a healthy smile,'* suggested another. There was no need to look further. *'Boost your efficiency,'* said the next one.

'No,' I said to the computer. 'I'm not clicking that reference.' I had a feeling I knew what the words really meant and that they had nothing to do with chewing gum.

I skimmed down several pages but it was more of the same. There was nothing I could see anywhere about the wrapping of chewing gum in silver paper and its association with serial killers. But how would I know for sure? How could anybody possibly search through eighteen million results? It would take a lifetime. Like with the door handles, I wondered if computers weren't sometimes just too helpful.

It dawned on me that I might not be going about things in the right way. I'd noticed that Jamal had typed different combinations of words in the browsing box when he was looking for specific items. 'The computer can't read your mind,' I remembered him saying. 'You have to try and help it.'

So I typed the words *'chewing gum killer'* and held my breath. This time there were only two-and-a-half million references rather than eighteen million, although it did still seem quite a lot. I clicked on the first link, but it was nothing like what I expected to see. Instead of a serial killer there was a video clip of two teenage boys in a shopping precinct. They were using chewing gum to play tricks on unsuspecting people. First one then the other blew bubbles, making them go bang and giving passers-by a surprise. One man jumped so much he walked into a litter bin by mistake. He staggered backwards, dropped his shopping and I burst out laughing. The clip ended. *'More killer gum pranks,'* said the message. I moved the cursor over the link and clicked. This time a boy was hiding in a gum-dispensing machine and catching people unawares. I laughed at that as well, it was so ridiculous. I couldn't believe how much effort they'd gone to.

I watched a few more clips. Someone had stuck some coins to the floor with gum and then filmed people who tried to pick them up, each time without success. A man asked for help to remove some chewing gum that had got stuck in his hair, which then turned out to be a wig and flew off. It did look funny. Another boy had somehow rigged his packet of chewing gum so that it gave people electric shocks when they tried to take a piece out. There were other practical jokes, too, that had nothing to do with gum. People playing tricks with hot water or buckets of ice, people knocking over wedding cakes, and people dressed up in funny costumes doing silly things in shops. All sorts of things, really. I chuckled so much at someone falling down a hole that my face hurt. And I forgot all about serial killers leaving secret messages. There was nothing about him anyway. It was simply people having fun. And I watched clip after clip and laughed and laughed and laughed.

I must have been giggling when Jamal called. It was probably why I didn't hear him knocking. I think it was only when I got to the end of a clip and was about to start another one that I recognised his voice coming through the letter box.

'Henry?' he said when I opened the door. 'Are you OK man?'

I brushed the moisture from under my eyes. 'I'm fine Jamal,' I said.

'So how you been getting on with that laptop? You have been using it, right?'

'Oh yes,' I said and tried to stop myself laughing. We walked through to the kitchen.

'And how was it then?'

'Great,' I said.

'Only I never seen you laughing before.'

'I just saw someone fall down a hole,' I said and burst out laughing again...

oOo

I was about to ask Jamal if he wanted some tea when I remembered I'd used up all the milk. I'd been so engrossed in the computer I'd forgotten all about it. So I said nothing. I expected Jamal to question me further about the laptop, but he ignored it. Instead he took the tablet from his bag, which soon had its familiar glow. Without saying a word Jamal proceeded to spin through several images until he'd found what he was looking for. Then he perched the tablet on top of a box and beckoned me to come and have a look.

'I got something,' he said. He seemed quite excited. 'I know who's in the picture Henry.'

'What, under the tree? In Parson's Wood?'

'Where they found that girl's body,' he said. 'I know who the people are.'

I felt my heart quicken and stared at the screen. The familiar image filled the page.

'It took me a while but I found out who they was.' He grinned.

'Oh my lord.'

'Remember I asked you about the cars?'

'Yes. But I said I didn't notice anything about them.'

'You might not have – but something did.' Jamal pressed his fingers together and made a click sound.

'I don't understand,' I said.

'Cameras.'

'A photographer?'

'Traffic cameras man, they're everywhere. You told me what time you was there, so all I had to do was check the local traffic.'

'How did you manage that?'

'You don't wanna know.'

'Don't I?'

He hunched his shoulders and made a slight noise.

'Was it illegal then?'

'Let's say the ends justify the means, eh? All's well in love and war or something.' He pushed the picture away and some words appeared. 'And once I'd got some names, one thing led to another.'

'Amazing.'

'The internet's a wonderful thing man. These things talk to each other more than what some people do. You just got to know where to look, and how to listen.'

I tried to read the words. 'Does it say anything about me?'

'Course.' Jamal expanded the page. 'There you are – Henry V. Henry. So you got two Henrys in your name, right? Didn't your mum think one Henry was enough?'

'It was my dad's idea.'

'And what's with the V?'

'Doesn't it say?'

'I'm just checking.' He flicked at the screen.

'Vespasian,' I said before he could respond.

'That's some name. I ain't heard that one.'

'He was a Roman emperor.'

'No shit. Dad again was it?'

'Mum I think. I never got the chance to ask.' The picture once again filled the screen. 'Who are the others then?'

'OK – these guys are the cops, right? Plainclothes, criminal investigation. The woman is Sergeant Wyatt and the bald geezer is Inspector Hillyard.'

'Yes.'

'You know them do you?'

'I've met them,' I said.

'Uh huh.'

'And that's Rose – Rosamund Bowyer.' I pointed at her picture. 'I do know her. Knew.'

'She was police as well. Don't look it though, eh?'

'No.'

Jamal swatted away a wasp which circled his head. 'Whoa!' he said.

'What's the matter?' I said.

'It's a wasp, man. That's the matter. Get away!'

'You mustn't frighten it,' I said.

'Frighten it? It's frightening me man.'

'Just ignore it and it won't hurt you.'

'Sure.' He flailed an arm in the insect's direction.

'What about this man?' I said. 'Do you know who he is?' I pointed at

Ginger Whiskers.

'Hang on.' Jamal referred to his research notes while keeping half an eye on the wasp. 'He's called Malcolm Feather. He's an army guy – or used to be an army guy. He ain't now.'

'And what about Sandwiches?'

'What?'

'This man.'

'Did you say sandwiches?' Jamal looked at me.

'Every time I see him he seems to be eating sandwiches,' I said.

'So you know him, yeah?'

'No, I don't really know him. Not as such.'

'Kenneth Reed.'

'Is that his name?'

'Yeah. He's a businessman. No, hang on that's the other guy.' Jamal picked out Cloth Cap. 'Nigel Smith they call him. I ain't sure what line of business he's in exactly. You could check though. Businessman can mean anything. I've got a friend who's a businessman and he don't look like that.'

Jamal proceeded to tell me about the rest of them. Miss Two Dogs turned out to be a retired teacher and the couple with the flask were the Reddings, who ran a mobile cafe. The only people Jamal hadn't been able to identify were the young woman and her child. She'd had her back to the camera when the picture was taken, while the baby was completely wrapped up and could hardly be seen. I found my mood improving with each name that Jamal read out to me, and didn't mind that there were two missing names and faces. I didn't think Chewing Gum was the young mother, or her baby. The murderer was a man, wasn't it? It was always a man.

'So what's the story with all these people?' said Jamal. 'I mean I know the names and where they are, but what's it to you?'

'I think someone in that picture is the serial killer,' I said. 'In fact I'm convinced of it.'

Jamal skimmed more images with his finger. 'That's a serious accusation Henry,' he said, not looking up.

'I know.'

'So why ain't the cops caught him?'

I shook my head. 'I don't know,' I said.

'Maybe they don't know what you know,' said Jamal. 'Cos you do know some shit, right?'

'Yes.' I dropped my voice to a whisper.

'And you think that he might know that you know, yeah?'

I nodded.

'And he's coming after you?'

'I'm sure of it.' I thought again about the chewing gum I'd found on the path and wondered if I should confide in Jamal.

'Course, you know there is a reason the cops might not have caught him, don't you?' he said.

'Tell me.'

'It's cos he's one of them. Have you thought about that?'

'A little bit.'

'They could be protecting their own.'

'They wouldn't, would they?'

Jamal pulled a face.

'Do you really think so?' I said.

'I dunno. You're the expert man. I'm just saying. It has been known to happen.'

I nodded.

'You ain't kidding about this are you?'

'About the murderer? No. I need find these people Jamal. I have to get to them before they get to me or anybody else. Have you been able to find out where they live?'

'Jesus Henry man, you hoping to catch him?'

'Something like that – I don't know. I just feel I need to do something, that's all. Do you understand?'

'Sure.'

'He killed my girlfriend. I think I told you that.'

'Yeah. Sorry about that other time – me asking if you was the serial killer. I'm not sure that came out right.'

'That's OK,' I said. 'So...'

'Have I got addresses and stuff?'

'Yes.'

Jamal sank to his knees and began rooting around in his bag.

'It was good of you to check that picture out for me,' I said. 'However you managed to do it. I know how busy you must be fixing people's computers and what-not.'

'Well you're lucky Henry. I've got a window in my hectic schedule right now as it goes.'

'So how much do I owe you for all this work you've done?'

Jamal shrugged. 'Nothing so far,' he said. 'It's all been on the house. Let's just say I ain't started the clock yet.'

'That's very kind of you,' I said.

He pulled out a folded sheet of paper from his bag and gave it to me. It contained a list of more than half a dozen names and addresses, including my own. I ignored the two policemen, Miss Two Dogs and the Reddings and just took down the details of the three lone men – Sandwiches, Ginger Whiskers and Cloth Cap. Cloth Cap was the one who lived nearest, so I decided I would visit him first.

'So are you gonna take the law into your own hands, is that it?'

'No,' I said. 'I just need to find the proof I'm looking for.'

'It's just the kind of thing they tell you not to do though, eh? Being a have a go hero. That's what they call them, isn't it?'

'Me? I'm not a hero,' I said.

'You don't need to be a hero to get yourself killed.'

'No.'

'Just watch out,' said Jamal. 'Don't do nothing stupid, will you?'

'I'll try not to.' I held up my fist again. 'We'll sort out a computer when I get back.'

Instead of placing his fist against mine Jamal took my hand and clasped it in his. 'Count on it man,' he said.

CHAPTER EIGHTEEN

Cloth Cap, or Nigel Smith as he was really called, lived less than fifty miles from me. It was close enough to both murder locations, so it would have been quite straightforward for him to have reached either of them. I'd stood near Cloth Cap when Lorna Coulson had been found. Why was he there? Was it to survey the aftermath of his handiwork, I wondered. And did he chew gum? And if he did, how did he dispose of it once he'd finished chewing?

I pondered my dilemma on the train journey. What on earth was I going to say to Cloth Cap when I met him? I'd need to remember to call him Mr Smith for one thing. Nigel seemed a bit too familiar. He might not even recognise me and I couldn't recall seeing him among the crowd outside Parson's Wood. It would have been handy if I could have studied that video tape one last time, just to have seen if Cloth Cap was there. I'd watched it so many times I could almost recount every detail, but I couldn't remember him. It was possible I hadn't given him an appropriate nickname. Sandwiches had his sandwiches and Ginger Whiskers had his moustache, but supposing Cloth Cap had been at Parson's Wood with his head bare? The thought had never occurred to me. But that didn't mean he hadn't been there, any more than it meant he wasn't on the train at that very moment, shadowing me, using his disguise of not wearing a cap. It made the remainder of my journey a nervous affair, and I spent my time checking the movements of the other passengers.

I alighted with most of the train at a town I didn't know. I lingered for a time in the booking office, and once everyone had gone I studied the map. Cloth Cap's home was situated somewhere along a road that stretched far out into the countryside. It looked to be at least three miles away, but I could also see that no buses went in that direction. I thought about how impressed Dr Singh would have been at all the exercise I was doing. She'd also told me it was best if I avoided unnecessary stress, which reminded me of the risks I was taking. But risky or not it seemed to be the best thing to do. I was living on my nerves at home, terrified of a man whose identity I didn't know. Well it was time to be proactive now and meet the enemy on his home ground. Always assuming it was him, of course.

The road was even longer than I thought. The map hadn't indicated the hills or the farmland or the lack of a footpath. The overgrown grass verges hadn't been trimmed all summer and made for slow progress, but I thought they would be less hazardous than walking on the gritty tarmac. Cars liked to speed down country roads, and I didn't want to fall victim to what would appear to the police to be a random accident.

I tried not to think too much about what would happen if I found myself face to face with Chewing Gum. If the killer called my bluff I'd be on my own. I had none of the modern pieces of equipment that might help me if my mission turned into a crisis. Most likely Jamal had some sort of device on his tablet that could have done the job for him without having to leave home. But I knew that even if I owned a computer I couldn't have stayed hiding behind my front door. This was something I had to do.

The open fields eventually gave way to woodland and larger houses, dotted among the trees. If Cloth Cap was a businessman, his business was doing well. The verges were more clipped here, and I felt a bit awkward about walking on what was clearly private property. I felt increasingly unprotected now, and exposed. There was no-one watching me with the possible exception of Chewing Gum himself. Chewing Gum might know my movements. If so, he'd be several moves ahead.

When the road took a sharp left-handed turn, I knew I was getting near my destination. Cloth Cap lived somewhere on the right. I kept hoping that when I finally saw the house I'd also see police cars in the driveway, with flashing lights and intercoms crackling. There'd be no need to stop if that was the case, my job would be done. I could turn around and go home without having to look over my shoulder. But there were no flashing lights or crackle.

I surveyed the scene from behind a large tree. Cloth Cap's house was quite a size and set some way back from the road. The only approach was by a wide gravelled driveway which went up to the property and some buildings beyond. There was no sign of any car, but there was a garage that might have contained several. A five-barred wooden gate was tied back, and there was nothing to stop anybody from walking in. But now that I'd reached my goal, I felt my nerve begin to desert me. It would be a mistake to ring the front door bell and simply introduce myself. Should Cloth Cap turn out to be Chewing Gum it might well be the last action I ever took.

I tried to convince myself that it didn't look like a serial killer's house. So I took a deep breath and began to walk up the drive. My optimism melted away with my first footstep. The sound of the gravel crunching underfoot was deafening. I did my best not to feel guilty or terrified and continued towards the house.

Despite the lengthening shadows there were no lights visible at the front, so I decided to follow the path around the side of the building. I would knock on the back door and say I was lost and ask Cloth Cap if he could direct me back to the railway station. If he got suspicious or gave himself away I'd just have to try and call his bluff. 'I know who you are,' I'd say. 'And I can prove what you've done. I told some people where I was going so if anything happens to me they'll go straight to the police.' It all sounded perfectly reasonable until I could hear Chewing Gum ask me: 'So why haven't you told the police yourself?' That was one question I didn't have an answer for.

I reached the end of the house and was heading towards the back door when to my horror I caught sight of a woman's face through the hedge opposite. I stopped dead in my tracks.

'Hello there,' she called. 'Do you mind telling me who you are?'

She passed through a gate and came walking over. She was a little older than me, wore a quilted jacket and wellington boots and was carrying a rake.

'I've come to see Mr Smith,' I said. I felt pleased I'd remembered Cloth Cap's real name.

'They're not here,' she said and came to within a few feet of me.

A man appeared behind her. He was dressed in boots as well and wore a thick woollen jumper with patches on its elbows and shoulders.

'This man says he's come to see Nigel,' said the woman. She kept her eyes fixed on me.

'Has he?' The man drew level with her and folded his arms. 'You've just missed them I'm afraid.'

'Ah.'

'They were called away. It was all very sudden.' The woman turned to the man. 'There was some trouble, wasn't there?'

'Yes,' he said. 'Most unfortunate.'

'Oh dear,' I said. I wasn't sure what else to say.

'There's no telling when they might be back I'm afraid.'

'That's a pity.' I fidgeted slightly as I watched them look me up and down.

'You're not the police are you?' The man squinted at me.

'No,' I said, quite taken aback.

'I'm sorry, I didn't catch your name,' said the woman.

'Where did you park your car?' said the man. 'I didn't notice your car.'

'I don't have a car,' I said.

'No car? It's more than three miles to the station. I take it you did come from the station?'

'We don't know you, do we?' said the woman. 'I think we know most friends of Ellie and Nigel.'

'I met him on my travels,' I said. 'And I was in the area so I thought I'd come and say hello.'

'I should have phoned if I was you,' said the man. 'Or don't you have a phone either?'

I wanted to leave that minute. They probably took me for a burglar or an opportunist thief who'd come to chance his arm. They most likely thought I was a weirdo as well, for not having a car. I wondered if the two of them had any idea what Cloth Cap got up to when he wasn't being a businessman or living in his big country house. But now wasn't the time to ask that particular question. It was rather time to go.

'I should phone,' said the man. 'Do you have your phone darling?'

The woman patted the pockets of her jacket. 'I must have left it in the kitchen.'

'Only I think we should call, don't you?'

'Yes. Yes you should call.'

I felt a faint tingling sensation on my skin. Some clouds of smoke had begun billowing their way over the dividing hedge from the garden beyond. 'Is that a bonfire?' I asked.

The woman glanced over her shoulder. 'Go and sort it out,' she said to the man.

'Well I'd better be off,' I said.

A thick plume of smoke rose up, and I could hear the odd crackle.

'Hurry.'

'I'll miss my train otherwise,' I said and without waiting for permission I turned and began walking. I kept expecting the woman to call out or chase after me but nothing happened, and less than a minute later I was on the road outside.

What had been going on there, I wondered, and what had the two of them meant by 'trouble'? Had Cloth Cap been arrested? If so, then why ask if I was a policeman? I surely didn't look like one. But then they didn't always, especially when they weren't police any more, like Rose.

I walked as fast as I could, all the time worrying that my journey would be interrupted by a police car, pulling over and asking what my business was and would I mind stepping inside the vehicle. It would have been summoned, no doubt, by Cloth Cap's guardians next door. In the event several vehicles passed me by, including a police car, but none of them stopped.

At the railway station I had another look at the network map. Sandwiches and Ginger Whiskers lived in opposite locations. I couldn't hope to visit both of them in a single day. But there was still enough time to see one of them. Sandwiches lived marginally nearer, so I chose him.

Sandwiches' home town was very different from the one Cloth Cap lived near. Industrial units lined the approach, and the houses were far more modest.

On the way an idea had come to me, so I made the railway station newsagent's my first post of call. Just inside the entrance I caught sight of the *Radio Times*. It was a Wednesday, already a day after publication, and that was the first I'd even thought about it. I ignored the magazine, made my purchase, and left for the area where Sandwiches lived.

It was unfortunate, but the information Jamal had given me regarding Sandwiches' address was incomplete. The computer had only listed his address as Ardwell C, which I'd assumed meant Ardwell Close. But after studying the map I could see that there was another Ardwell C – Ardwell Crescent. And that on nearby Ardwell Road was listed an Ardwell Court. Fortunately all the Ardwells were in the same part of town, and not too far from the station, so once again I began walking to my destination.

I made mental notes as I walked, keeping an eye out for anything unusual, however it might present itself. I needed to have my wits about me. There were far more people here than there had been in the last place and Chewing Gum could be hidden among them, watching me. I did my best to look as though I knew where I was going as I continued towards the Ardwell streets. Then, at an intersection, I became disoriented. The road I'd hoped to take was blocked. A trench for a water or gas main repair had been dug, fenced off and abandoned, and a detour sign pointed to the road ahead. But how could a sign know which way I wanted to go? I wondered if I should follow it or ask a pedestrian if they knew the way to Ardwell Close? I was struggling with this quandary when my thoughts were interrupted by a voice.

'Can I be of any help?'

I turned round. The man who'd spoken, and who was already half way across the road and coming towards me, was Sandwiches himself.

'Only you look lost.'

Now, suddenly, I had no idea what to do. Here was the man I'd come to investigate at touching distance. But I could hardly say outright that I'd taken it upon myself to investigate the Chewing Gum murderer. I pressed the piece of paper that carried his partial address as deep into my pocket as I could.

'Where are you trying to get to?' he said.

My mind whirred, desperately trying to think of an answer. I remembered passing a corner shop on the edge of a housing estate and blurted out the name. At that moment I couldn't think of any other. 'Jubilee Street,' I said.

'Jubilee Street?' His eyes looked into mine. If he knew me from our previous meetings there was no flicker of recognition. 'I don't know anywhere by that name. Are you sure that's right?'

'Yes,' I said.

'We've got a Jubilee Stores not so far away.' He pointed. 'You weren't thinking of that were you?'

I wasn't really thinking of anything in particular. My mind had gone blank.

'What was the number?'

Sandwiches lived at number thirty-eight, I remembered that much. So I knew I mustn't say thirty-eight. Any other number would be fine. 'Twenty-five,' I said.

'Twenty-five? Like a Silver Jubilee?' Sandwiches chuckled.

'I suppose,' I said. I could feel my heartbeat racing.

'I should like to live at that address – wherever it is.'

I somehow managed to smile.

'Sorry I can't be of any help,' said Sandwiches.

'Well, never mind,' I said. I was keen to get away, uneasy at my poorly chosen lies and worried that Sandwiches might ask to see proof of the place I was looking for. But I was also determined not to return home empty-handed, so despite feeling awkward I kept calm, fumbled in my coat pocket and pulled out the object I'd bought in the newsagent's. I took a stick of gum wrapped in silver paper from its slim packet, and tried to stop my arm from shaking as I held it in front of Sandwiches. 'Would you care for a chewing gum?'

'That's very kind of you but it's not for me.' Sandwiches bared his teeth. 'Dentures, I'm afraid.'

'Oh,' I said. I unwrapped the stick and popped it into my mouth.

'Anyway, as I said, I don't really think I can help you with your search,' said Sandwiches. 'What was it again, street or road?'

I chewed for a few moments and tried to recall which word I'd said.

'Street,' I mumbled.

'No.' Sandwiches shook his head. 'I can only wish you good luck.'

With that he walked away. I made off in the opposite direction. There was no reason to find 38 Ardwell C now. I'd established to my own satisfaction that Sandwiches was not Chewing Gum. Besides, I could hardly follow the man back to his house, could I?

When I returned to the railway station I could see that the train timetables were against me. My trip to see Ginger Whiskers would have to wait for another occasion. Tomorrow would be fine, I told myself, and headed home.

CHAPTER NINETEEN

When I got home I could see that I'd missed Jamal. He'd dropped off a computer leaflet for me and ringed a few of them in marker pen. Some of his choices took me quite by surprise. It seemed he'd changed his mind about the Shensu. Maybe they'd suddenly got better. It made me smile when I noticed that the leaflet bore the same address as the old electrical repair shop.

By nine o'clock the following morning it had brightened up a bit and I was looking forward to seeing Susan. It would be a chance to mend some fences after our last meeting. Her bad mood might have passed, but just to be on the safe side I wrapped my dirty trousers in a bin-liner and taped it shut.

There was no telling when Susan would show. I hoped she'd come early because I couldn't go to Ginger Whiskers' house until I'd handed over the washing. While I waited I grabbed a broom and began tidying up at the front. It had been windy in the night and some twigs and litter had blown in. I was relieved to see that there were no further parcels of gum. But as I reattached the polythene sheets over my collection of paperbacks a chilling thought came to me. I'd shared rather a lot of information about the murders with Jamal, but what if I'd misjudged things? Young people were always chewing gum and messing about with knives. I stood for a moment and considered the possibility that Jamal was the Chewing Gum killer for all his denials about liking gum. No, that was exactly what Chewing Gum wanted, to sew seeds of doubt and make me suspicious of everyone. It was Jamal who'd been worried about me being the murderer, not the other way round. Unless that was all a double bluff. No, of course it wasn't. Jamal couldn't be Chewing Gum, the very idea was ridiculous.

I went back to the kitchen and switched on the television. As I watched the news I realised I'd lost touch with current affairs. I had no idea there'd been a motorway pile-up in Scotland, nor an unseasonal heat-wave in

Belgium. Both stories rather highlighted the lack of news about the serial killings. Poor Rose seemed to have been forgotten; Rose who I hadn't been able to mourn properly. When Chewing Gum had been caught it would be a different matter.

I'd be more prepared for my visit to Ginger Whiskers. As a former military man, he'd know how to use a knife. He'd be well ordered in his habits, too – just the sort of person who wouldn't casually discard his used chewing gum but who might dispose of it with – well, military precision. I was pretty sure I had some maps of his local area somewhere. I guessed they'd either be in the living room or one of the units upstairs. They'd certainly take some retrieving, wherever they were, but it would be a better use of my time while I waited than messing about with a pan and brush.

A wall of boxes blocked the doorway to the front room so I soon gave up that particular mission. It might be better trying upstairs.

On the way I stopped at the front door to squint through the frosted glass. There was no sign of Susan, nor, thankfully, anyone else. I'd need to keep an ear out for her while I was searching. Susan did have her own key but I didn't want her to let herself in. I thought it was only fair to explain exactly what was inside the taped-up bin-bag.

I found many things in the unit but no maps. The tea chest also proved a dead end. I was surprised though, when I checked, to see that the wardrobe in the corner was still completely empty. It could definitely make room for a computer, I thought to myself, not to mention some of the overflow from the kitchen.

By the time I went downstairs again, the morning had gone. The one o'clock news was now in full swing. Another self-inflicted crisis had erupted in the farming industry. The empty fields looked just like the ones I'd seen yesterday through the carriage window and reminded me that I should be in a train, en route to Ginger Whiskers.

The afternoon news also made me think of food. Susan wouldn't offer me lunch now, not at half-past three. I'd have to feed myself. I opened a tin of sardines and spooned them onto a slice of bread. While I ate I had a look at Jamal's brochure. I tried to work out why he'd recommended the computers he had done. He'd ringed a Shensu P50, which seemed odd considering how uncomplimentary he'd been about it. The Williamson TD2020 had been circled as well, or at any rate, some of the name. Perhaps it was something to do with the futuristic number. The D1 E-Z just looked ugly and I couldn't understand why Jamal had picked that model at all. He seemed to have changed his mind quite radically since his last visit. Two of the ones he'd previously praised he'd left unmarked. Circling the word 'Now' in the tag line 'Open Now' only made matters more confusing. I'd have to have a word with Jamal next time I saw him.

I'd run out of milk, too, but couldn't very well go to the shops when

Susan hadn't come. Even if I was only away for fifteen minutes she'd be sure to call when I wasn't at home. There was no point writing her a note, I knew from bitter experience she never paid any attention to them. Time, meanwhile, was rapidly slipping away.

I felt very frustrated. Why had Susan chosen today of all days to go and see that solicitor? So much for making an early start to see Ginger Whiskers. I wondered if I should just forget about Susan and head off to the station instead. I made one more attempt to enter the living room. When I realised I was going to need a torch if I hoped to see anything, it came home to me how much of the day had already gone. I felt cross that my trip to Ginger Whiskers' house would have to be postponed again. I could hardly visit him at night.

It might be starting to get dark but it wasn't too late to have my washing done. I slipped on my coat and scarf, double-locked the front door and walked as fast as I could to the phone box.

Where are you? I muttered while Susan's phone kept ringing, before the beep sounded and her voice informed me that she was unable to get to the phone and would whoever was calling please leave a message.

'Hello Susan,' I said. 'It's me, Henry.'

I paused for a moment, half expecting the phone to be picked up.

'You know how I hate these things.' How many times had I said that? 'I presume the fact you haven't answered means you're on your way over. In which case I'd better cut this short and get back, because I don't want to miss you.'

I could always call Susan on her mobile. I found another coin and tried to remember her number. The phone rang twice before I heard a voice.

'Hello?'

It belonged to a man. I'd used my last coin and dialled the wrong number.

'Sorry,' I said, as Susan's number popped into my head.

'Henry?' came the reply.

'Jamal?'

'Yeah man. So what's new? How did them trips go?'

'I haven't finished yet.'

It would take too long to explain – that would need more money and more time, neither of which I had right now. Susan was probably pulling up outside the house at that very moment, about to discover that I wasn't at home.

'I was going to call round,' said Jamal.

'Yes,' I said. 'Thanks for that, but I thought we'd agreed on something else.'

'I ain't with you man.'

'That computer leaflet you dropped off at my house.'

'What leaflet?'

'The new one,' I said. 'The one where you marked off your favourites.'

'I don't know nothing about that.'

'The Shensu.'

'The Shensu's rubbish. I already told you that.'

'That's what I thought.'

'Listen Henry, I'll be round in the morning. We can check one out then, OK?'

'OK.'

'Take it easy man.'

I walked back home as briskly as I could. My head was in a muddle. There were so many things going on it was no wonder I'd got the phone numbers mixed up. I still hadn't worked out exactly how to get to Ginger Whiskers' place. That was going to have to wait till the morning now. But that would mean postponing Jamal. I couldn't understand what he'd meant about the leaflet. Unless of course a rival computer wizard was trying to capture his business. None of it would have happened if Susan hadn't chosen today to turn up late. Everything had gone out of the window now because of that.

I rounded the last corner that turned into my street and saw at once that Susan's car wasn't there. Had I missed her? I'd only been away from the house – out of sight of it anyway – for ten minutes. It was plenty of time for her to have called, seen that I wasn't in and gone home. The washing was still there at any rate. Perhaps once I'd sorted out a computer I should think about investing in a mobile phone. That would have removed all the uncertainty about what time Susan was coming and when she'd left home and whether or not she'd taken a detour via the supermarket. And with Chewing Gum still on the loose – who knew when having a mobile phone might even save my life? It was high time I got myself sorted out. Tomorrow morning, Jamal had said. Ginger Whiskers could wait till the afternoon.

It was a bit of a struggle getting through the hallway into the kitchen. Being out of breath must have made me clumsy, because as I pushed past the piled up things a bag dislodged itself and fell into the gap with a clatter and a smash. That was all I needed. I couldn't remember what that particular bag contained exactly, although the crunching sound indicated broken glass. I stooped down to inspect the bag's contents, but then decided against it. There were more important things to do now than search through an unknown bin-liner for breakages. It was obvious that Susan wasn't coming. Perhaps I'd misjudged our row last time and she'd taken more offence than I thought. Well, there was only one way to find out. If Susan wouldn't come to me, then I'd have to go to Susan. I scrambled over the fallen bag and picked up the bin-liner containing my dirty clothes. It was properly secured, so it should be safe to take on the bus. And if I should encounter Chewing Gum while I was carrying the bag... Well, I could wait until the murderer was upon me and then tear the bag open. The foul smell might give me the element of surprise, and allow me time to escape. There was only one problem with the plan that no amount of soiled trousers could conceal. I didn't know what Chewing Gum looked like – and by the time I did it might be too late.

A visit to Susan's house at this hour meant that I'd most probably bump into Derek. Susan's husband usually made himself scarce when I called round, going upstairs to mess about on his computer. But sometimes he'd stand there doing this or that, which always made me feel uncomfortable. I know he doesn't like me. It's the little things that make it obvious, such as throwing out my coat and pretending he's done it by accident or not making enough coffee when he knows I'm there. He never signs my birthday card either. It's always Susan who writes them – putting 'and Derek' after her own name. Well it was my sister I was visiting, Derek would just have to put up with me. I made a mental note not to pass comment on Susan's non-arrival. That would only set Derek off. Poor Susan – she really did deserve better. Derek might have a good job, but that wasn't everything. I felt sorry for Christopher as well. I wondered if I ought to make a detour via the shops and buy some sort of gift for him. The problem was I was bound to buy the wrong thing – either something Christopher had already got or something his parents considered inappropriate. The catapult I'd given him for his eighth birthday had been very badly received. Ever since then Susan had provided me with a list of suitable gifts at birthday and Christmas-time, along with the repeated instruction that whatever it was shouldn't be too expensive. I know how touchy she can be when it comes to the subject of money. I decided to by-pass the shops.

The walk from the bus-stop on the main road to Susan's house was a long one. The estate had sprung up in the late 1960s and been designed with cars in mind. The planners had assumed that all the residents would drive so there wouldn't be any need for a bus-stop. What about the poor person struggling with a large bundle, I thought to myself? The bin-bag was awkward to carry, and every few minutes I had to readjust my hold, being careful not to catch it on my zip. If I punctured the bag, Susan would never let me in.

A pair of living room curtains closed as I walked past, and the street got darker. The un-shuttered windows provided the only source of light, now that the sky had turned a deep-blue above the rooftops. Along with no buses, there were no street-lamps either. If Chewing Gum attacked me here, nobody would see.

Suddenly without warning, a shape came hurtling from the shadows accompanied by an ear-splitting shriek. For a split second my heart stopped and I stood rooted to the spot, then as my eyes adjusted to the half-light, I saw it was nothing more than a boy on a bicycle. There was another boy behind him giving chase, yelling and swinging a stick in the air. A moment later a car swung into the road, its headlights blazing as it drove past, and I could see the boys were no more than Christopher's age. The sudden glare caused me to blink and shield my eyes, clutching at the bag with my spare hand.

I took a deep breath. I was seeing Chewing Gum everywhere, even when I couldn't actually see him, and now my mind was playing all sorts of fiendish tricks. Chewing Gum wouldn't come at me like a wailing banshee. He hadn't become the most wanted man in the country by behaving like that. But however much I might reassure myself something nagged at the back of my mind, and I became gripped by a feeling of unease that I couldn't shake. It began with me thinking that perhaps I should have bought Christopher something, for all that his parents might protest. The boy deserved some sort of gift. Did he have a bike? I couldn't remember. Boys his age needed bikes, though they shouldn't be riding them in dark streets. I noticed my heart was thumping. Why was I getting so worked up about a bike? Something about my phone call with Jamal nagged away at me too. I didn't like the idea of a computer war brewing on my street. Unless it was something more than that.

All the while I walked I kept expecting Susan to surprise me. She'd pull alongside me in her car any minute, and be her usual crotchety self. But that expectation decreased with every step. And by the time I could see her house, dead ahead, I was actually feeling quite anxious. There were lights burning in all the houses – but Susan's alone was dark. Her car was on the drive, so where was she? And where were Derek and Christopher? As I got nearer I could see that the curtains were drawn, just as they had been on my last visit. But there were no chinks of light escaping from the edges of the window, and nothing from the hallway. To all intents and purposes the house looked abandoned.

I walked up the short drive and was at once bathed in the brilliant glow of a security light. I pressed the doorbell. Nothing. I waited, then pressed it again. There was no response.

I smiled to myself at my foolishness. They were out shopping, that was it. They'd taken Derek's car and all gone to the supermarket together to do the weekly shop. They'd probably be back any minute now. I rubbed my hands. I couldn't just stand there in the meantime though. It wasn't as warm in the evenings now as it had been. I'd be better off sitting inside while I waited for them to come back. They'd understand. Well, Susan would.

The security light went off and once again I was in the dark. I didn't have my own key to the house, but I knew they kept one hidden for emergencies under a large plant pot. Hoping that it was still there and that I could find it, I dropped to my knees and began groping about in the darkness, which soon turned to bright light again once the security sensor caught my flailing arm. I scrambled from one blank pot to the next, hoping that an inquisitive neighbour wouldn't come out and ask me what I thought I was doing, and that I'd find the key before Derek got back. Eventually I managed to locate it, tucked beneath a planter that housed a browned conifer.

I picked up my trousers and let myself in. My first impression when I entered the gloomy hallway was that I'd been wrong about there being nobody in the house. I could hear voices, and prickled with embarrassment. As soon as my ears adjusted though, I realised that the voices came from a radio. That struck me as rather curious. Susan might have forgotten to switch off the radio, but Derek wasn't like that. Or had they taken to using the radio as some sort of back-up to the security light? Perhaps a casual burglar might think twice if he placed his ear to the window and got the impression there was someone at home. There was no need for it now though, so with the bin-liner wedged under my free arm, I headed for the kitchen.

I fumbled with my hand behind the door frame and eventually located the light switch. What I saw when the lights came on made the radio seem unimportant. Susan was seated at the table, slumped forward, with just a bottle of wine and an old video recorder for company. 'Oh Susan,' I said with a sigh.

I wasn't completely blind. I'd suspected that things weren't perfect, but had they got so bad that Susan needed to drink herself senseless? It looked like she hadn't stopped at just one bottle either, because she seemed to have spilt most of it in her drunken state. A pool of wine lay in front of Susan across the table and had dribbled onto the floor. It took less than two paces for me to realise that it was not wine I was looking at, but blood.

'Aah!' I recoiled in shock. After a few moments, I'm not sure how long, I recovered myself.

'Susan,' I said, hoping she'd reply. 'Oh Susan.' I crept closer to her.

'No no no please.' I kept repeating the words. My limbs were shaking.

I moved around the table, avoiding the blood on the floor. I took as deep a breath as I could and tried to look at Susan.

She was dead.

I howled. I squeezed the bin-liner tightly, crushing it against my body then let it fall from my hand. It landed on the kitchen floor with a dull thud.

And then I started crying, and great fat salt tears rolled down my cheeks. Only then, through my burning eyes, could I begin to take in the picture. There were spatters of blood all over the kitchen table, and marks on the floor, too. There was a handprint – no, two handprints on the wall by the calendar. And Susan had trodden in her own blood before she'd ended her days at the table.

Another drop splashed onto the floor. This was recent, wasn't it? Trembling, I inched my way forward.

'Oh God Susan, how did this happen?'

Had Derek left her and taken Christopher with him? And after they'd gone she couldn't bear the thought of living without them so she'd killed herself. Is that what this was about?

Of course it wasn't.

I made myself look at the last thing I wanted to see. There were deep cuts on Susan's body, to her neck and I presumed through her clothes. My sister hadn't taken her own life – no-one killed themselves like this. No, she'd been subjected to a savage attack – murdered in her own home by a knife-wielding maniac. I'd finally had my wish, hadn't I? I'd always wanted to see just what was under those white tents. Well it was something like this. Was I satisfied now? My sister was lying there dead. It took all I could manage not to be sick at the thought. I moaned instead, and a solitary tear fell to the floor where it mixed with Susan's blood.

I reached out a quivering finger and touched my sister's skin and whimpered as it made contact. She was still warm. She hadn't been murdered all that long ago.

I felt light headed. Susan's killer might still be in the house, waiting. He'd set a trap for me and I'd walked into it. But this was wrong, so wrong. It was me that Chewing Gum wanted, not anybody else. If anything it should have been me lying dead across that table, not Susan. She'd done nothing to deserve this.

I stepped backwards and switched off the radio. It was hard to think straight above the commotion. I had to inform the police about what had happened. They could catch the killer while the trail was still fresh. But I'd been questioned as a suspect – they'd think I was responsible. My sister's death was just too much of a coincidence.

I heard a noise outside. There were cars at the front of the house now. I couldn't stay a moment longer. I had to get away. Trying to control my shaking fingers, I unlocked the back door. As the cold night air rushed in, I paused for a moment in the doorway. This was no way to say farewell. But what could I do now? I could hardly give Susan a goodbye hug. It was hard enough looking at her. Whatever else might happen to me in the future, I'd never see Susan again. For years I'd tried to preserve the memory of countless victims of tragedy – well, my own sister wasn't going to be forgotten. That I could promise. I'd do everything in my power to find the sick individual who was responsible for Susan's murder, but to do that I needed to stay free.

The noise at the front was a commotion now. I had to go, and quickly. Staying wouldn't help anyone. It was too late for Susan, and if I wasn't careful it would be too late for me as well.

Steeling myself I dashed across the half-lit garden and began scrambling my way over the flimsy panelled fence that separated it from the house behind. My foot kicked out some of the rough wood but I somehow managed to pull myself over, landing in a pile of wet grass cuttings on the other side. They'd be after me soon. Chewing Gum or the police or whoever it was would be on my tail tracking me down. I had to get as far away as possible and give myself time to think.

I scampered across the garden brushing the cut grass from my face as I ran. A bright light fizzed and blinded me momentarily. I stumbled through a collection of plastic garden toys as I went from light into darkness, passing through the small side gate and onto the unlit road.

Perhaps I'd left a bloodied footprint behind, I thought. I hadn't looked to see whether or not there was a mark on the floor, nor had I checked for any discarded gum. I told myself I should have gone upstairs to see if Chewing Gum was there. If I'd been a little braver I might have grabbed a kitchen knife and searched for the killer. But supposing Chewing Gum had been up there, what then? The serial killer was an expert not just at using a knife, but killing people with one. I wouldn't have stood a chance, and the clues I knew about the his identity would have died with me. Maybe Derek and Christopher were up there, throats slashed, murdered in their own rooms. No. Derek's car hadn't been there. Everything suggested that Susan had been on her own. There hadn't been any sign of an obvious struggle, not by the front door, anyway. The back door was still locked from the inside and there'd been no broken windows that I could see. No, Chewing Gum had been let in. It pained me to think of it. Poor Susan. She'd had a miserable time of it recently, in life as well as in death.

I found myself walking on a street I didn't recognise. The roads curved first one way then the other, and it was hard to know in which direction I was headed. All I knew was that I had to keep walking and trust that my path didn't lead me back to Susan's house. The police would set the tracker-dogs on me soon, looking for my scent. That was the most likely thing. It wouldn't take them long to find it. I'd left my smelly trousers behind. The proof that I'd been to my sister's house was lying in a black plastic bag next to a pool of Susan's blood. I cursed my stupidity.

There was a sudden screech of car-tyres behind me and a flashing of lights and I panicked. I spotted a narrow pedestrian cut-through between two houses and dashed down it as fast as my body would allow. The car couldn't follow me there. I emerged on another twisting road which I crossed into a second alleyway. My legs ached and my lungs felt like they'd burst. If my pursuer didn't catch me my heart would probably give out.

That was a risk I'd have to take. I couldn't stop now.

Beyond the alleyway was the hum of a busy street, and in the distance I caught sight of a bus. Instinctively I headed towards it. The number didn't matter. I just had to get away – to put as much distance between me and that terrible place as possible.

With only one thought on my mind I chased after the disappearing bus. It seemed to speed forward and then, to my delight, I saw it signalling. It was going to stop. My hopes raised I spurted blindly across a side road and only narrowly avoided being flattened by a fast braking car. I stopped, breathless.

The car's window lowered.

'Mr Henry?'

I looked into the dark interior of the car. I tried to speak, but when I opened my mouth the words wouldn't come out.

'Henry?'

It was Wyatt.

CHAPTER TWENTY

'Get in the car.'

It was said gently, but it was an order nonetheless. And when I didn't move, Wyatt repeated it.

'Henry, get in the car.'

She shuffled some papers from the passenger seat and dumped them in the back.

'Come on.'

A van drew up behind Wyatt's car. In the burst of light I could see that it wasn't a police vehicle she was driving, but her own. I climbed in and with a shaking hand clipped myself into the seat.

'You're lucky I was in the area,' she said.

The car was held up at the junction, while she waited for a gap in the traffic.

'Yes,' I said, finally able to speak.

'A bit off the beaten track here aren't you? I mean this isn't your neck of the woods is it?'

'No.'

I realised that she couldn't know about Susan. That meant the police hadn't found out about her yet. Either that, or nobody had told her.

'Bloody traffic,' she said.

I wondered if I should say anything.

'Where does it all come from, that's what I'd like to know.'

'My sister...'

'Look at it.'

'She...' I paused. 'She lives not too far from here.'

Without waiting for a break in the traffic Wyatt weaved her way across the busy road. Cars passed by in both directions, beeping horns and flashing their headlights. Susan would have flapped her arms and apologised to every single one, I thought. The detective sergeant just ignored them.

'Your sister?' she said.

'Yes.'

'Does she now?'

I noticed it wasn't just my hands that were shaking, my legs were as well. I tried to keep them still and hoped Wyatt hadn't noticed. There was a mark on my trousers too, that looked new. It was impossible to tell what it was under the flashes of street lighting. Could it be blood – Susan's blood? And where was Wyatt taking me?

'Where are you taking me?' I said.

'Where do you think?' she said.

I don't know, I thought. She'd turned my question back on me and I felt as though I wasn't entitled to ask another one. With any luck Wyatt was taking me home. I could work out what to do next once I was there. As long as she wasn't taking me back to Susan's house or the police station I'd be safe. Maybe it wasn't the police who'd been following me. It couldn't have been, not if Wyatt didn't know what had happened. Assuming it wasn't all a bluff on her part. I tried looking at her as discreetly as I could, hoping she might say or do something revealing. But the traffic was heavy and Wyatt seemed preoccupied with that and she paid no attention to me. So if it wasn't the police who'd been after me that meant it must have been Chewing Gum – Chewing Gum in his car. I was tempted to ask Wyatt how far the police had got with their investigation, and the breakthrough they kept talking about.

'How..?' I was about to say the words but stopped. They could have been about to re-arrest me.

'What's that?'

'Nothing,' I said. 'Never mind.'

We were held in traffic, stuck behind an enormous van.

'Removals,' said Wyatt. 'Who moves house at this time of day?' She turned towards me. 'I look at that and I can't help wondering what's going on – that's the police mentality. You can't switch it off. They could be doing anything – going home, travelling overnight, working late. And all I can think is – what funny business are you up to? You find yourself suspecting the worst when most of the time there's some perfectly innocent explanation. Do you follow?'

I grunted a reply.

'I called by your house the other day,' said Wyatt. 'You weren't home. I was hoping to drop off those VHS tapes of yours.'

My old tapes. I'd had nothing to play them on since the police had wrecked my old video recorder. But Susan had dug one out for me, just like she'd promised she would. I could picture it on the table, and the blood next to it.

'Are you all right?' said Wyatt. 'Only you seem on edge.'

What could I say? Did I tell her that I'd just come from my sister's house and that not half-an-hour ago I'd seen her hacked and slashed and lying in her own blood? That the Chewing Gum killer was after me? If I revealed all that now and showed the police all the things I'd collected – I'd just get into further trouble for withholding crucial evidence.

No, I was most certainly not all right. Not after everything I'd seen and experienced. But it wasn't just about me. There was the bigger picture to think about – the one that encompassed justice; the one where I could stop running because I didn't have to run anymore; the one where they caught the vicious serial killer who'd murdered all those innocent people and who'd taken the life of my girlfriend and now my sister. A tear welled up in my eye which I prodded gently with my finger. The police could take care of things now, they were there to help. Yes, they might question me again, but I hadn't really done anything wrong. The truth would come out in the end anyway and that was what was important. It was time I unburdened myself. Once I'd done that I could start to deal with all the grief and the guilt and the pain. I just needed to keep calm. If I kept calm then everything would be all right. Everything.

'It's my sister,' I said. 'Susan.'

'Go on.'

'She saw me after you... that is, after you saw...'

'After we questioned you?'

'Yes. And I told her that I knew who the serial killer was – thought I knew.' I tried to control my breathing, but my lungs still hurt from running.

'But you didn't say a word of that to us.' The car had picked up speed, and raced through a light. 'You didn't think to share that information?'

'I know, I know,' I said. 'I should have said something, I know that.'

'So what happened to your sister?'

An ambulance tore past in the opposite direction, its lights flashing and klaxons blaring.

'Susan?'

'How did she react when you told her what you knew,' said Wyatt.

'I can't remember exactly,' I said.

'Was she worried?'

'She should have been. And it's all my fault.'

My eyes were filling up with tears now. I couldn't see anything – how much my body was shaking or how much my clothes were covered in bloodstains.

'And what name did you give her Henry?'

I snuffled.

'When you told her who the killer was.'

I gave a sigh and rubbed at my prickling skin.

'Henry?'

'I didn't tell her a name. All I said was that he'd been leaving clues as he went and I was the only person who knew that. Because the police – you – didn't seem to know anything.'

'But you did, eh Henry?'

'Yes. Yes I did.'

'And instead of telling us you kept it to yourself. Because you thought 'Well, if I go to the police station and tell them everything I know then they might not let me out in a hurry. They might just say 'hold on a minute, there's a lot of evidence here that points to this man and it looks very conclusive.' And that's before they mention all those bits and pieces you've gathered on your travels. Something from here, something from there...'

I pulled myself upright. 'Hang on,' I said. 'How do you know about that?'

'Little things that have fallen on the ground. You'd be amazed what the cameras can pick up. You followed us around everywhere Henry. Almost like you were checking up on us. Lorna Coulson, Tabitha Williams.'

'I didn't follow you to Parson's Wood,' I said. 'I was there before you.'

'Hillyard and me were first on the scene,' said Wyatt. 'Before anybody. We just kept it quiet to avoid any panic, until we were certain.'

I couldn't feel my legs shaking any more. I couldn't really feel my legs at all.

'And all this time you've been looking over your shoulder, wondering if the killer knows that you know.'

The car picked up more speed. The world outside passed by in a blur.

'Where are we going?' I said.

'Living in a state of constant fear.'

We were racing now past shops I recognised. I wanted to call out to her: 'You can let me off here, I'll walk the rest of the way.' But just like my legs, my tongue felt numb and useless.

'When of course what you should have done all along was come and seen us. Somebody who's committed no crime has nothing to fear Henry, surely you know that. Because if you can't trust the police, who can you trust?'

She was looking at me now and there was a smile on her face. I couldn't tear myself away and for a second our eyes locked as we hurtled through the night time traffic.

'You don't need to worry,' said Wyatt. And as she spoke I noticed for the first time the motion of her jaws. 'I'll see you're taken care of.'

Then without another word Wyatt pulled a piece of chewing gum from her mouth. I watched in horror as she took a square of silver coated paper and began to fold it neatly and precisely around the gum. I looked for the split second it took for everything to make sense, and then I moved. In an instant I'd unclipped my seat belt and opened the car door.

'Henry!'

Wyatt yelled and grabbed at me with her free arm. I pushed her away and thumped her with as much strength as I could muster. She swore at me and for a moment lost control of the steering wheel. The car veered into the fast moving traffic and almost smashed into a vehicle on the inside lane which had to brake sharply to avoid a collision. Behind us first one car then another screeched and squealed and swerved. But I wasn't really paying any attention to the traffic. I was gripped by one thought and one thought only – the desire for self-preservation. To remain in the car would mean certain death at the hands of a knife wielding serial killer.

So I jumped.

The traffic thundered.

The brakes screamed.

Wyatt yelled.

And I hit the road with a crash, my leg slipping from under me as my body slammed onto the unforgiving tarmac. A car passed to my left blaring as it went by. An articulated lorry boomed its horn as it dodged to the right. Wyatt's car, with its door swinging, slipped and slowed, but there was speeding traffic on either side and it was swallowed up by the roundabout. I rolled over, into the kerb, the skin scraped from my hand and arm and pain shooting through my hip and left leg. It would no doubt feel much worse in the future. But at least I had a future. I was alive. I'd come face to face with the Chewing Gum killer, and survived the encounter.

CHAPTER TWENTY-ONE

I pulled myself onto the narrow strip of kerb which skirted the edge of the roundabout. I had to head off quickly, regardless of the pain. It would only be a matter of seconds before Wyatt had done a full circuit and caught up with me. I couldn't afford to wallow in my good fortune. The killer wouldn't give me a second chance.

The slip road that filtered traffic into the roundabout seemed the obvious avenue of escape. Wyatt would have to defy every known traffic law if she wanted to follow me that way. Of course there was no guarantee that someone who'd already killed – how many was it? Five? Six? Wouldn't just do as she pleased and plough through the oncoming traffic in her hunt for the one man who knew her secret. Not that any movement, let alone flight, was going to be easy for me. Each step was agony. My hip was at very least badly bruised, and as for my leg... Was that what a broken leg felt like? It made walking difficult and running impossible.

The serial killer was a man, they'd kept on telling me, always a man. Or was that what I'd been telling myself? I couldn't remember. But I'd become fixated on the idea and it had turned out to be a blind alley. Perhaps everyone else thought the same thing and that's why Chewing Gum had got away with it for so long. No, I had to stop referring to her as Chewing Gum. She wasn't Chewing Gum anymore. She was Wyatt. The serial killer was Detective Sergeant Wyatt.

I ducked into a doorway to rest. The pain in my leg was barely tolerable and I knew it was only going to get worse. Still, I had to consider myself fortunate the injury had been to my leg and that there was nothing wrong with my head. It had been a close thing though. If the articulated lorry had hit me I'd have been little more than pâté now – a stain just before the roundabout.

I continued shuffling along the road. I ought to go to the hospital. As soon as I'd got my bearings I could head towards it. But Wyatt would presumably be waiting for me outside the A&E. In which case it might be best to forget the hospital for now, just like I had to try and ignore my own discomfort. There were far more important considerations than the pain threshold. I had to make it home somehow. If I didn't do that it wouldn't matter what state my leg was in. Wyatt had probably thought the same thing, of course, and there was every chance she'd go there. She'd been to the house before. Once with Hillyard and then again when she'd left her trademark gum on the front path. Returning my tapes, did she say? Come round to kill me, more like. As soon as she'd checked the A&E department she'd go straight round to the house and wait outside the front door for me, knife at the ready. For once in my life I had no desire to go home.

But unless I did go home I was helpless. My money was there for one thing. Not to mention all the other bits and pieces that might help me survive.

The other option was to drag myself to the nearest police station and tell the desk sergeant everything I knew. I'd have to come clean right away – tell them I'd been a suspect in the serial killing case and questioned before someone provided me with an alibi and they'd let me go. But it would be an uncomfortable conversation. They wouldn't want to hear that the real killer had been under their noses all this time and what's more she was a serving police officer. This same officer had murdered my sister as well, not long before I'd gone round to her house. And now that she was aware that I knew her identity, the police station was the only safe place I could go. The trouble was, if I told the police that they'd lock me up as soon as look at me. At best they'd think I was a nutcase. At worst they might think I was a cornered serial killer trying to wriggle off the hook before the net finally closed round me. So I discounted the police station. The police couldn't help.

Whatever I chose, the critical thing was to keep out of Wyatt's sight. In my current condition I couldn't hope to get away from her if she found me. I'd be easy meat.

There was somebody who might be able to get me out of this scrape though: Jamal. I could phone Jamal and tell him what had happened. I could ask him to meet me at such and such a place – near the library perhaps – and give him instructions about what I'd like him to do. First off I'd give him my keys and send him round to the house to fetch my things, like bank details and stuff. I'd need to fill him in on all the gory details though, that only seemed fair. But I knew I could trust Jamal. He wouldn't blow my cover, I needn't worry there. The main danger was that I'd be risking Jamal's life sending him on an errand like that. Look what had happened to Rose and Susan.

It was then that the reality hit me. I no longer had any change. I could picture Jamal's number, that was the worst thing. I'd dialled it before thinking I was calling Susan. But I only had three coins in my pocket, all coppers, and they weren't enough to make a phone call. It was frustrating to think that I could have been in the very street where Jamal lived without even knowing it. He'd never mentioned where his home was and I'd never thought to ask him. How I wished we'd had a conversation about it.

I was going to need luck now. As tempting as it was to stay away from the house I knew I had to go back. Apart from money, there were all the mementoes I'd gathered – the ones Wyatt seemed to know about. They were my insurance policy now. I'd collected every one as my way of trying to help others. Now it would be their turn to come to my aid. In the end I would have to take them to the police. They could be as suspicious as they wanted, but I had to ensure that Wyatt didn't get to me first and then remove my treasures. I owed it to Jacqueline, Lorna, Tabitha, Rose, Susan and anyone else Wyatt had killed. Their lives had already been destroyed, but their memories couldn't, mustn't, be allowed to wither away. There were about four hours till daylight. I just had to stay safe till then. A clear head was what was called for now. Heaven only knew what had set Wyatt off on her killing spree, but I wouldn't be permitted to mess up her plans. I'd need to play her at her own game if I was going to get home in one piece.

I couldn't exactly describe myself as calm, but knowing that I'd uncovered the identity of the nation's most notorious serial killer did give me a feeling of relief. At least I knew who Chewing Gum was now. There was no need to look at every person I encountered with suspicion, nor continually glance over my shoulder, frightened for my life. I thought back to my interrogation at the police station, and all those hours I'd spent watching the murder case unfold on television. All those suspects – me included - and my instincts had been wrong. Not just with regard to Chewing Gum's identity, but I'd completely misjudged the character of the two investigating police officers. I'd taken an instant dislike to grizzled, shiny headed DI Hillyard, whose face was set in a constant frown. No wonder he was always so cross looking. He was the public face of the biggest murder investigation in the country. A detective inspector who hadn't got his man – or in this case, his woman. Did he have any inkling, I asked myself, about his partner on the case. Or was it doubt that caused him to frown? DS Wyatt had seemed much nicer. She'd offered me a cup of tea. Once or twice she'd even managed a smile. And all the time she was a murdering psychopath. I'd been interviewed by the serial killer herself. She hid her dark side well, but how had I managed to get it so wrong? I recalled sitting in that bleak interview room with Wyatt, wondering if I should tell her about the chewing gum I'd found. It was only Hillyard coming back that had stopped me. I was glad I hadn't said anything. I'd have been signing my own death warrant.

The long and difficult journey home gave me plenty of thinking time. I wouldn't need to pay that visit to Ginger Whiskers after all, always assuming I kept one painful step ahead of Wyatt. All told, I'd rushed to judgement a little early on quite a few people – Mr Shields from Environmental Health, Jamal, Tattoos, Sandwiches, Cloth Cap, Hillyard. Just about every male of my acquaintance. What a monumental error that had turned out to be.

Wyatt would be outside the house now, waiting. Most likely she was chewing her gum, with the knife in her hand. So I couldn't go in by the front, not while she was there. The rear of the house was trickier to get to. I could access it via Tattoos' garden, but that was just as visible from a parked car, wasn't it? Even then there was the problem of the kitchen door. Without a key I'd have to force it open or smash the window. The noise would wake the neighbours, who'd then call the police. I'd be afforded some protection then. I could tell the police I'd locked myself out, and was sorry about all the fuss, but while they were there they might as well hear what I had to say. And I could show them my boxes of treasures and finally tell them about the chewing gum. But supposing it was Wyatt who took the call. What if she said 'Leave it to me, I'm in the area.' And she came to investigate. That would require a diversion of some sort. If Wyatt was there, sitting in her car waiting, I'd need to find some means of drawing her away.

It took me an hour of painful trudging through the streets before I finally figured out what I had to do. Wyatt thought she knew me. How I lived and how I acted. Well, I could show her that she didn't know Henry V Henry at all. She wouldn't be expecting me to be devious or cunning, would she? But that might just help me. This wasn't the time to do anything obvious. Cunning was what was called for now. I found a phone in the shopping arcade that was still working, and dialled the emergency number.

'There's a fire,' I said. Where exactly was it? I told them it was at the school, the one that wasn't too far from the house. There hadn't been any reports of a fire. No? Well this was the first one. And where was I calling from? Not far from the school – the burning school. There were people in it as well, I told the operator. I'd seen them when I was walking my dog. Yes, I knew it was late but my dog hadn't been able to sleep. My skin prickled as I heard myself say the words. I reminded myself that I wasn't playing a game and that I had to be careful not to give myself away. There was an ominous pause at the other end of the line. Were they tracing the call or looking for proof that I wasn't making it up? Was someone about to call my bluff? There was a click on the line and then the voice at the other end came back.

'Thank you for your help sir.'

And that was that.

Would they come, I wondered. They couldn't assume it was a hoax.

People's lives might be at risk if it wasn't. And if there was a report of a serious fire and a crime then the police would hopefully be called as well as the fire brigade. If Wyatt was nearby, which I suspected she was, then she'd be obliged to go and offer her services. No. I was kidding myself. There was no guarantee at all that Wyatt would pitch in. I just had to hope, that was all. Still, I'd done what I could – the first part of my plan, at any rate.

I needed some other form of diversionary tactic though – something that would make me not look like the normal Henry V Henry that DS Wyatt was used to. The first thing that I noticed was a box. That would do, I thought. I could carry a box. Wyatt wouldn't expect to see me carrying a box. There was no shortage of them lying around outside the shops, all different sizes. Then I caught sight of something else lying in a doorway, and that gave me another idea. Next to the charity shop, just beneath the sign asking people not to leave any items when the shop was shut, was a mound of plastic bags. Judging by their shape, I suspected they contained clothes. What if I got changed and put some of them on? Wyatt would be searching for me in the clothes that she'd last seen me wearing when I jumped from the car. She wouldn't be on the lookout for me in disguise. I tore open the first bag and pulled out a floral patterned skirt. Wyatt definitely wouldn't be looking for me in anything like that. I held it up for a moment and wondered if I had the courage to dress in women's clothing for the remainder of my journey home. I decided that I didn't. There were some acceptable clothes though – a pair of striped slacks, a cardigan and best of all a raincoat. Wyatt would never think to look for me wearing a raincoat.

I began taking my clothes off, all the time looking around in case anyone should come. I'd been at school the last time I'd taken my clothes off in public. I didn't like doing it then, and I didn't much care for it now, but it had to be done. Removing the shirt was no trouble, but my trousers proved to be a different story. They were only half way down my legs when I felt an excruciating pain, which only increased when I took off my shoes. The new trousers proved to be far too small, and went no further up my leg than my bruised thigh. I shook them off as best I could and dressed only in cardigan, pants and socks began rooting through the other bags. It was infuriating. I had more than enough trousers at home, not to mention a filthy pair I'd abandoned at Susan's. Even they'd have been preferable to standing half naked in a charity shop doorway at two in the morning.

I tore open another bag, and just as I did so I heard a voice call out.

'Hold on a second.'

I shrank back into the shadows of the doorway.

'What are you doing?' It was a woman's voice. Was it Chewing Gum? Wyatt?'

'I'll only be a minute.'

It sounded as though the first voice was walking towards me. I squirreled as best I could under the bundle of clothes and tried to lay as still as possible.

'Come on!'

'Wait!'

I heard a belch and then the sound of a zip.

'You can't do it there,' someone else shouted.

'I think there's a tramp under here.' The voice was directly above me now.

'It's a charity shop.'

'A tramp. Dirty bastard.'

And then I heard the unmistakable sound of a man urinating, before he staggered into the night, accompanied by his friends and laughter. It wasn't Chewing Gum.

Once I was sure the coast was clear I opened another bag, which was wet, and searched through that. Finally, on my fourth bag I found a pair of elasticated nylon shorts. Wearing football shorts was something else I hadn't done since school, but I had no other choice so I put them on.

I noticed that my foot seemed to have doubled in size since I'd taken off my shoes, and I suspected that putting them back on again would cause me no end of pain. I'd have to leave my shoes behind and walk the rest of the way in stockinged feet. I began refilling the plastic bags, adding my own discarded clothes and shoes as I did so. Near the chemist's shop I picked up an empty box that had once held containers of talcum powder. I lifted it onto my shoulder, and began the last stretch towards home.

The klaxons would be ringing soon, I told myself. At least, with any luck they would be. But with each step, the only sound I could hear was the raincoat flapping around my bare legs. I wondered if it might have been a mistake not to have opted for the floral patterned skirt, or perhaps something more matronly. And was the cardboard box a useful addition to my costume or nothing more than a nuisance? My legs felt cold and uncomfortable but my foot felt worse. I could feel the pavement through my socks and I weaved from side to side as I limped along. My disguise had better work, I told myself. Escape would be next to impossible should the need arise.

The fire brigade must have worked out it was a hoax, I thought, as I neared the turning to my street. They'd have had a look at their computer maps or whatever it was they did and seen that there wasn't any fire. It was too late to turn back now, though, I was committed. And where else would I go in any case? I braced myself for the sight of Wyatt waiting for me. Would she laugh at my uncovered legs and socks as she went for me with her knife? A corrugated cardboard box wouldn't offer me much protection.

While I was mulling over the possibilities of what I ought to do I became distracted by a sound in the distance. It started out as a small noise that grew steadily by the second. Then I realised what it was and I saw, coming in my direction, not one but two fire engines. They whizzed past me, followed in quick order by several police vehicles, all noise and flashing lights. Momentarily overcome by guilt, I pressed the talcum powder box to my face as they went by. It looked like my scheme might have worked after all – at least in bringing out the emergency services. But had it shifted Wyatt? I peered cautiously around the corner. There were cars parked in the street, as always – but I didn't recognise Wyatt's amongst them. Still, I couldn't afford to be careless. Not when I was so close to my sanctuary.

As painful as my foot was, I almost skipped the last remaining yards to the house. Once inside I'd barricade the door behind me and wait there until morning – nine o'clock seemed a reasonable time – and then I'd go straight to the police station. It would be safe then. Of course Jamal might pay me a visit before then, or... I suddenly became aware of the terrible reality of what had happened and that the one person I wouldn't see would be my sister. It had only been a few hours since I'd found Susan's body, but I'd been on the move from that moment. There hadn't been time to think about what it really meant. I was tired now – the hours and the injuries were starting to take their toll. All I could think about was how grateful I'd feel when I finally closed the front door behind me. I could rest then.

I began muttering under my breath as I shuffled and scraped my bad foot for the last few yards. Please don't come now, I kept repeating to myself. Please don't come now. If Chewing Gum – Wyatt – found me now it would ruin everything. But to my relief there was no-one waiting by the door or lurking behind the bookcases in the front garden. I fumbled for my keys and my fingers shook so much it took me a few seconds to open the door. As I locked it behind me I breathed a huge sigh of relief. I was home now – safe and secure at last.

And then I switched on the hall light.

CHAPTER TWENTY-TWO

Click.

Nothing.

Click click click.

Still nothing. What had happened to the light?

Click click.

The bulb had gone. That was all I needed. I'd forgotten how awkward it could be getting about the house in the dark.

I struggled through the hallway, which seemed narrower and more restricting. I stumbled forwards, only stopping when my good leg made contact with the bin-liner which blocked my path. I reached down to calculate its size, jabbing my hand on what felt like broken glass in the process. I took a sharp intake of breath and pulled my hand away. Had I drawn blood? It was hard to tell in the murky half-light.

It was only with some difficulty that I managed to get past the bag. First thing in the morning I was going to have to sort that out, I told myself. Someone could hurt themselves on it. I sucked my finger. I might have done so myself.

There was another light switch at the end of the hallway tucked behind one of the stacks of boxes. I couldn't remember when I'd last used it, let alone seen it, but I'd lived in the house a long time and still remembered where all the fixtures and fittings were, even if most of them were covered up. I slipped my hand behind a cardboard box and fished for the switch. It was always possible there was nothing wrong with the bulb and that a fault had developed in the switch by the front door.

Click.

Nothing.

The bulb must have gone then. At least, I hoped it was just the bulb. I tried turning on the light in the kitchen but the result was the same. Perhaps the fuse had blown. That happened sometimes. But if that was the case then why was there no standby light on the television, nor any hum coming from the fridge? There was no electricity at all, was there?

Had there been a power cut? I recalled the time a few years back when the television and video had blinked off in the middle of the news and it turned out there'd been a fire at the substation. So perhaps that was what had happened. But I saw light coming from a neighbour's bathroom window and that told me it wasn't a power cut this time. I tried to suppress the terrible thought that Wyatt had broken in, cut the electricity cables and was lying in wait for me. No, there was another explanation, and I suddenly remembered what it was. I'd had a final reminder from the electricity company, informing me that unless I settled my outstanding bill then my supply would be terminated forthwith. I'd meant to go to the post office. I was going to write a cheque and clear the arrears. Only there'd been a murder that day or a news report or some other distraction and that had blown me off course. And I'd stacked the letter in a pile with all the other ones and forgotten all about it and now I was suffering the consequences. They'd gone through with their threat and cut me off. There was no electricity.

I groaned at the inconvenience of it all. Even if I settled the bill in the morning I wouldn't get the supply reconnected before Monday at the earliest. I'd have to last the whole weekend without lights, TV, radio, cooker, fridge... And that was on top of everything else, like staying clear of Detective Sergeant Wyatt.

It was a good job I was prepared for emergencies. I had a torch. It might be dark but I knew exactly where it was. I kept it in the cupboard under the kitchen sink.

It took me a minute or two to negotiate my way through the kitchen to the cupboard. The boxes all seemed much bigger in the dark and closer together. I leaned against the sink and took off my new raincoat, preparing for what I knew would be a difficult manoeuvre. Once I'd steadied myself I bent my injured legs until I was kneeling on the kitchen floor. A few seconds of groping around inside the cupboard was all it took for me to realise that I was going to be disappointed. The boxes of soap powders, the floor cloths, the tins of shoe polish and assorted sanitary products were all wet to the touch. It didn't smell very nice either, and reminded me of my trousers. The drainage trap must have developed a leak, and it had steadily dripped dirty water over everything. The torch, which was directly underneath the trap, was soaking wet and useless. The batteries had rusted through. The box of household candles had somehow escaped the dampness; the nearby box of matches unfortunately had not. So that was it then. I'd just have to sit in semi darkness until morning came.

Thump.

I jumped. What was that?

It was a noise of some sort.

I stood still and listened. What had it been? I knew all the noises in the house – the humming of the fridge, when the electricity worked – the churning in the pipes and the cistern; the creaking of the floorboards; the gurgle in the tank as the water heated up. The thump hadn't been any of those familiar noises – not one that I recognised anyway. I tried to convince myself that it was only a noise, but that didn't work. A month ago, perhaps less, I might not have noticed a thump from upstairs. But with all that had happened to me and those around me – with all that I knew... No, I didn't want to think what the noise had been, but much as I might try to I couldn't stop myself.

It could have been the newspapers. A pile of them might have tipped over. Or it could have been a heavy object of some sort falling onto the floor. I had plenty of those all over the house. But papers and objects didn't just move of their own accord. And there was almost no empty floor space upstairs for them to fall onto, even if they did. I tried to control my breathing and the pain in my leg, which I'd momentarily forgotten but was now back and worse than ever. I told myself it was probably nothing, and that noises in the dark always seemed louder. But I still felt I ought to check and see what it was. I didn't particularly want to, but I knew that I wouldn't be able to relax even for a second if I ignored it. The light was poor, almost nonexistent, but I had a good idea where things belonged and I'd be able to tell at once if something was out of place.

I went back through the kitchen and struggled once again past the awkward bundle that blocked the hallway. The injuries I'd sustained jumping from Wyatt's car didn't make it easy. But clambering over a bin-liner would be child's play compared to the job of getting up the stairs. Every single step would require that I place my full weight on my worsening leg and foot, while I hauled my body up eighteen stairs. I was finding it difficult enough walking on a level floor, but each stair had a hazard of its own, being mostly half filled with piles of papers and magazines. It would be like trying to climb a mountain, and just like a mountain, once I'd got to the top I'd have to come back down again. I'd be in agony by the end of it. Was it worth the pain, just to investigate a bang? The more I pondered the problem, the less sure I was that I'd even heard the noise in the first place. I wondered if it was the pain or my situation that was causing my mind to play tricks on me.

I stopped by the front door. There was freedom outside. I could unlock the door and in a minute I'd be out in the dark night air. I wouldn't need to worry about any bangs out there. Then I remembered that the keys were still in the pocket of my raincoat, which I'd left by the sink. I thought about how relieved I'd been when I arrived home and locked the door behind me. I hoped my relief hadn't been misplaced. What if there was someone in the house with me? Well – not so much a someone, more a Chewing Gum. A Wyatt. I tried to tell myself not to be so silly and keep frightening myself, but it wasn't easy.

I gripped the banister post and shifted onto my good leg. It eased the throbbing sensation for a moment, but I knew the pain would only increase once I began climbing the stairs. There was, of course, another thing I could do.

'Hello,' I called out. 'Is there anybody there?'

I needed to be more decisive. So I cleared my throat and tried again.

'I know you're there. And I know who you are. I think you'd better come out now.'

I squinted upstairs into the gloom. There was no answer, and no thump. Whoever it was – if there was anybody at all – would have heard me. I looked again at the front door. Open it, the voice in my head was telling me. Go and get your keys and open it. Things don't just go thump for no good reason. Chewing Gum is in here, not out there. This is your chance to get away. Yes, I answered back. But what if I'd been wrong about the noise and Wyatt was outside waiting for me? I'd have walked into a trap then and all because of a stupid sound I'd imagined. An overbalanced heap of something or a bag that had fallen over. Nothing, in other words. I wasn't going to be betrayed by one of my possessions falling onto the floor. I steadied my breathing. The last time I'd seen Wyatt she'd been out there, not in my house, and as far as I knew that was still the case. I had to go and put my mind at rest.

I dragged myself up the first step, and then the second. It was painful each time I lifted a leg, or put my weight on the other, but after a few stairs my climbing had acquired a steady rhythm. There might have been more sounds that I'd missed, I told myself. But over my laboured breathing and thumping chest, it was almost impossible to hear anything. Nine, ten – I counted each step as though I were scaling a peak. What untold damage was I doing to my body? People often ended up with disfiguring limps because they ignored pain and mistreated broken bones. Thirteen. Still, there was nothing I could do about it. Not now, when I'd climbed so high. If it was Chewing Gum – if Wyatt had found her way into the house, then I was as vulnerable now as when I'd been out on the streets. No, I was more vulnerable. Wyatt could do anything in here and I'd be helpless. I'd be 'taken care of' – isn't that what she'd said? I had a pain in my chest and I felt sure that my legs would give way, but with one last heave I finally made the summit.

'Hello?' I called again, but I didn't imagine anybody would answer. Or at least I hoped they wouldn't. And to my great relief nobody did. Once I'd got my breath back I shuffled along the landing. The thump had come from the back bedroom. I saw at once what had happened and my heart lifted. It was the cat. Henry the concrete cat must have somehow slipped free from its bin-liner and come crashing to the floor. I tried to reach down and pick it up, but found my bad leg was less willing to bend than it had been by the kitchen sink. The cat would have to stay on the floor. I pushed it against the wall with my good foot. It wouldn't do to leave it in the middle of the doorway where someone might trip over it. Someone? Me. Nobody but me.

I flopped down against a pile of boxes, exhausted. After all my hard work it had just been the concrete cat. What a silly thing to be frightened about. I was too on edge, that's what it was. I'd allowed myself to get too worked up about nothing. Of course Wyatt wasn't in the house, the whole idea was absurd. I should have thought about it more logically from the start. The door was locked and the windows hadn't been broken. I'd have noticed the draught if a window had gone. And how was Wyatt supposed to have got in? Down the chimney?

I made my way back to the staircase and began the slow, painful descent. I'd been an idiot. Punishing myself with one torment after another. Surely I'd suffered enough without torturing myself further. I'd lost Rose, I'd lost my sister – I might well have lost my own life earlier that night. If I wasn't careful I'd end up losing my mind.

I wasn't sure if it was because the sky was getting a little lighter, or because my eyes had adjusted to the darkness, but with each step it felt that things looked much less gloomy. The long, dark terrifying night was finally coming to an end. Everything would be coming back to life soon. People would be waking up, getting dressed, making breakfast and preparing to go to work or enjoying their time at home. It was Friday. Only one more day till the weekend. Everyone was in a better mood at the weekend. The thought of all those people rousing themselves from sleep made me realise just how tired I was. I'd been awake for twenty-four hours now, in which time my sister had been murdered and I'd suffered all manner of indignities and stressful situations. It was all starting to catch up with me.

As I neared the bottom of the stairs my foot slipped on a loose sheet of paper. I clutched the banister in time and winced as the pain shot through my leg. I scolded myself. Just because daylight was approaching there was no need to be careless. I'd survived the longest night of my life. It wouldn't do to break my neck now. If that happened I'd be another statistic – the one they always quoted about home being the most dangerous place of all.

There was a leaflet on the front doormat. Or at least, it appeared to be a leaflet. It was hard to tell in the murky light. I hadn't noticed it when I'd come in, my mind had been on other things. I stepped on the piece of paper and dragged it towards me with my foot, further aggravating my leg when I bent down to pick it up. I could just make out the electricity company's logo. No doubt there was a cheery message, telling me they'd called while I was out but that they'd still cut me off. I decided against filing it away with the other leaflets on the stairs. In fact, I thought, when everything had settled down and gone back to normal again, it might be time for a full scale sort out. I'd have a computer soon and the world at my fingertips. If I wanted to have my sash windows replaced or my drainpipes done I could look on my computer. Still, it would have to wait at very least until the electricity supply was reconnected. I couldn't do very much of anything until then.

More importantly there was Susan to consider. It was still hard to accept the awful thing that had happened. The image of her, slumped at the table, was one I'd never forget. But that wasn't how I wanted to remember her. Susan deserved better than that. And what would happen to Christopher? The poor boy. I'd been about the same age when I lost my own mother. It was something – well, it could really have an effect on a person for the rest of their lives. I'd been lucky in that I'd somehow found the strength of will to overcome the hardship. There was no telling whether Christopher would be so fortunate. I'd do my best for him of course. Derek might not like it, but I was Christopher's uncle when all said and done. Anyway, it was the least I could do. Not that any amount of money could ever change what had happened. Money never did.

I wondered what the time must be. Was it half-five or nearer to half-seven? It was impossible to tell. There was only one clock that didn't run off the mains and that was upstairs. I had no intention of going back up there again, at least, not in a hurry. I fought my way past the blockage in the hallway. There was no real reason to go to the kitchen but it felt like the best place to be. I could sit there and wait, and when the time was ready – perhaps when I heard my neighbour's door slam, or people in the street – then it might be safe to go to the police station. I squeezed through the kitchen doorway. Until then I'd sit tight. And if Wyatt came hammering on the door pleading with me to let her in I'd tell her where to go. As long as I stayed in here I was safe.

Safe...

No.

That was when I caught sight of it. The light was still poor, but what I could see was utterly unmistakable. An enormous knife – the kind they used for carving meat – had been thrust into the top of a cardboard box. It was just like the one I'd seen in the interview room and I had no knife like it. I stared at it for a moment before my brain finally registered what it was that I was looking at, and that now I was anything but safe. But that wasn't all that I could see. Because even in my abject terror I noticed something else that told me everything I thought I knew about the killer was completely wrong. In fact, I'd been about as wrong as it was possible to be.

I had to get away, as fast as I could. Now. I inched to the edge of the kitchen then remembered that the front door was locked. My keys were in my raincoat pocket on the far side of the room next to the sink. I could grab the coat and get to the front door in less than a minute. I felt sure I could suppress the pain for that long. So without taking my eye off the knife I took a step across the cluttered floor. And then I took another. A few more steps around a few more boxes and I'd have the keys in my hand. I took another step, but as my foot touched the floor I felt a strong arm grip mine and something sharp jab against my neck.

'Hello Henry.' The voice breathed into my ear. 'And where do you think you're going?'

CHAPTER TWENTY-THREE

'Well?' said the voice. 'What's the matter? Cat got your tongue? Come on Henry, you've let me down.'

'I was just...' I mumbled a few words, then without thinking I tried to pull myself free.

'Steady.'

The grip grew tighter on my arm.

'This thing has killed, remember.' The point pressed into my flesh. 'Or was it the other one? I forget. Either way Henry – two knives. And all it takes is for one of them to get jealous. Well, you know what temperamental things they are.'

'So it was you,' I said. 'Sandwiches.'

I looked over at the box. Beside the knife was an upturned shell of wrinkled kitchen foil, which enclosed the remains of a half eaten sandwich.

'Sandwiches.' As he spoke a few crumbs tumbled down my shoulder. 'Is that what you've been calling me?'

'Yes.'

'Huh.'

'You're the serial killer.'

'It would be silly of me to deny it now, wouldn't it?'

I screwed my eyes shut. All that time, all those journeys, all that stress. And it turned out the killer was Sandwiches. It hadn't been Chewing Gum. It had never been Chewing Gum. The chewing gum I'd found had never been anything other than chewing gum. I'd made a terrible mistake.

The murderer began sniffing, loudly. 'You've wet yourself, haven't you?' he said. 'That's what fear does Henry, it robs you of dignity.'

'It wasn't me,' I said.

'Then that's even worse,' said Sandwiches. 'I wouldn't have thought it was the weather for shorts by the way. It's autumn Henry, almost winter. You are an odd one and no mistake. By the way, I'm curious – did you ever find Jubilee Street? I looked and looked but I'm damned if I know where it is. My guess is you were barking up the wrong tree.'

I felt the knife against my neck. This is what had happened to Rose, and Susan, and the others. It was a horrid way to die. And the knowledge that the same thing would happen to me at any second only made it worse. I'd failed. I'd tried my best, but I'd failed.

'Funny you coming to visit me like that,' he said.

The knife jabbed into my skin again, and I winced.

'A little bit of freelance investigating, was it? I'll bet that stuff with the chewing gum had something to do with it. Now what was all that about, eh?' He laughed. 'Ah well. We all make mistakes, don't we? I'm used to people not seeing me. I look ordinary. It's a gift in many ways. No-one notices you if you look ordinary.'

I steeled myself for the final plunging of the knife, and tensed my neck muscles. They'd offer no resistance to a blade of sharpened steel. All I could do was try and make my final minutes count for something. If I was going to die, I didn't want it to be in ignorance. 'Can I ask you a question?' I said.

'Feel free,' said Sandwiches.

I wanted to know why this evil man had killed my sister and my friend. I wanted to know what had possessed him to embark on a campaign of sadism and misery; why he'd ruined the lives of people he couldn't possibly have known. But the words didn't come out like that. 'How did you get into my house?' I said.

'Is that all?'

I felt the pressure ease on my neck.

'Easiest thing in the world Henry,' said Sandwiches. 'Well it is when you've got a key. All this garbage you've got piled up in here – you couldn't even see whether your door was shut properly, could you? Careless I'd call it. I saw you leave it open. Didn't know that, did you? I'd come to check you out. Jumped over the garden wall. And then, wouldn't you know it, some kids did the same thing. I heard them coming over so I hid in that old fridge you've got out the back. It's a good job it was there, so thanks for that. They turned out to be a right bunch of hooligans, breaking your glass and everything. I'm not surprised you came and shouted at them. Course, if you'd stopped and had a proper look around you might have seen me. They very nearly did. I couldn't believe my luck when you rushed off. I mean that was more than I could have hoped for, especially when you didn't shut the door behind you. That meant I didn't need to break in. I could just drop off the knife, lock the back door and take the key. I bet you didn't even know it was missing. It was me who told the police about the knife of course. We had some fun and games with that, didn't we eh?' The knife jabbed against my neck again. 'Happy now?'

'No,' I said.

Sandwiches let go of my arm and thrust his hand forward. On the flat of his palm was my back door key.

'Take it,' he said.

I didn't move a muscle.

'Go on, take it. It's no use to me anymore.'

Cautiously I took the key from his outstretched hand.

'There, didn't hurt, did it?'

'No.'

I noticed that the knife was no longer pressing against my neck.

'Just look after it for next time,' said Sandwiches.

And then he giggled – softly to begin with but it soon built up into a full blown laugh. I didn't need to ask what he found funny. He was laughing because there wasn't going to be a next time. He'd worked it all out down to the very last detail. I did my best to calm my nerves. That was important. The calmer I was, the less agitated Sandwiches was likely to be and that might just keep me alive a bit longer. By rights I should have been dead by now, I knew that. Sandwiches was a serial killer – he wouldn't have sat with his other victims and taunted them. He'd have had his way with his knife and then moved on. But for some reason Sandwiches felt compelled to talk to me. Well, I'd oblige him. With any luck I could keep him talking until someone arrived. When I heard a knock on the door, or the flapping of the letterbox I could call out for help. The newspaper boy came around nine. No. He didn't any more, I'd cancelled the papers. After all those years of endless newspaper deliveries, I wasn't going to get one when I needed it most. The postman didn't get here much before eleven and that was hours away. I'd never be able to keep Sandwiches talking till then. But I could try.

'You killed Rose, didn't you?' I said.

'Your lady friend, right?'

'Yes.'

'Guilty.'

'And Susan.'

'Susan?'

'My sister.'

'Yeah.' Sandwiches gave a sigh. 'They're my last two. Well...'

I could sense him move away from me. I wondered if I dared to turn around and look at him, but decided against it.

'Still, you can't say I didn't warn you,' he said. 'You got my note, didn't you?'

'No.'

'You sure?'

'I think I'd have remembered,' I said.

'It was a leaflet for computers. I was quite pleased with that. I'd rung all the words for you – spelled it out. I thought you liked clues.' His hand held out the leaflet. 'You see?'

I peered at the folded sheet of paper.

'It's all there if you know how to look.'

Suddenly I could see only too clearly what the note said. The words spelled out a message. '*Open Now*' from the leaflet's banner – the word '*Now*' was circled. Shensu. The first half of the name had been highlighted. The same was true of Williamson. The D1-E was self explanatory.

'Now She Will Die,' said Sandwiches.

'I can see it,' I said.

'So what can I say? I'm a man of my word, if you'll forgive the pun.'

'You enjoy it, don't you?' I said.

'Oh, I hate myself afterwards Henry, is that what you want me to say? That I'm filled with self loathing? Let me tell you – the feeling doesn't last. I've always managed to get over it. By the way I know exactly what you're doing. You're thinking 'If I keep talking, perhaps he'll forget what he's come here for.' Nice try. As if I'd do a thing like that.' He paused for a moment. 'But I'm happy to talk. Let's be honest Henry, talking is all you've got left. You messed up good and proper, didn't you? All that running around, all those trains and buses – goodness, you did some travelling. Now what was all that about, eh?'

'I was looking for you.'

'I should be flattered.'

I could hear him shuffling about behind me. What was he doing?

'And you found me, didn't you? Yet you were none the wiser.'

'I made a mistake,' I said.

'Your Rose knew though. She found out. Turns out she wasn't such a lousy copper after all.'

I tensed at the mention of Rose's name. I wished there was something I could do, something that would even things up in my favour. But I was a prisoner in my own home, at the mercy of a sadistic killer. He was toying with me, but clearly didn't want to kill me just yet. Sandwiches was keeping me alive for a reason.

I tried to concentrate on my breathing. It seemed steadier now, and my heart rate slower, in spite of all my problems. I'd used up all my energy worrying about things and lived in fear of almost everything for weeks. Now I'd finally been snared and it had all caught up with me. I was too exhausted to be afraid.

'I need to sit down,' I said. I looked ahead at the kitchen chair. 'I hurt my leg.'

'That's unfortunate,' said Sandwiches. 'Go on then.'

I hobbled forward and sat on the chair.

'Is that better?' he said.

I looked up and got my first proper glimpse of the serial killer.

Sandwiches was slight in stature and though the light was still poor I could see that his skin was pale and his right eye had a tic. For a mass murderer he cut an unimpressive figure. How dare this man kill my loved ones, invade my house and now threaten me.

'Why don't you just kill me and have done with it?' I was surprised to hear myself saying the words.

'Oh Henry Henry Henry Henry Henry. What sort of a question is that?'

'Why don't you just kill me and have done with it?' I said them again.

'You know they're calling me the worst murderer in Britain. I expect you're aware of that. Worst murderer though Henry. It's enough to make your blood boil, isn't it? I'm up to six now. Six. I think it's six. I could have missed one.'

'Why don't you just kill me and have done with it?'

'I think that makes me the best murderer, don't you?'

'Why don't you just kill me and have done with it?'

'You're starting to annoy me now,' said Sandwiches.

He wagged a finger at me. 'There's no subtlety to you, is there? Living in your stupid rabbit warren of a house with your bags full of shit, terrified of letting anything go. You're sick in the head. You can't make value judgments, that's your trouble Henry. You can't tell the wheat from the chaff – the chewing gum from the sandwiches. When did you last make an important decision, eh? Look at this place – I mean look at it. Your whole bloody life is a shambles. You're so busy being a nosy little bastard you can't even keep your electricity sorted. Jesus, what I wouldn't do for a cup of tea right now. I don't know why I expected things would be any different. You're a walking mess Henry Henry Henry. And you know what? No-one's going to miss you.'

'I don't believe you're the worst murderer,' I said and stared at him. 'You're not even close.'

'That's not true.'

He brandished his knife. I tried my best to ignore it and keep talking.

'Other men have killed more,' I said.

'I've killed six,' said Sandwiches. 'And I haven't finished yet.'

'Neither have I,' I said.

'I can make you stop.' He bunched and unbunched his fists, his knuckles showing white on the hand that gripped the knife.

'Others have done it better.' I wasn't sure where my defiance had come from – but it had come, regardless.

'You're doing this all wrong,' he said. 'This isn't how it works. I'm the one in charge here – me.'

I sat there, impassive. I thought about asking Sandwiches once again why he didn't just do what he'd obviously come to do, but decided not to.

There was no need to antagonise him. He clearly hadn't expected me to show any fight. Well, I was fighting in my own way. With any luck Sandwiches would make a mistake. And if he did I just had to hope that I'd be ready.

You know what really makes me sad Henry...' He began toying with his knife. 'Is that you don't even know who I am.'

'I know your name.'

'Names don't tell you everything. You call me Sandwiches – I suppose I should be grateful you didn't call me twitchy. People have done you know. They can be very cruel.'

I didn't say anything.

'So my real name doesn't mean anything to you?'

'Should it?' I knew it was Ken or Kenneth something, but I couldn't recall the rest.

'All right then – what about the name Siobhan Douglas? You remember her all right don't you? I can see it on your face.'

I could feel myself tensing as he said the name.

'She has her mother's surname, perhaps that's why you didn't make the connection. Tragic Siobhan Douglas, the girl who had everything – according to the papers. Except she didn't, did she? She didn't have the things that seem to matter so much to people – like self confidence. I can't tell you how many times we told her what a pretty girl she was but it didn't seem to matter any. She was bullied you see Henry. Picked on by other girls – confident girls, slim girls, prettier girls. They needled away at her. Because girls are like that. They're not like us men Henry. Oh no. We just cut straight to the heart of a problem, don't we?'

He ran the knife down the side of the nearest cardboard box. It burst open, and a few things fell out onto the floor.

'You know what happened of course. In the end she couldn't take any more.' Sandwiches took a deep breath. 'It was my wife who found her Henry. Dangling from the banisters. She'd kicked two of the pictures off the wall in her struggle. I don't know if that means she had a last minute change of heart. She never said. And who knows what goes through someone's mind at a time like that?'

I fidgeted on my chair. His eye was twitching more rapidly now, I could see. Perhaps that happened when he was about to use the knife. I had to stay calm. If I stayed calm I might just have the faintest chance of saving myself – and everybody else.

'Of course it turns into a circus, doesn't it? A human tragedy like that. The world and his wife want to tell you how sorry they are. As if bunches of flowers and cards do any good. But of course you know all that. You were stood there with all the others, gawping like it was a spectator sport.'

I opened my mouth to speak, but no words came out.

'What Henry? A little titillation was it?'

'What's all that got to do with you killing people?'

'Was it?'

'No.'

'Then what?'

'I didn't know she was your daughter.'

'You haven't answered my question.'

'I thought I might be able to help in some way.'

'Help? Standing by my front gate is helping is it? Rooting around, poking your nose where it isn't wanted.'

'I never saw you at the house.'

'You didn't know I was her father Henry.'

I rubbed my tired eyes. A tiny glimmer of light had begun to appear at the kitchen window. In an hour or so, perhaps even less, the darkness would have gone.

'Her mother went to pieces. Started acting strange. She threw all Siobhan's things out – couldn't bear the sight of them. Made her too upset. One day I came back and everything was gone.' He clicked his fingers. 'Just like that. I wasn't happy Henry, I wasn't happy at all. Especially when I found out someone had been taking things.'

'I wanted to preserve her memory,' I said.

His shoulders slumped. 'We all cope in our own way I suppose. Helen did her thing and I decided to do ... mine.'

'Killing innocent girls,' I said.

'You don't know they were innocent Henry. Did you look in their eyes?'

'They weren't the ones who'd bullied your daughter.'

'I couldn't very well go for them now could I?' He laughed. 'I'm not an idiot. If I'd shat on my own doorstep I'd soon have had the police round, wouldn't I? As it was I had you instead.'

I wondered if I should sympathise with Sandwiches for his loss, or lecture him about what he'd done. I decided to keep quiet.

'We drifted apart soon after, Helen and me. I say drifted, I think she was gone by the end of the month. Marriage is about togetherness isn't it? A problem shared and all that. Well you tell me Henry – how can a husband share something like that with his wife, eh?'

I didn't say anything.

'I moved to a new town. Too many bad memories – I'm sure you understand. And Helen moved to a bungalow. No stairs.'

'And you killed again.'

'I was making my mark. But each time there you were like some sort of ghoul. So I watched you and followed you. After what happened at my house I wanted to see what you were doing. I soon got the idea it must be you who'd taken it. None of the others ever took anything, you see. Only you Henry.'

That was why Sandwiches had come before, and why he hadn't killed me yet. I understood now. I'd taken something that incriminated him, and presumably he needed me to tell him where it was.

'The heat was starting to build up Henry. And I kept wondering to myself, what's his game? Rooting through my dustbins, collecting crap. I had an idea it might be blackmail, can you believe that? So I thought I'd come and pay you a visit. And I took one look and thought – here's a feller who can take the rap for me.'

'It wasn't in a dustbin. I've never gone looking in dustbins.'

'I'd gone through every last bit of stuff Helen had thrown out looking for the damned thing. But could I find it?' He shook his head. 'Of all the things you could have taken Henry.'

'You'd thrown it away,' I said.

'My wife threw it away. She was upset.'

'It was in a box by the gate. Just lying there. I couldn't believe her parents had got rid of such a nice thing that belonged to their daughter.'

'Well that's just it Henry, and it's why I want it back. You see it wasn't Siobhan's brooch, that was the problem. It belonged to a girl called Shannon something.'

'You don't even remember, do you?' I said.

'It's not my job to remember. I leave that to other people.'

I shuddered.

'I thought Wyatt was on to me that time. Of course she wasn't Wyatt back then, she was still Johnson, wasn't she? I've never really got used to her not being Johnson.'

Johnson – I remembered the name as he said it. She'd been involved at Bradnam Common after Rose had been moved aside. She'd made a statement had DS Johnson. It was there in the papers up in the loft. I'd had all the information at my fingertips but I hadn't really seen it. Johnson, or Wyatt, had been there on every occasion, chewing her gum and looking for evidence. If I'd said something, if I'd just said something...

'It won't be long before the paperboy gets here,' I said. 'He usually comes around nine o'clock. Sometimes a bit before.'

Sandwiches grinned and shook his head.

'You've cancelled your papers Henry. I have done my homework you know.' He pressed a finger against the point of his knife. 'I had you down as a crank at first – like the van bangers and the other nutters. As I said, I couldn't be absolutely sure you'd got it. Not until she turned up at any rate.'

'Rose.'

'She came calling one evening. I didn't recognise her at first. She'd rather let herself go. And she told me she'd seen something of mine – something I'd lost. It was the brooch Henry. She knew about the brooch. No-one else would have recognised it, 'cos they kept it out of the papers, but she was a policewoman. She knew all about it. How you'd found it at my house. Well, it didn't look good, did it? The brooch that tied me to another girl's murder. And I couldn't have her going to the police, could I? Crazy as she was they were going to listen to her.'

'No.' It was all I could say.

'I was hoping she might have it with her, but no such luck. Her bag was empty.'

I tried to haul myself to my feet.

'Steady on Henry, watch your leg. You'll do yourself an injury.'

'I don't care,' I said.

Sandwiches shook his head and smiled.

'So if she didn't have the brooch, that meant you'd still got it.'

'You've been lying haven't you?' I was shaking with anger. 'It's all just words.'

'You tell me I'm wrong. You've got my brooch.'

'This has never been about your daughter's death for a second, has it? You just wanted to make believe you had some excuse. You were already a murderer before she killed herself. So you killed those girls, you killed Rose and you killed my sister for the sake of a brooch.'

'It was your fault Henry. You led me to her.'

'No.'

'I thought you might have left it with her. But we had a little chat and it turns out you hadn't.'

I got to my feet. If there was pain in my leg I couldn't feel it at that moment. I was consumed by an emotion that went way beyond anger.

'Sit down,' yelled Sandwiches.

I stood rooted to the spot. The murderer walked over to me, sticking a hand in his jacket pocket as he weaved between the boxes. Then he took a length of blue-coloured plaited nylon cord from his pocket. He stood in front of me and tugged at the cable with both hands. I could see that it had already been fashioned into a makeshift noose.

'You got insurance Henry? Don't bother answering. Of course you haven't. This happens to be my insurance policy.' He began fiddling with the loose end of the nylon cord. 'It's all very well being a notorious serial killer Henry, but they all end up behind bars eventually, don't they?'

The nylon fibres made a scratching sound as they rubbed against one another.

'Well this one won't. Because someone else is going to be unmasked as Britain's worst – or best – murderer. That someone is you Henry.'

I didn't struggle as the noose was slipped over my head.

'There, that's better,' said Sandwiches. 'Now let's have no funny business. I need to be on my way soon before things start warming up. All I want is the brooch and then we'll call it quits, eh?'

'Then you kill me.'

Sandwiches tightened the cord. I felt it bite into my neck.

'No, I'm not going to kill you Henry,' he said. 'You're going to kill yourself.'

CHAPTER TWENTY-FOUR

'Now you know how this thing ends,' said Sandwiches. He tugged at the cord and I choked in reflex. 'For you, at any rate. Move.'

He jabbed at me with his knife. I lurched forward, and picked my way through the collection of objects which had spilled onto the kitchen floor.

'You know you won't get away with it,' I said.

'Your girlfriend said exactly the same thing. And look what happened to her.'

'You won't.'

'Perhaps. Perhaps not. But you'll never know will you Henry?'

He ran the cord between his fingers while I tried to splutter a response.

'Hurts, doesn't it?' said Sandwiches. 'So why the rope, I bet you're wondering. Well, the thing is Henry, if I kill you, then it just looks like another murder, doesn't it? And where will that get me? I need your death to mean something. An apologetic suicide seems the best solution. It certainly gets me off the hook. I'm picturing the scenario here. After all the terrible things you'd done, you'd had enough – so you took your own life. That should wrap everything up. The police have a mind it's you, don't they? Your girlfriend's dead and now your sister is. And when they find your body and a suicide note, that's case closed. The public can rest easy again. And I can go back to being the grieving father. You've only got yourself to blame really. If you hadn't picked that brooch up, just think how many lives you could have saved.'

The rope was starting to hurt now, like a collar that was far too tight. I'd black out soon, that was the first stage. Was Sandwiches right? Supposing I hadn't picked up the brooch or the gum, would things have turned out any different? The people I loved might still be alive. But others would be dead. And where would it end? No, he was wrong. He'd have kept on killing because he enjoyed it too much to stop. Sandwiches was a sick man to start with.

'She knew, didn't she?' I spluttered.

'Your girlfriend told me as much – weren't you listening?'

'I meant Siobhan.'

'Eh?'

'She knew.'

'Knew what?'

'Everything.' My voice was rasping. 'She didn't kill herself because she was being picked on. She did it because she found out about you.'

'No. No, that isn't true.'

'She knew what you'd done.'

'She couldn't have known about the brooch.'

'Can you be sure?'

'Be quiet.'

'Think about it.'

'I said be quiet.'

Sandwiches pulled the cord tighter around my neck, then gave me a shove for good measure. I jerked backwards and steadying myself turned round to face him. I saw what he was wearing and stifled a laugh.

'I was right,' said the serial killer. 'You are a nutcase. What's so funny?'

I was choking and couldn't speak.

'Tell me.' He loosened the nylon cord.

'I was admiring your coat,' I said. The words came spluttering out. 'I was just thinking how much nicer it would look with a full set of buttons.'

Sandwiches ran his hand down the front of his coat. He touched each of the silver banded wooden buttons, before stopping at the gap where one of them was missing.

'I went back to look for it,' he said. 'But it had gone of course. So that's something else you owe me.'

'Why should I–'

My next word was cut off as the cord was pulled tight.

'The button and the brooch,' said Sandwiches. 'I want them back. I'll be here till doomsday looking through this rubbish and I haven't got that long.'

I tried to swallow, but all I could manage was a selection of noises. I had to think now, and quickly. Time was ebbing away, so I had to make the most of what was left. Perhaps I might be able to wrestle the blade from Sandwiches. I could knock him over and turn his weapon against him. I'd got newspapers upstairs with lurid accounts of how a mugger or some psycho had come to grief on their own weapon. But they were the exceptions, because most of the time whoever held the knife had the advantage, and didn't give it up lightly. Sandwiches possessed physical strength, too, and I suspected that even if I hadn't got an injured leg I'd probably come off second best. I'd die where I stood – among the boxes and bags in my hallway. And what would they make of me when I was gone? I'd be the man with a loft full of newspapers and a house full of junk. They'd call me a weirdo, most likely. 'He kept himself to himself.' That was the phrase they generally used. And I'd have died for nothing, just like all those other people would have died for nothing. No, I couldn't use physical strength. There was only one thing I could do now. I could lie.

'In there,' I said.

'What?'

Sandwiches eased the pressure on the cord.

'The brooch,' I said.

'Where?'

'In there.'

I nodded my head and felt the blue nylon rubbing on my neck. It was strong stuff. Unbreakable.

'What? In that bag?'

'Yes.'

'And the button?'

I indicated the bin-liner which had tumbled to the ground and blocked the hallway.

'What's it doing there?'

'I meant to put it somewhere safe,' I said. My heart was beating fast now, but I had to stay calm for my plan to work. Not that it was so much a plan really, more a ridiculous idea that had popped into my head. But at this stage it was all I'd got.

'Get them for me,' he snapped.

'Me?'

'Who else?'

'I can't bend down,' I said. 'Not with my leg.' I shuffled on the floor until I was directly behind the squat shape of the bin-liner.

'Move out of the way then.' Impatient now, Sandwiches shoved me and I stepped over the bag as best I could.

'You'd better be telling the truth,' said the killer, and pointed his finger at me, before thrusting his hand into the bag. I tensed. There was a crunching, grinding sound for a second, a moment's quiet, and then a scream.

At its first utterance I knew what I had to do. I moved down the hallway as fast as my body could manage, and made for the front door.

'You cut me! You cut me!'

Sandwiches' voice was a high pitched squeal. Blood was pouring from a gash in his right hand, while a long shard of glass dangled from his forearm. In the poor light, I could barely see it, but I could hear the dark liquid spattering onto the black plastic.

'Look at my hand!' he screamed. 'You bastard!'

I tugged at the front door but it refused to budge. I pulled at it again and remembered that the keys were still in my raincoat pocket, in the kitchen. There was nowhere else to escape but upstairs.

I slammed my foot on the bottom step and a jolt shot straight through my leg. The pain, which I'd been suppressing for some time, was suddenly impossible to ignore. I cried out and held onto the banister to steady myself, then began to climb. At that moment, Sandwiches turned his attention towards me. His hand flashed between the banister spindles and grabbed the nylon rope which trailed behind me. He tugged at it, my leg shot out from under me, and my knee crashed onto the step. A cry was stopped in my throat as sheaves of old papers and cards went tumbling and fluttering down the stairs. I grunted instead and yanked back at the tightening blue cord, causing Sandwiches to fall back onto the bloodied bin-liner with a crunch. He gave a blood-curdling yell then hauled himself to his feet and stuck his other hand through the wooden spindles. I tried to push myself up with my good foot, but my sock slipped on some loose sheets of paper. Sandwiches stabbed at it with the glass, which was still gripped in his hand. The spike slammed down, but somehow missed my foot and connected with the stair. The jarring shock caused Sandwiches to let out another shriek and fall back again, the blood gushing from his wound.

Using both hands I hauled myself onto the next step. There was no time to reflect on my pain or what might happen – escaping upstairs was all that mattered. I'd be trapped there, of course, but provided I reached it there were surely things I could use to fight back. But I'd need to get there very quickly if I was to stand any chance.

Sandwiches was at the foot of the stairs himself now, moaning and mumbling. I didn't dare to look back to see how far he was behind me or how much blood he'd lost. I just tried to keep on climbing. I expected at any moment to feel a stabbing sensation in my leg, or a hand clutching at my ankle. It felt like the thumping, snarling sound of the wounded serial killer was coming closer every second.

Finally, with one last effort, I scrambled onto the landing and looked around for a weapon of any sort. There was a metal pole that I'd flung on top of some boxes a while back, but it still had the curtains attached. If I tried to go at Sandwiches with it, the killer would most likely grab the fabric and pull me towards him.

Only one doorway offered any possibility of escape – the back bedroom. I limped towards it, my leg stiffening with every step. Somewhere on the stairs I could hear Sandwiches grunting. And then I heard another cry – someone calling my name. It was hard to make out above the noise of the climbing killer, and I thought I might have imagined it. But then I heard it again.

'Henry.'

And it was followed by a banging on the door.

'Henry!'

It was Jamal.

He wouldn't be safe, I thought. When Sandwiches had finished here he'd seek him out. I couldn't let that happen.

'Henry!'

'Get away, it's not safe,' I yelled.

Sandwiches was nearly upon me now. Desperately I looked around for something, anything, I could use. I caught sight of the concrete cat and with an agonising effort bent down and picked it up. I staggered to the top of the staircase, holding it above my head.

'Come on Henry,' I said before flinging it at the scrambling figure of Sandwiches. The concrete cat struck him firmly on the shoulder then bounced down the stairs and finished by the front door. For a moment Sandwiches lost his footing.

'Henry! Open the door, man.'

I disappeared into the back bedroom. Perhaps there was something useful in one of the drawers. I'd looked in them only the other day. But I couldn't remember. It was too late now anyway, there was no time to check. All I could do was retreat further into the last possible hiding place that was left – the wardrobe. I undid the catch, climbed in, and closed the door behind me.

It was only as the darkness smothered me that I realised I'd not set foot inside the wardrobe since my father had shut me in all those years ago. I'd been terrified then. But this time I was in a place beyond fear. When I was a boy of eight I'd sat huddled in the corner with only Mother's jumper and a black and yellow scarf for comfort. I had nothing like that now. Yet as I sat in the dark awaiting the inevitable, I felt strangely serene. The sounds, too, seemed to have melted away. Was I imagining the quiet? Had the banging on the front door stopped? Maybe Sandwiches had given up the pursuit – or collapsed from loss of blood. I had no idea. I couldn't hear anything other than the beating of my own heart.

But then my senses were suddenly awakened and I felt something brush against my cheek. It was soft, like Mother's jumper had been. Is this what happened at the end, I wondered. Was I slowly losing my mind and finding some memory to make the last few moments feel somehow less awful? The feathery sensation began to extend to the other side of my face, and then I noticed it on my hands and my bare legs. And as the feeling spread across the remainder of my exposed skin, I realised that what I could feel, and now hear, was the beating of wings, and the massing of insects. Suddenly it all made sense – the regular sightings, the endless complaints from Tattoos – these were a very particular kind of insect. I was covered from head to foot, I now knew, in wasps. They must have built their nest in the dark recesses of my old wardrobe. And they were everywhere now.

They were in my hair and in my ears, beating, humming and clambering over one another in an insect orgy. A feeling of revulsion overwhelmed me as the wasps swarmed across my skin, their bodies pulsing in rhythm. I began to tremble as I waited for their first strike. But then from somewhere I recalled a wood, and sunshine, and a picnic with my little sister and the sound of my mother's voice. She was there with me, telling me not to be afraid. That I just needed to stay calm and relax. The wasps wouldn't hurt me if I did that. They didn't want to hurt me. Wasps only hurt people for a reason, I just needed to remember that. So I screwed my eyes shut, and did as my mother told me. I breathed as deeply as I could, relaxed, and gave myself up to them.

And then the ground thundered and shook and the air was filled with a shrieking, wailing sound. Finally with a roar the wardrobe began to shake. Then the door juddered and burst open, and I saw daylight and a screaming Sandwiches. There was blood cascading from his half-glass hand and a look of madness on his face. He stood and stared at me for a moment, perhaps trying to make sense of what was in front of him. But whether he could see me, or whether he just saw countless wasps, writhing and crawling all over me, I have no way of knowing. All I saw were his hands in the air and the skin and blood flapping around the glass, and all I heard was the scream.

And nothing was the same after that.

It could be that the scream acted as a signal to the wasps, for it had barely died before they began to fly, singly at first but then growing rapidly, until their number swelled first to hundreds and then into the thousands. But rather than scattering, the wasps instead began swarming all over the mass murderer. They twitched and fluttered across Sandwiches' skin, congregating around his bleeding wound to begin with, then crawling into his ears and nose and mouth, creeping down his collar and heading up his sleeves. And then the screams turned to a shriek of terror.

'Get away, get away! Get off me!'

He flapped and twirled and slashed his glass shard through the emerging sunlight, as more and more wasps continued to settle on him. But while the wasps had colonised me in a benign fashion, they were not so kind to Sandwiches. He yelped and shrieked as the wasps started to sting. And with each pitiful cry the assembly grew larger and larger, until finally he was covered from head to toe in wasps and screaming for dear life. Unable to stand the torment a moment longer, Sandwiches moved away from the wardrobe. I watched as he tottered towards the bedroom door, extending an insect covered hand to steady himself. And all the while, above the buzzing and the beating of the wings, were the howls of the man in agony underneath.

I shuffled a step behind. Sandwiches turned briefly to look at me and tried to say something, but the wasps swarming around inside his mouth made it impossible for him to speak. He staggered on to the landing, dropped to his knees, and with a final gurgling sound fell headlong down the stairs. As his body plunged head over heels there was another crash, as the front door splintered and cracked and gave way. Two policemen, wearing body army, tumbled through, as Sandwiches' body came to rest. No sooner had it done so than the wasps, now several thousand strong, rose as one and departed in a cloud through the open door.

I stood on the edge of the landing and looked down at the prostrate figure of Sandwiches. Wyatt was there now too, I could see. And beyond on the garden path, standing by a bookcase, was Jamal, his jacket pulsing with light reflected from the police vehicles behind. I could hear chatter now too – crackling intercoms and cackling bystanders in the street. I looked again at Sandwiches, just to be certain. Two paramedics were crouching over him now, but there was nothing they could do. The twisted body told me that the serial killer had murdered his last. It was over.

CHAPTER TWENTY-FIVE

I snipped away the last remaining stalks of grass that were still poking above the rest. When they were finally trimmed to my satisfaction I struggled to my feet and stood back to admire my handiwork. Was it absolutely even? Was everything in its rightful place, just where it should be? No. But then nature was like that. It did what it wanted, in its own way, and behaved in ways people didn't properly understand.

I bent down again, slowly this time to protect my leg. It still hurt, after all this time, and I winced as my knee made contact with the ground.

'Sorry for making such a fuss,' I said and took a deep breath.

'The doctor told me I probably wouldn't be able to play football again. I had to laugh. I told him I hadn't played football since I was at school. Could you imagine me playing football? He's new, that's why. It's not Dr Singh anymore. It's Dr Meredith. Dr Singh's left the practice. I'm not sure if you knew Dr Singh.'

I took a small cellophane bag from my pocket and scattered the contents onto the grass. Then I took the pointed end of the shears and made a few indentations in the ground.

'Yellow crocuses I thought. The blooms are quite fragile and don't last long but they are lovely. And I got some aconites and dwarf narcissi. That way there's going to be colour from January all the way into spring.'

I began poking the bulbs into the holes I'd fashioned, pressing the soil back around them.

'I'm not sure which ones are which though. I think the big ones must be the dwarf narcissi, but I could be wrong. We'll just have to see what comes up in the New Year, won't we?'

A tear began forming in the corner of my eye. I brushed it away with a muddy finger.

'Now look what you've made me do,' I said. 'I was managing fine until then.'

I stood up again, leaning on the stone for support. It was a good grave, there was no denying it. The setting was pleasant, and the site looked to be well maintained. I couldn't recall Susan ever expressing an opinion about whether she'd prefer to be buried or cremated.

'We never got to talk about that, did we?' I said.

But then, people never did talk about such things when they were in their thirties, did they? They had their whole lives ahead of them. Why waste breath discussing it?

Flowers. I should stick to talking about flowers today. I'd told her before about what had happened to her killer and what the police response had been and how sorry I was. I was never going to stop being sorry. But there was no point going over all that again. Not today, anyway. That would just open up old wounds.

Black marble. Derek had taken charge of the headstone, too.

'I'm glad he did though. I shouldn't have been able to talk to you here otherwise.' I put my hand against the side of my mouth. 'I didn't tell him about the crocuses.'

I talk quite a bit on my visits. I've never said too much about Rose but then I don't really know what to say. I don't expect I'll ever understand why she never told me the truth. Some things even a computer can't tell you.

It's all right to talk. People are allowed to do that here, as long as they aren't too indiscreet or loud. No doubt casual observers who knew nothing of Susan's life would look at her dates, calculate her age and say to one another: 'She was only young.' And then they'd probably try to work out what 'Cruelly taken from us' meant. Derek had chosen those words as well, so far as I knew. And when people got home, if they still remembered and bothered to look her up on the internet, they'd see what had happened to Susan Mullings, née Henry. And that yes, it was cruel.

'It took me two journeys to move all the newspapers,' I said. 'If the van driver had offered to help me lift them I expect we could have done it in half the time. But apparently you have to pay extra if you want the driver to do any heavy lifting and that all needs to be sorted out beforehand. Still, it's done now. And I probably needed the exercise. Not that it's easy with my leg. Sorry. That's me making a fuss again. It has made me think I should learn to drive though.'

I brushed some grass trimmings from my hand.

'It turned out there was another wasps' nest in the loft. A huge one. Right at the back, under the eaves. I only found it when I cleared the last of the newspapers. They chew up the paper Susan and transform it into a home. They're amazing things.'

The sun emerged from behind some clouds.

'Did I mention the charity shop last time? I'm not sure if I did. I've been taking my books in and some of the other bits and pieces I've had lying around. The garden's clear now, you wouldn't recognise it. Anyway, they've been getting quite used to me there, I think that's what it must be. We've been striking up conversations when I've dropped stuff off. Well you'll never guess but they've only gone and asked me if I want to help out in the shop. Just a couple of days a week, they said, to start with. Then we'll see how we go. They've got some stuff there though Susan. The stockroom is piled high from floor to ceiling. It'll take some sorting out, I don't mind telling you.'

I bent down again and poked a hole in the centre of the cropped turf.

'I went to Parson's Wood again earlier in the week.'

I fumbled in my inside pocket, took out a small object and dropped it into the ground, compacting the soil on top.

'I'm one of the Friends now. A few of us have been clearing away some brambles so we can replace the old fountain. Even Jamal has promised to come along and give us a hand. Just as soon as he's back from his holiday.'

'I'll come again soon Susan,' I said. 'There's someone else I have to visit now.'

I adjusted my woollen hat and stood up. Then I tightened the knot in my favourite black and yellow scarf and walked out through the open gate.

ABOUT THE AUTHOR

Simon Bullivant graduated from University College London with a degree in Art History, and after several jobs which had nothing to do with art, or history, he began writing comedy. This eventually led to a career in radio, and then television.

Following a three year tenure on Radio 4's 'Week Ending', he co-devised a comedy panel game for BBC radio called 'They Think It's All Over', which was later adapted and modified for television, where it proved to be a huge success, enjoying audiences of eight million and more at its peak. He wrote for the show, and ended up its producer.

In 1996, he helped create 'Never Mind the Buzzcocks' for the production company Talkback. He was a writer and producer on this show during its near twenty-year run on BBC2.

Simon Bullivant has also been a writer and occasional producer on such shows as 'Mock the Week', 'A League of Their Own' and 'Argumental', not to mention a hundred other shows that in many cases have been rightly forgotten.

Simon has co-written a number of comedy books, and his anthology 'The Bumper Book of Slightly Forgotten But Nevertheless Still Great British Olympians and Other Sporting Heroes' was published in 2011. 'The Uncommon Prison of Henry V. Henry' is his first serious work.

OTHER PUBLICATIONS
FROM OUEN PRESS

Other crime thrillers...

IMAGINE GHOSTS TELLING TALES IN FRONT OF SMOKY MIRRORS *by S.L.Masunda* – is a fictional memoir exploring a writer's quest for literary recognition. The atrocities he commits in the name of ambition become increasingly gruesome, but we are drawn back in time to reveal pivotal moments in the writer's life that challenge the reader to seek out redemption for our hero turned killer.

MAY ALL YOUR NAMES BE FORGOTTEN *by Michael Connor* – a fast moving crime thriller set in south London, containing as many pointers for budding telesales staff, prepared to break the rules, as it does for the ordinary citizen seeking to avoid being hustled.

Biography...

THE SOHO DON *by Michael Connor* is a biographical narrative about a London gangster whose unique power was strongest in the 25 years after World War II - a very powerful read. The Krays said he feared no-one, and was the one man they truly respected. Likened to Graham Greene's period thriller *Brighton Rock*, and the style of Truman Capote's *In Cold Blood*.

KNIGHT: Yorkshireman, Storyteller, Spy *by Greg Christie* is an epic tale of an extraordinary man who reinvented himself as artist, soldier, newspaper reporter, film critic, intelligence officer. A major inter-war novelist whose work was lauded by the literary establishment of the 1930s – but overshadowed by his biggest hit – a little pot-boiler he sold for $10,000 he called *Lassie Come-Home*.

Rites of passage...

CODY, THE MEDICINE MAN AND ME *by Alan Wilkinson* – a trip across the USA transforms into the ultimate voyage of personal discovery. Attempting to establish the truth of his baffling ancestry, Ray West struggles to prepare himself for a reunion with his estranged twin brother – old rivalries quickly resurface. **A showdown brews – but ultimately only one of the brothers can ride off into the sunset.**

THE CLEANSING *by Michael Connor* – weaves a powerful plot, full of vivid encounters and fascinating characters. It depicts the harsh reality that still faces many, particularly the women, in Africa today. .

Short story collections...

LAST CALL & OTHER SHORT STORIES *including Ouen Press Short Story Competition Winners 2015* – a variety of fictitious working-dogs portrayed in many different circumstances as their 'jobs' dictate or their conditions demand; a collection of compelling tales that reflect that vast, often unfathomable melting-pot of human emotions and intention.

JOURNEY THROUGH UNCERTAINTY & OTHER SHORT STORIES *including Ouen Press Short Story Competition Winners 2016* – featuring physical and emotional journeys, endured and enjoyed, with humour and courage – each one a testimony to a place, or an event, or a sentiment.

TASTING NOTES & OTHER SHORT STORIES *including Ouen Press Short Story Competition Winners 2017* – a complex and diverse menu of science fiction, art, humour, the spying game, magical realism, celebrity cooking and much more, expertly crafted to tantalise and entertain.

All books available in paperback & ebook from Amazon
www.ouenpress.com

www.ingramcontent.com/pod-product-compliance
Lightning Source LLC
Chambersburg PA
CBHW071159260626
47162CB00003B/1106